READING THE CEILING

Dayo Forster

SIMON &
SCHUSTER

London · New York · Sydney · Toronto

A CBS COMPANY

First published in Great Britain by Simon & Schuster UK Ltd, 2007
A CBS COMPANY

Copyright © Dayo Forster, 2007

1 3 5 7 9 10 8 6 4 2

Simon & Schuster UK Ltd
Africa House
64–78 Kingsway
London WC2B 6AH

www.simonsays.co.uk

Simon & Schuster Australia
Sydney

A CIP catalogue record for this book is available
from the British Library

ISBN-13: 978-0-7432-9571-0
ISBN-10: 0-7432-9571-4

Typeset in Granjon by M Rules
Printed and bound in Great Britain by
William Clowes Ltd, Beccles, Suffolk

For my family –
my excuse for those weekends in Watamu

Contents

Prologue

1

Girl

In the slit between my bedroom curtains, I see a long triangle of sky more grey than blue. The light changes with each sweep of my eyelids. At this time of year, when the harmattan blows straight off the Sahara, not even the wide expanse of the River Gambia can add enough wet to stop it in its tracks. It has coated with dust the mosquito netting on my window.

Today is my birthday. It is also the day I have decided to do The Deed.

'Remember, they are only after *one* thing,' my mother says. She advises me to stay aware of what men want; that I need to practise light prancing, à la Muhammad Ali, keeping my butterfly just out of their reach. Keep myself. For what? At eighteen, why do I need to keep to the butterfly dance? Why exactly?

'Otherwise everyone will think you are loose, cheap.' That's the answer my mother would give.

Ma thinks of me as a child-woman who does not know her own mind, and is easily influenced. At university, I'll be beyond her reach, I'll be able to do what I want. There's only one thing that's stopping me from throwing off childhood. And I plan to deal with that today.

Osman's radio starts a low-volumed griot wailing. The plucking of the *kora* strings adds texture to a mellow baritone voice. I find it strangely comforting as the sound soaks into my skin. Today the singer tells of Sunjata Keita, a warrior king whose exploits in the savannah have been erased by tropical sand and hot winds. But whose history is played on, retold over the years in the memories passed through mouth and ear of the people who hold our past in their heads. The griot sings:

> *The Sunjata story / Is very strange and wonderful.*
> *You see one griot, / And he gives you an account of it one way,*
> *You see another griot, / And he gives you an account of it in*
> *another way.*

Sunjata's life – one story that is now told in different ways. The radio moves and a clanking joins it as Osman picks up his kettle. The griot continues:

> *Cats on the shoulder / The hunter and the lion are at*
> *Naarena.*

A minute later, I hear Osman at the tap. The water gushes into the kettle, sounding hollow against the metal, then the gushing is drowned by the weight of more water.

Osman is our family's night protector. He is paid to watch while we sleep. Now he has to greet the day with sleep-soaked eyes before getting ready for his real job, shifting sacks of rice, flour, or sugar at the port. A few ships dock this week, conjuring jobs for men with muscles who don't mind the work being irregular.

4

Both sides of this watchman deal are grateful. Osman gets extra cash for his family in Mansakonko, halfway up the river. My mother sprinkles in additional tight-lipped help when his unexpected emergencies arise. Such as:

1   the new baby has malaria
2   the middle boy was sent home because he didn't have his school uniform
3   the mama's leg isn't getting better from that dog bite.

In exchange, my mother gets the security of a man about the compound. Someone who can run to our rescue if a gang of toughs ever smash their way into the house. In case any of her emergencies arise, unexpectedly or otherwise, our muscular, manly, hired Osman is around.

So, here I am, one in a household of four females protected in the night by a wiry thin-faced man from Mansakonko. The drumbeats of other kinds of danger are in my ears while my sisters sleep, dreaming how my mother wants them to – like butterfly dancers.

The flame-coloured cockerel at the Salanis' is shrieking hoarsely. Its loud, nasty echoes fade into still air. My mother is soon awake. I hear her shuffle past, her bedroom slippers muffled against the tiles in the corridor. A yell out of the window: 'Ozz-maaaan. *Demal jainda mburu.*' Go and buy some bread.

'How many?'

'*Nyeta.*'

Number of hot, stub-ended loaves needed for breakfast: three. Number of unloose women left in the house: ditto.

I plan to be loose today. But who with? I've been making up a list but find it scary to think through the options knowing I have

5

to decide on *one*. My possibilities begin with Reuben. Why is he on the list at all? If the idea comes creeping that I need him as a fall-back, my failsafe option in case it turns out that the others don't want to be chosen, I will swat it away. He's there because, well I guess, because he fancies me. I'm not exactly breathless with desire, but a list is a list and therefore – it needs entries. So he stays. With one of his front teeth showing bigger than the rest, jutting halfway up his gum. With his thick-framed glasses that darken whenever the sun casts shadows over his even-toned, blunted oval of a face. Reuben has a plank-flat bottom and wears brown Crimplene trousers. A former Boy Scout, he's not ugly, but he's not what you could call a catch. Reuben does not know how to angle his arms and legs properly when he lounges on the low school wall. He's not yet safe in his own body. I wonder how he'll be about touching someone else's. But how can I ever know that kind of thing about someone without trying him out?

Another option is Yuan Chen. Last term, everyone at school kept saying he was my boyfriend because we were always together during break, but he's not really. He can seem sexy if I try. His Chinese father came over to teach our farmers how to grow paddy rice. Then he stayed and his wife eventually came over and they stayed some more. When our government got tired of Mao-style paddy farms, his parents started a restaurant called Green Bamboo where they cook a lot of white rice.

Last year, he asked my friend Remi and me over to his parents' restaurant as my birthday treat and he made sure we got a platterful of freshly fried spring rolls which are my favourite. I watched his lips form the words: 'Good spring rolls need pastry so thin you can see through it. The filling has to be cold so it doesn't stretch the pastry and make it tear.'

Maybe it was then that he started to creep into my conscious-ness as a Possible. He knows how to be careful.

Remi protested that those instructions were not clear enough. 'They never turn out right, even if I leave the stuff in the fridge overnight.'

He laughed, eyes bending up at the corners, his floppy black hair brushing his eyebrows.

'To cook,' he says, 'the oil has to be really, really hot so it singes brown almost as soon as it reaches the pan.'

I think he'd be gentle. When we were at the beach after Tunji's party, with me in my strappy dress, Yuan and I were leaning against his car as we waited for the others. It was quite dark as the moon was not yet up and stars pinpricked the sky's velvet. There was a bit of a breeze off the sea and when I said I was cold he took his sweat top off and put it around me. He tucked me in under his shoulder and it felt kind of cosy.

I don't want to wait for this falling-in-love business, or aim for passion, even though everyone everywhere – books, films, magazines – makes it seem like the ultimate. I want to get this sex thing over and done with so my life can move on. Some of my friends have done it – Amina and Mahmoud behind the school kitchens when we were thirteen and in the third form. She needed to go to the nurse for a spare uniform as stuff had leaked onto her skirt. I remember her walking funny all the way to the gate.

When we stand around after school waiting to be picked up, or sit tight in each other's bedrooms painting our nails, talk often turns to university and work, or . . . boys and men. Amina says sex can be mysterious or straightforward, it either makes you feel fantastic or is as simple as what dogs do. Her cheeks climb up her face, her deep dimples show as she talks. It seems as if she's defying life itself, as if the choice has been hers all along. She's able to brush off what my mother, and probably hers, might think. She's started to claim life in her own way.

7

Remi's found The One in Kojo. She doesn't want to go to university herself, but is willing to go with him when he starts medical school. They mess around but she says they might as well wait until they're married. That will be soon, and sex will be something to look forward to.

Moira also wants to wait for the right one, she won't do it until she's sure. She has a crush on Idris, who bounces on and off my list. When we've talked about him, she does that 'oooh, he's so cute' thing. I can see that Idris obviously has the experience. And everyone seems to like him. Moiras giggle and Aminas look him up and down. Remis ignore him. The shape of his back, his shoulders in his white school shirt as he walks away down a corridor catch my eye. I tend to keep very still inside, not wanting to let any smoochy type of longing jump free. Sometimes I ache to be noticed by him, for him to show he wants me. Yet at other times, I feel like I'd just be another pair of knickers in his drawer, taken simply because I was there.

And the largest mango in my pile? The biggest *bonga* on my stall? My best friend's father, Frederick Adams, forty-two years old with a pot-bellied future, a short full beard, hair closely trimmed to his head, and fingers that make my skin sing. Nothing much's happened yet, of course. Just one leaning-over-to-open-the-car-door touch. Just one let-me-introduce-this-youngster-to-Motown dance.

'I bet you youngsters don't know about this kind of music. Want to dance?' he'd said at my cousin Tunji's wedding. He touched my arms to show me the dance step. Even after he'd moved his fingers, I could feel where they'd been. He's on the list because I think he might teach me quickly. This is so obviously one of the things that will have to remain secret, be doubly hidden and buried from my mother (and Remi), with me having to pinch my words. But just the once with him might be enough.

8

It's almost as if I can see a list of names in my head, with passport-size photos alongside, each taken in a studio with a full glare of lights, so that as I peer into each picture, I can see the pimple above Reuben's eyebrow, notice that Yuan's eyes are set slightly too close together, linger over the pout in Idris's lips, observe the sheen on Frederick Adams's face. I can choose whether to put a tick, a question mark or an x against each name on my list. It's in my power, it's up to me.

My mother knocks on the door and enters with my birthday greeting. Behind her, breeze blocks filter the day's early sunshine. As a child, I've sometimes seen Ma thin with worry, when her ribs have poked out of her side like the ridges around the seeds in a tamarind pod. But as her school has become more successful, she's filled out more. The skin over her cheekbones is smooth and even-coloured. This I have inherited from her, along with a hairline that starts high up on her forehead. We look alike – we just don't think the same way.

'Ayodele, who would believe you're as old as eighteen?'

'Morning, Ma.'

'I'm just going to make you some *akara* for breakfast. I've sent Osman for some bread.'

As I sit up, part of the sheet covering my body slips to show half a boob and an entire nipple. Upstanding and free, the nipple looks like the eraser end of a wood-wrapped pencil when tickled by air. My mother's smile freezes into a half-frown. Displays of flesh in teenage females, especially her own daughters, are always a worrying sign, regardless of whether I am safe in bed at home or not. 'Cover yourself up' has greeted every excess shoulder, leg or chest exposure. 'You can't go around looking like a *chagga*.' A slutty whore. Today, her look does the job. As I pull the sheet up to cover myself, the smile returns. My mother firmly believes in cloaking one's body's treasures.

9

'I'll tell you when they're ready to eat,' she says.

As my mother closes the door, a memory slips in to sit alongside me and remind me of when her Good Behaviour Snippets began in earnest. It must have been when she was suddenly shocked into blood reality that I had left my childhood behind. I hadn't been at all amazed about my sudden thrust into womanhood, just plain disgusted by what followed.

I was not prepared for the red gush, at my very first dance at Amina's house. I had on my blue dress with the full skirt and tight waist. Slightly off-shoulder and specially tailored by Isatou's mother, in whose garage I had spent a couple of afternoons watching the tailor in order to hurry the dress along. At the party, I stood up and made my way into Amina's kitchen to ask for a drink. On the way back, I noticed a couple of fifth formers, who usually ignored me, whispering together and throwing a few looks my way. Soon after, Amina's mother appeared at my shoulder.

'Come with me, dear. Your dress is soiled, can I give you something to use?'

What did I know of blood then? There had been no pain, yet she said, 'The red splashes are a confirmation of you becoming a woman.'

She must have talked to my mother on the phone because Ma had a pack of sanitary towels ready when I got home.

'You know what to do now, don't you? Use these supermarket bags to throw away the used ones. Wrap them in two bags. You'll need to take them out to the bin with the heavy metal lid so the cats don't get to them.'

And what I was left with were these heavy things between my legs that chaffed the skin they rubbed against. And they smelt. My first party was over, and only my cousin Tunji had asked me to dance.

*

Soon, I'll be leaving home, no longer a child. Like everyone else who wants to go to university, I have to go abroad. My mother's headmistress salary doesn't go far – Ma can't afford to pay overseas fees, so I've applied for scholarships. The Senegalese government may pay my fees at the University of Dakar, or the British Council my place at the University of London. I cannot control where I'll end up studying, but at least I will have a say in something else today – the who, the where, the when.

As I try to drift back into sleep, the green baized door in the kitchen bangs shut, waking me up for sure. Ma starts her clatter in the kitchen, and plans are afoot for today's meal. I make my way towards her noise. She has a bowlful of *akara* mixture ready.

'I couldn't wait,' I say. 'I've come to help.'

The beans were soaked, peeled and pounded yesterday, so all I have to do is to drop teaspoonfuls of cream-coloured mixture into sizzlingly hot oil and watch them deepfry. My bean balls puff up well, get themselves russet-coloured without burning, as if they are keen for me to have a breakfast worthy of a birthday.

When Osman comes back with the bread, my *akara* is resting in a covered calabash on the side and the fried onion and pepper sauce is sputtering in a small saucepan. He stands outside the door, stiffly holding a batch of loaves wrapped in an old flour bag.

When we were little, he gave all of us pet names. Mine was after my favourite orange-coloured forest fruit, my twin sisters were Solom Solom and Saydame, after theirs. These were all fruits that were best bought up-country and we'd beg him before he went home to bring some back for us, rushing to him with a clutch of hastily grabbed dalasi notes in our hands. 'I want fourteen,' I might say, 'so I can eat one for every day of the Christmas school holiday.' Taiwo would ask for her *solom soloms* unpeeled, Kainde would ask him to remember to find the biggest, creamiest-tasting yellow *saydames*. 'And don't forget,' my sisters would chorus, 'bring us two bags each.' And Osman would nod and tickle us under our chins and arms, and we would wriggle and squeal.

He's become afraid of me. He no longer jokes or calls me Little Cabadombo.

When I open the door, I stare at his face, more out of curiosity than anything else. His eyes are focused on my feet. When I glance down, all I can see is a line of brown sugar ants following a crack in the cement pavement, heading for some nest buried underneath. '*Jere jaiffe*,' I say as I reach for the loaves. I take longer than I need to, touching his fingers and easing the bag out of his hands. I know I have this ability to make some men uncomfortable looking at me. And it's getting stronger. I have sometimes caught thick stares – the baobab juice kind, sticky and textured – that flick away the moment I turn to face them. Even from Osman.

Osman's always done a bit of the gardening, tending the tiny kitchen plot behind our L-shaped house, trimming the ever-sprouting casuarina hedge that shields us from the street, and supervising the sometimes unwieldy branches under which we had doll picnics and twirled on rope swings.

Osman used to help us climb mango trees, or catch avocados that we threw down from the glossy-leaved trees in the back garden. He used to help us light fires in charcoal burners so we could roast maize or bake groundnuts in their shells. If we were really dirty from playing in the muddy puddles outside the gate during the rainy season, he'd hose us down after we stripped to our knickers, shivering as we stood on the driveway, waiting until we could dash up to the front door and be tutted at by Nimsatu, the househelp, for bringing in grit with our wet feet.

The last time Osman helped us was after we'd been dancing in a July downpour, sheets of grey pelting our bodies. As was usual at the time, with Ma struggling to run her nursery school, we were at home under Nimsatu's care. I knew Ma had to work hard because we didn't have a father so I took charge whenever I could. I phoned Ma to tell her what she needed to buy on her way home, and sorted out squabbles between my sisters when twinship proved too hard for them to handle.

Osman asked us to leave our wet things outside. My T-shirt got stuck as I tried to pull it over my head so I walked towards Osman for help. He'd done the same for my sisters. But as the neckband squeezed my ears tight and I bowed my head to make it easier to yank it off, my mother drove in through the gate. I hardly had any breasts then, they were barely the size of a *mampatang*. With one sour look in my direction, my mother barked at me, 'Get inside at once!' And to Osman, 'Wait here, I need to speak to you.' She'd followed me into the house, 'You are growing up now, and you're no longer a little girl.' And she'd sent me off to have a proper shower.

I talk to Osman in a different way now. Today I tell him, 'I'm going out tonight. Taiwo and Kainde will be at the cinema with some friends. My mother wants you to come to work early, before it gets dark so there'll be someone at the gate.'

Then I turn into the kitchen with the bread resting against my chest spreading a soft warmth. I reach for a knife and slice a chunk off one of the loaves. I cut through the soft vertical vein in its side, then slobber in some onion sauce before stuffing in the crispy bean balls.

Ma flaps her way into the kitchen to check on her *Satiday soup*, into which she's flung dried *kuta* from the deep Atlantic mixed with tripe and rump steak from the cows at Mr Pratt's farm up the road. Later she'll add some chopped greens from our backyard and the okra I bought at the market yesterday. The okra are in a huge bowl of water next to a chopping board and as she starts to get them ready she says, 'You should have chosen larger ones.

These tiny little ones you bought will take ages to top, tail and chop.'

I hate market errands.

The only part I enjoy in making the soup is when I get to melt the oil, so I ask, 'Can I do the palm oil now?'

'Yes, you can. But you do need to concentrate a bit more on how you do it. Soup's not just about palm oil. It's about all the ingredients. Unless you learn to get the details right, you'll never be able to make proper food in your own house.'

I go outside to collect the tin. The oil, usually stilled into a waxy orange when stored, has been left outside in a sun bright enough to turn the edges soft and red. I use a large metal scoop to ladle out eight spoonfuls and drop them into the furiously churning pot with the beginnings: chunks of meat mixed with *peppeh en yabbas*, raw chillies and onions which my ma has ground in our wooden mortar. As there is so much water in the pot, the oil separates into swirls of orange, as if hesitant about mingling with what's already in there.

Ma is proud of her cooking. Depending on the type of soup she intends to make, she can add various enhancements – crushed *egusi* seeds, fermented tamarind, or a large grey segment of crystallised soda. She would be surprised to find out I've paid any attention at all to what she tells me: 'When I make *egusi* soup, I like to mix it with a bit of green. Some of your grandmother's Yoruba friends used to make it with no greens but I think that looks too coarse. *Egusi* needs balance.'

Or, to explain the mysteries of adding the right touch of okra, she says, 'To stop the okra from cutting in the soup, I'm going to add a largish chunk of *lubi*. I know your aunt in America uses bicarbonate of soda but I think her soup lacks depth. Flavour is what brings your cousin Tunji round here on Saturdays.'

Her secret, she says, is letting the soup come into its own. The meat has to soften, the *egusi* has to blend, the oil has to turn. You simply cannot hurry it along.

My mother has tried to teach me what she knows about managing men. I guess being deserted twice by the same man in one life has limited her experience. She never told me my father ran off with his secretary when I was four (and my sisters were two), came back home with his tail curled in regret and promptly died a year later, of a stomach tumour. I twisted the truth out of Aunt K a few years ago.

Ma does say, 'All men have two faces – the one they show you before they get what they want. This first face is attentive and caring. Then the coarse settles in and that's the face that stays for the rest of the time you know them.'

She tells us marriage is a battle. 'You have to find some way of storing up your kindness in an armoured case. Otherwise your man will leak you dry and you'll find you have none left – not even enough for your children.'

I don't remember my father. I used to make things up about him when I was little. That he would hear from the ground whenever I fell down, thinned my skin and then squeezed beads of blood out to show the hurt. Sometimes I dreamt he was sitting next to me as I slept, telling me about something that happened in heaven. Now, I wonder how life would have been different for us if he hadn't died. My friends' fathers are hardly ever at home, pre-ferring the company of their beer buddies. Some of my mother's friends have husbands with parallel unacknowledged families, chockful of stepchildren who everyone knows about but who are ignored in public.

I'm outside, tending to a freshly lit charcoal stove, when Remi's father drops her off. My mother is hovering, distracted from dismantling a huge chunk of smoked fish, by the noise of the car. He says, '*Unakusheh*.' You're hard at work, well done, keep it up.

And with a few well-placed how-dos and goodbyes, Frederick Adams, the number 4 on my list, drives off in a cloud of Peugeot-disturbed dust. Leaving his daughter, my best friend, behind to discuss our plans for tonight.

I holler to my sisters, 'My jobs are done – the charcoal is lit.' It's their turn to see to the cooking of the rice as part of their 'training'. Hard work, elbow grease and general busyness are advised to discourage loose thoughts. And also to help to prepare the female teenager for a well-kept house of her own one day. I do my big sister thing and complain to Remi, 'They are probably in the bathroom again, messing around with *my* makeup.'

Tonight Remi, Amina, Moira and I will celebrate my birthday at the newest disco in town. I didn't want a home party so we've organised this between us instead, and invited some of our friends. Remi is styling my hair in the garden when my mother's childhood friend, who we call Aunt K, short for Kiki, short for Katherine, arrives. Her noisiness is announced at the iron gate where, instead of knocking or, more sensibly, simply swinging the unlocked door open, she shouts aloud, 'Kong kong kong,' her imitation of door knocking. I don't understand how she's stayed friends with my mother. They are as different as Kingston's Chalk (boxed and imported from England) from Anchor Cheddar Cheese (tinned and shipped from New Zealand). Aunt K takes pride in 'not having let herself go'. She regularly loiters around young people, 'sucking up their spirit' and 'keeping her mind young'. She knows what music we like and listen to, whereas my mother's tastes stopped with Jim Reeves, who tragically died in an aeroplane accident, 'too young, too young – too tragic, too tragic'. From the newest Senegalese *pachanga* to the haHAhaHA of

'Staying Alive', Aunt K dances with her arms raised, adding some nifty footwork as she twirls her sturdy rectangular body around.

Characteristically, she walks up to us with a sway in her hips. 'This is me at the very end of my prime. Can you imagine what I could do with a young body?'

She makes a shape with her hands, starting from an imaginary bust, palms placed slightly upwards and flat, outlining down to a thin waist, then a bulge of curvaceous hip before narrowing again. In reality, Aunt K is wide-bosomed and big-bottomed, representing herself in a new character symbol for some odd European language, her own compacted percentage sign, a half-reflected capital B.

'Here you are,' she says to me as she bends down to kiss my cheek. 'Happy birthday.' She hands me an envelope. 'I didn't know what to get you, and decided you'd probably like to choose something yourself.' I open it to peek. I've got a wad of money to spend.

'Thank you. Hochiemy's got some new things in, I'll go and have a look,' I say.

'So. Where are you going tonight?'

'Ocean, the new disco on the cliff by the junction.'

'Ah, young people, this is a good time of your lives. Staying out late. Going dancing. You know of course that I used to COM-MAND the floor,' she continues.

We know the routine now and mimic the perfect body shape with our hands, and shout out 'COMMAND' when she pauses for effect.

She loiters at our home salon, curious to know what we are up to. She watches us for a minute before launching into options for my hairdo.

'How about hot-tonged curls at the sides with a middle parting – that would suit your face,' she says, and pulls out some of the

17

pins Remi has just spent an hour putting in, yanking some of my hair in her enthusiasm. I yelp.

'Hmm,' she goes. 'Or you can make some ringlets here.'

Now she jabs at the back of my head. 'I can see them dripping down if you hold here like *this*.' She scoops all the hair off my face now, with a 'Got any hair slides?'

She pauses, weighing our silence.

'No?'

We shake our heads.

'Well then, what shoes are you wearing?'

When I asked my mother whether I could go to that first dance at Amina's where I revealed I was a woman while still a child, Aunt K had put in a word for me. She'd said to my mother, '*Bo*, Millie, you have to leave young people to find out for themselves what life is about. We can't always be watching, always advising.' My mother had been taut with indecision. 'I don't know what kind of people will be there. She wants to stay out until *ten* o'clock.' But Aunt K had worked out the logistics, who I could go with, who would bring me home. Among my mother's circle of friends, she is someone who can be relied on.

Out in the garden, the sun cools into evening. The breeze off the sea starts to wiggle the leaves of the mango tree above our heads. We gather up our things and move inside for the final stage of preparations. I'm not very good with eyeliner yet, the pencil drifts in my hand and I never seem to be able to do the upper eyelid. Remi's better at it so she does mine for me, making my eyes look mysterious and grownup. We decide that the false eyelashes Aunt K brought back from America look ridiculous and cannot be left on. Remi laughs, 'All right for pop stars who need to define their eyes, but not when people will be looking at you up close.'

'Yes,' I reply, 'ordinary people like us have to use what we've got as well as we can.'

The phone rings and I dash to the living room to answer it. It's my sisters' friend, saying they're on their way over for the cinema pickup. When I turn around, I see Osman watching me through the side door. Without sunlight to illuminate his face, and the distance of a wall and glass between us, he's mostly shadow. He does not move.

I'm wearing my pink bra with lacy edges and a sheer pink slip. I can feel the power of my body, the twang it has been creating from when my *mampatang*-sized breasts expanded to the size where I can push them up with this special bra. There's a hint of a shadow on my chest. I guess that it both scares and pulls men. I think it might be possible to learn how to call the ones I want. When I want. Should Idris come off my list and Osman come on it?

I have to think practical. I need to be sure I can make my plan work. I know both Yuan and Reuben will be borrowing cars from their parents so that should be relatively easy. I've had to think harder about the Frederick Adams option. Remi's negotiated a pickup at one. Her father said, 'I want to make sure you get home without getting yourselves into trouble.' I will have to say I want to pick up my sports bag and kit from Remi's room so I can start to keep my new eighteen-year-old promise to stay fit. If that sounds too lame, it'll have to do. I don't have any other ideas.

My life needn't unroll in the way my mother's did. None of her friends seem to have ended up with the version of man they originally wanted, judging from their shared complaints. They suffer the poor specimen they landed with, as if none of them had figured out that their bodies could be wielded without leaving it all to chance. Clearly, they never saw that in the midst of trying to find out who they could become, they could aim beyond what

19

they saw around them. They were satisfied with the usual end point of women, the finale of man-searching: a rubbing-along marriage or, at best, a partner you could occasionally talk to about the children. I want different.

I turn away and head back to my bedroom to put on my clothes. Remi looks stunning in a tight-fitting shift dress with tiny little silver sequins all over, making her seem all shimmery. She's small and compact with good curves – bum and boobs all perfectly proportioned. She's jolly, smiles a lot, everyone likes her – from great-grandfathers to children. I put on my clingy velvet trousers over legs I think are a bit too thin, then ease my sheer top over my underdeveloped chest. As I twirl around I catch my eyes in the mirror. Serious, large, dark-rimmed. Almost overpowering my face, which today co-operates with the smooth flicked bob that Remi styled.

We use the corridor as our catwalk. Taiwo and Kainde sit with their backs to my door and knees drawn up close to their chests.

Kainde says, 'Can I borrow that top when we go to the fifth-form dance?'

Taiwo says, 'How do you know Ma will let us go?'

I tell them going out at night is a privilege to fight for. 'I was fifteen before Ma let me go to my first dance.'

Kainde says, 'We'll be fifteen in a couple of months. Aunt K said she'll talk to Ma.'

'Well then you'll have to wait and see,' I say. 'Check this out.'

Remi and I lengthen our strides and put some sway in our walk. Our audience watches and claps.

I am ready and waiting for Remi to finish her final touches in the bathroom. I lie back on my bed, forming support for my head with my hands to protect my hair, my elbows sticking out.

Remi already has a proper boyfriend, and is sure she wants to get married soon and run her own household. She can cook and clean, and does not seem to mind doing either. We've known each other since we began stealing cashews together when we were six. She's always loved the drippy juicy part, which stained our clothes unless we ate with care. I liked the planning part, the thinking through of probable exit routes from newly discovered cashew tree sites. She knows pretty much everything about me. Yet in this, we are different. I'm ready now. I long to . . . lose something I've always felt was valuable, and exchange it for . . . well, I'm not quite sure exactly, but for something else. Not with any dour, mysterious, handsome men who need to be won over by my charm. Instead, I have to choose from a ragtag of misaligned teeth, pot bellies, turn-the-best-side-for-the-photographer kind of men-boys. I don't need them to promise commitment or anything, I just need someone to show me It. And move me from where I am now to the other side of knowing.

My eyes play on the ceiling. I find myself picking out patterns, reading the ceiling just as we used to when my sisters and I were little. My ceiling's boards have been repainted white, but rainwater, eager to leave behind a memory of itself, has sploshed new stains on it. I can see a bra with enormous cups and wriggling straps. Also a leg, with well-toned thigh, bent at the knee, lying open, suggesting the other leg is also flung sideways, welcoming entry. A mouth in a grimace. An eye wide open in shock. All my fears, worries, traipsing across my ceiling, watching me watch them.

A life beginning has many paths before it; but older people – women like my mother – they can only see the one path that brought their lives to the now. Cats on my shoulder. I can choose to be the hunter or the lion. What will my story be?

STORY ONE

Reuben

2

Choice

The sudden change from the warmth of bodies, noise and gaiety to a brash ocean wind squeezes my skin closer to me. I rub my hands over my arms, flattening the landscape of hair-tipped bobbles, only to have them peek up again in protest at the cold. My toes cling to each other as I crunch my way past the dread-topped coconut palms, past a few occupied benches shrouded in capsules of shadow. The bathrooms are at the back of the club.

A girl is leaning against the row of sinks. Her cigarette is tucked into a holder and her hair is pulled back off a face you would want to look at again. She drags her eyelids down and, keeping them closed, turns her back to me. Smoke wisps upwards and she says clearly, to the occupants of the first cubicle, 'You'd better hurry up in there. Someone's come in.'

I had started the beginnings of a smile but now it's shrinking. What it would have been is paused and reversed, so I can regain my face, keep it to myself, carry myself past her to a cubicle at the far end of the room. I walk past tiny scuffles, and little *unhs*.

The door won't shut. My pee seems to come out all in a rush, too quick, too loud. When I open the tap, water gushes out and splashes onto my dress. I look at the girl out of the edge of my eye. She has not moved. The cigarette is almost at the filter. The grunting has not stopped.

Outside, one of the capsules of shadow splits into two. I cannot see who it is at first. Then the girl says, 'It's getting a bit cold. Let's go back in.'

Remi's voice.

He says, 'Let's sit out here for a bit longer. I'll keep you warm. Stay close.'

By the time I walk past them, they are locked into each other again, like a self-involved octopus. They do not notice me.

Back in the club, I cannot see anyone I know. I move into the shaded dark, edging along the wall, past clumps of people. A few scattered pairs have parts of their bodies touching. The song changes and I hear Amina's whoop as she drags Yuan to the dance floor. It's not a tune that needs close contact.

Oh. I'm going to Barbados.
Oh. Going to see my girlfriend.

She flings her arms around Yuan's neck, pulls his head down, and kisses him on the lips. He's not pulling back. He's not struggling. They stay intertwined for a long time. My heart squeezes itself tight and my eyes drum. Sadness, anger, bitterness, rage, all flash by, strobing with the disco lights – black, shiny, acid blue, blood red. Using my hands behind me as a guide, I find the rough wall to lean on, to watch from.

I attract the attention of a few beer-stuffed young men, who detach themselves from their gang only to stumble towards me and my frosty cracked smile, and then stumble back towards a raucous re-welcome into their group.

The song ends. Amina drags Yuan off, leading him by the hand. Why? She can choose whoever she wants. Surely she must know. Why? He's told me before he doesn't fancy Amina. And today of all days!

I know what I have to do today. I will choose and I will do it.

Reuben can drive. I direct him all the way. Will you take me home? Why don't you stop here for a bit? Shall we move to the back seat? I have the good sense to take out the condom in my disco bag.

I sleep through much of the next day, getting up late in the afternoon to have a second shower. I think about taking a walk, but when I go outside, Osman is sitting there on his little stool, with his radio pressed to his ear. The newsreader is announcing in Wolof, 'The president will be leaving soon for the second leg of his meet-the-people tour. He will be visiting Mansakonko . . .'

'*Nanga deff*,' I say as I walk past him towards the gate.

'*Jama rek*,' he replies.

I catch his scent as I walk past – it's the roughness of old palm wine ground into stale, unfiltered cigarettes. Reuben's had been straight out of a bottle. Outside the gate, the idea of trudging through the dust, up to the shop for a Coke and a breath of fresh air does not appeal any more. I turn around and go back to my room.

When Reuben rings, I don't want to speak to him. I don't want to speak to Yuan or Amina either. They leave messages with my sister Kainde:

Ring Reuben when you get out of bed. He will be at home.

Yuan rang to say he looked for you last night and that Amina told him you'd left. He waited for you anyway until they closed the disco, in case you came back.

Amina says Yuan was looking for you everywhere yesterday. She left him at the party, waiting for you because he wanted to take you home. She says you should ring her back immediately.

Remi rings but does not leave a message.

While the phone rings and Kainde collects my messages, I stay in my bedroom. The curtains are still flowery blue. The walls are still yellow. And the stupid sun is still washing the air with heat.

'What's wrong?' asks my mother the next morning.
  'Just tired,' I reply.
  'What's up with you?' says Taiwo.
  'Mind your own business,' I answer.
  Kainde continues to write down my messages. She knocks with a murmur of explanation, and then shoves pieces of paper under the door.
  'Thank you,' I reply to each one.

I feel empty. Reuben has not brought knowledge.

Remi's reaction is what I would have expected.
  'Lord have mercy! With Reuben!'
  She shakes her head, covers her eyes with one hand. She opens her mouth, closes it again. She holds her chin with her left hand to ponder, and then asks, 'What was it like?'

28

I twist my mouth in response. Yes. With Reuben.

'When my dad came to pick me up, he thought you'd want a lift. He wondered who you went home with. And whether your mother knew.'

'So what did you say to him?'

'That I didn't know.' She pauses and scratches her nose. 'But I thought Yuan was the one. How on earth did you end up with . . .?'

She shuts up when she sees my face.

On one of the days when I spend more of my time in my bed than anywhere else, Aunt K comes around. I hear her way down the corridor, talking to Kainde.

'*Watin do am?* What's wrong with her? Boy trouble? You say *boy?* Let me go talk with her.'

Her footsteps accompany her comments to Kainde. 'There are certain things in life you shouldn't hurry along. Look at Aunty Beedi – it wasn't until she was in her fifties that she found someone to settle down with. That's the kind of thing that's enough to make anyone live long. Look at her, she's just like a young girl now. Her face is fresh, she's always giggling when I meet her out shopping.'

She stops outside my door. '*Which borbor dis?* Which boy? You don't know? She didn't say? You're her sister – you should talk to her. I won't always be around, you know.' She raps on my door, three sharp ones and says, '*Comut dooyah*. Open up. I have something to say to you. Might as well let me in now, or I'll shout it out in the corridor. Right here where I'm standing.'

I get up to let her in. My door has been locked, key-locked, all day.

After Aunt K leaves, my mother delivers two weak taps on my door.

29

'Yes, Ma,' my dry throat scrapes out in answer.

She enters my room and says, 'I heard Kiki in the corridor. About you having boy trouble. I've talked to you about this kind of thing before.' Her voice sounds odd, a bit higher in pitch than usual. Ma breathes deep at the end of her sentence.

'I'm OK. It was just Kainde telling tales.'

'So there's nothing I should worry about? Nothing I should know?'

'No, Ma, nothing.'

'Don't forget what I've told you.'

'I know, Ma, men are only after one thing.'

'That's right. And when they get it, they don't stay.'

At the door, she grabs the handle. She goes out but her footsteps do not go away. How can she ever begin to understand what it's like inside me? I scowl at the shadow of her legs falling in two thick lines on the little crack of air under my door. She stands there as I listen to her listening for me.

Amina barges into my bedroom the next day. 'Why didn't you ring me back?'

Her arms move to rest on her hips, akimbo. I know what she's staring at. My hair is sticking up on end. My eyes are puffy and my cheeks ashed grey. I am in a pair of tartan flannel pyjamas.

'What's up with you? Yuan's going stirfry crazy. And here you are looking all rough.'

'You're good friends now, are you?'

'We talk. He's pretty cool.'

'I saw you kiss him at the disco.'

'Oh. Is that what this is all about then?'

Her raised eyebrows. Her scrunched-up face with the questioning look. Her you-stupid-girl shake of her head. 'I know you like him. There are lots of men and boys out there. I don't need Yuan.'

I burst into tears.

'Look, you know I fool around. I kissed him on a dare, that's all. It means nothing.' Amina throws herself onto the end of my bed, and leans on one elbow watching me sob myself into my pillow. 'Pull yourself together. It's not the end of the world you know.'

Three days later, I start to come out of my room more often to face the world with its bright shining sun. Reuben calls on a day I'm closest to the phone and I pick up.

'Ha-hallo. That sounds like you, Ayodele,' he starts.

'Yes, it is.'

'I've been phoning . . .'

'And I've got the messages.'

'Ah I wondered whether you'd like to go for a *charwarma* or something?'

'Not today, thanks.'

'Perhaps another time?'

'Perhaps.'

By Thursday the following week, my head is in a twist. I chose the guy I didn't want, and am now ignoring the one I did want. I feel stupid.

We are about to go for our end-of-year, end-of-school picnic party. This is our very last time together as a class. I am late on purpose, having asked Amina and Remi to save me a seat. Although we were all allowed to bring one guest, most of us haven't bothered. Remi has invited Kojo, her boyfriend, and he will be driving up to meet us later.

Reuben finds me as soon as I arrive and comes up to grin and mumble a few words.

'You're looking nice,' he says, but his eyes do not quite know where to look on my body. They jump from my face to my boobs, then my feet. He stares at my leather flipflops while I think up an answer.

'Thank you' is the best I can do.

His eyes flicker back up to mine and then stare past my right ear towards the main school entrance, where our rowdy, chattering friends wait. 'Which bus are you going in?'

'That one. With Remi and Amina.'

His hands find his pockets. 'Just wondered, whether. Um. You'd like us to sit together?'

'Thanks but the others are waiting for me.'

His eyes shift past my face to a spot beyond my left ear. 'See you then.'

Most of us are wearing jeans, khaki trousers or shorts. Amina's version of our teenage uniform is tight, tight, dark, dark drainpipe jeans with a loose T-shirt screaming 'babe'. I see her clambering into the bus, squealing about something or other, as she usually does.

We are going to a tiny village up past Pirang. Mrs Foon, one of our teachers, has relatives who own a farm by the river. The bus drivers are waiting for their final instructions. Everyone is trying to find someone they'd like to sit next to. Stragglers jostle for improved bus seats. An hour later, we're crammed into the two buses. They ease out through the front gate, past COAST HIGH SCHOOL written out in red china grass against a patchy bit of lawn, onto the road to start our journey. We're taking everything we need for our party. There are plastic sacks of ice stuffed into metal bins for our drinks. A couple of car batteries to power the music and small speakers. Half a tin drum, cut lengthways, that will be our BBQ. Bags of charcoal. Lots of crates of soft drinks with a few stray ones of Julbrew beer – our teachers have acknowledged that we are, after all, now officially Grown Up. We have cane mats and *malans* to spread out on the ground. There are vats of seasoned chicken, and half a sheep, potatoes, plantains, baskets of mangoes, and drifts of lettuce leaves.

Moira, Remi and Yuan got into the bus early, and picked the best spot – the row of five seats in the back.

I sit next to Amina, who declares, 'Could not find anyone young enough to invite who wasn't coming already, so I came on my own.'

Remi says, 'Why am I not surprised?'

'Yeah,' Yuan says, 'you mix in different circles, Amina.'

'And those friends won't want to come to a boring sixth-form party,' Moira adds.

I know Yuan senses something is different about me. He leaves his eyes on my mouth when he looks at me. I find I cannot keep my eyes on his whenever they meet.

We drive past groyned beaches and sleepy casuarinas, past huddles of stalls by the roadside at Serrekunda, and newly built Amadiya mosques. The road is fine until we get past Brikama, when it becomes dusty tarmac with many generous potholes, accompanied by two parallel lanes of laterite carved out on either side by weary drivers. Rain-worked ravines hurry across the road. The bus tilts over each bump.

There's talk of university, some drifting towards us at the back before being snatched away by wind through the open windows.

'I've had enough of studying,' says Remi. 'Kojo will have to earn all the money.'

'So he becomes a doctor and you become a wife?' asks Amina.

'Any problem with that?' Remi asks, her voice sharp.

Moira sighs and asks, 'And you, Yuan, what will you do?'

'I've applied to a couple of universities in America to please my parents, but as I keep telling them, Europe will be a lot closer. I'd rather go to England.'

'I know I won't be able to go to England without a scholarship, even if I get the university place,' I say.

'All this England, England. Why not try further afield? I want to go somewhere where no one else is going, like Italy or Singapore,' says Amina.

'I want to work, start earning some real money,' says Moira.

'I wonder where we'll all end up,' I say.

Elsewhere on the bus, there are occasional bouts of laughter, raucous shouts across the aisle. 'Pipe down,' says Mrs Foon, 'you're almost grownups.'

We turn to stare out of the back windscreen. An outrider in a security service uniform speeds towards us flashing blue. His motorbike steadily gains on us, stirring up a blanket of red dust. It appears he wants us to get off the makeshift laterite road, and stop on the potholed tarmac. The driver turns the engine off in protest.

The outrider pulls up next to the driver. 'Get off the road, the president's coming.'

'I'm already off it, so he can stay in the middle.'

'Don't be cheeky. The president needs a smooth ride. Get back on the tarmac.'

'That's not so easy here – look at that huge hump at the side.'

'Get off soon, and show proper respect. Or the next outrider will make sure you're sorry.'

We crowd on the driver's side of the bus, gawping at the leather-booted man in a moonscape helmet.

Amina stands up on her seat, her tight-packed rounded bum hovering north of Yuan's head. She yells out of the window, 'Is Mr Bojang in the car with the president?'

The outrider turns to her and replies, 'What's it to you?' before gunning his engine and giving us a blast of processed petrol.

'How do you know a Mr Bojang, in with the president?' Yuan asks.

'I get around.'

It doesn't take long to squeeze the story out of her.

'I met him at Landing's a couple of months ago. He happens to like schoolgirls.' She puts on her cheeky grin and her eyes spray sparks of merriment. 'He thinks his power and money will buy him anyone.'

'But you showed him otherwise, right?'

'You bet. Men are so stupid – not you, Yuan, you are perfect. They think a flash of dalasi and a flag with the president's seal are all it takes to sniff a girl's underwear.'

'You should be careful. What if he'd turned nasty?'

'Nasty? In a place as public as Landing's? No chance. I teased him a bit, let him buy me a drink and then went off to close-dance with someone else. Soon enough, some skinny girls were on to him. They looked young, so I think they diverted his attention from me.'

'All these stories, Amina!'

'I bet you have a few of your own. Go on, tell.'

'I'm sure our lives will never be as exciting as yours,' says Yuan, looking at me.

We have arrived at the farm, and hauled our communal picnic into the shade of an enormous mango tree, with huge glossy leaves and coarse-thighed buttresses off its trunk. Remi and Moira start to spread out mats and pillows, trays and cups.

A few fishermen are offering boat rides off a shaky-looking jetty – built of planks made from the insides of coconut palm, sodden with brackish water. Tongues of river lick the sides of the canoes, hollowed-out trunks that can take three or perhaps four slim people at a time. Amina and Yuan dare me to join them. We leave the other two to the unpacking.

The boat trip itself is without incident. The fisherman uses a long pole to ease us away from the bank. Stretches of bare mangrove roots above the surface of the water breathe in air without a shudder. Once we are in the little tributary, with greenery tight on both sides, voices from our picnic site get rubbed away by our distance. All we can hear are bird noises. Clusters of river oysters have crusted onto the mangrove. The fisherman splashes his paddle past a group of women up to their waists in water. They wield large blades, prising the oysters off with hands thickened from years of doing the same thing.

Even Amina falls silent, letting her hand trail through the water.

'Watch out, it might be sweet enough for crocodiles,' Yuan says to her.

'Don't be silly,' she replies, but she takes her hand out, sprinkling the river water at Yuan.

She makes it all look so easy, this freedom around boys, this mucking about.

When we get back to the jetty, the others get out first as they are nearer the front. When I stand up, the canoe suddenly tips to one side.

'*Togall*!' shouts the boatman.

'Move your weight!' yells Yuan.

Do I sit, stand, move or keep still? In the seconds it takes me to decide I don't quite know what to do, the boat loses its balance under me. I fall backwards, away from the jetty, into deep water. It is thickly brown. I cannot feel which way is up. I cannot see the bubbles I blow out. I thrash about at first, and manage to bring my head above water, but when I open my mouth, all it seems to do is swallow. I know I can swim, but it takes a full sharp-edged minute before I can convince my body it needs to let the water carry it. Then my foot touches something hard and slimy. A scream boils free from my body. My arms start to punch the water again, my feet kicking.

'Try to get to the boat,' instructs Yuan.

I see the long shape of the boat's bottom alongside me. Relief swamps the fear. The boatman, who was also flung into the river, appears next to me. My legs kick the water and my arms find a stroke. The jetty comes closer.

They help me out – Yuan and Amina each claiming an arm while the boatman tries to boost my feet with his hands.

I sit in a pair of borrowed *malans* all afternoon, one tied round my waist as a skirt, the other in a halter top. My clothes, which Remi wrings out, are lying on a nearby bush, drying in the sun.

Mangrove roots in the river can feel like the skin of crocodiles.

We stay in our tight little group, lounging in the shade. Mrs Foon waves a hand. Reuben walks by several times on his own, making a track to and from the jetty. Kojo eventually arrives in his father's old snub-nosed Peugeot 504, his exhaust giving a little fart when he turns off the engine. He walks towards us.

'Here he is,' Remi announces, 'our ride home.'

Yuan greets him with 'Hey man, you've missed all the action.'

'What action? Tell me more, but first get me something to drink. That road's a killer.'

Moira says, 'Ayodele got soaked.' Everyone piles in to elaborate.

Yuan concludes, 'She looks calm, don't you think, for someone recently rescued from being crocodile food.' Their heads all swivel round to look at me.

The barbecue tin drum is now hissing with mounds of oysters

piled on the ash-rimmed coals. I stand up to make a pretend curt-sey. 'I'll get us some river food to celebrate my resurrection.'

Armed with a tin enamelled bowl piled with a mountain of barbecued oysters, I make my way back to the group, only to find they are still discussing the intricacies of how I lost my balance – how I looked flailing about in the water, my swimming technique, and my final last lunge towards the jetty. Fuelled by the empty green bottles beside them, Amina and Yuan are miming my actions, as if scripted.

'Why don't you talk about something else for a while? How come Amina knows someone who works with the president, for example?'

'That's not half as interesting as falling into a river when there's a perfectly good jetty to get off onto,' protests Amina.

'Good point, Ayodele,' says Yuan. He shakes his index finger at Amina. 'Girls like you should leave men like that alone.'

'Why?'

'Go on, someone, fill me in,' says Kojo.

With relief, I summarise. 'On the way here, an outrider ordered us off the road. As he drove off, Amina asked about a certain Mr Bojang. Then she told us that she'd met him at some club. Which is worse? That or swimming with crocodiles?'

'Some of the men in this government are absolute bastards,' Kojo says.

Amina tries to clear her name. 'Hey, I only tried to pass on a hello to someone who would not remember me. It was a joke.'

'Do you know there's rumours of a Mr Bojang who tells doctors what to put on death certificates?'

We all freeze, as in how we used to when small and playing musical chairs.

Amina breaks into the disquiet. 'Like I said, I've only met him the once. Don't take me too seriously. It was only a joke.'

Kojo has the last word. 'Men like that cannot be joked around with.'

The early bus is ready to leave. I notice Reuben shuffling near the door, looking around with his hands in his pockets, shoulders hunched. When I think he might notice me looking at him, I turn away and reach for my bottle of beer.

The moon settles into the night. What breeze there is is muddied by the large mango trees standing in its way. We are leaving later with Kojo. Amina is given the chore of explaining our plans to the teachers supervising the tidy-up in preparation for the second departure. We help to spill hot coals and scatter them onto sun-hardened laterite. Empty bottles clink together as they are put back into the crates and loaded onto the bus. We commandeer a few bottles from the vats of cold water before the dustbins are emptied and the plastic bags of our litter loaded in. When all is done, the last bus starts up. We allow the quiet to hang over the trundle of the engine as it turns out of the gate.

The noises change. The bird sounds are fewer, longer, lower.

'What about snakes?' says Amina, her voice tangled and squeaky.

We burst into delighted laughter. And the laughter and lightness carry the rest of the evening.

Eventually I say, 'Should we go now?'

Yuan replies, 'Don't want to.'

'Should we stay till morning then?'

Amina echoes, 'Don't want to.'

We knot ourselves into a drift of conversations, starting and ebbing. University crops up again. And what we intend to do with

39

our lives. We talk about the moon, about whether mermaids will come this far up the river, about crocodiles and oysters. The night is stretching itself thin, with no one wanting to break up the easy company until the sky starts to lighten, and we agree that yes, indeed, it is morning after all.

3

Heartbreak

Our Sunday evening descends into the bitter dark that comes with the clocks being turned back. Trails of summer had been left in the autumn days when leaves gusted off the trees. Now, even those occasional days have been shut away with cheap time wizardry. We have turned up the thermostat to compensate for the drizzle-drenched winds outside. Six months hasn't been long enough to get me used to the inconsistency of English weather. It's been long enough to help me shed the disappointment of Reuben – who I chose on a whim only to find myself in a muddy pool of self-pity. Sometimes, when I think of what he would have expected of me – I shudder. Me, to declare him as my boyfriend and allow him to claw my body. And to drift towards marriage with thorough approval from both families, having achieved the rare magic: '*Krio titi marraid Krio boy*.' Thank goodness I could leave.

My Uncle Sola is out. He's been gone since he left earlyish this morning in search of the Sunday papers. We did not wait for him to come back and eat with us. Aunt Abi has kept a portion of his food warming in the oven on low.

There is a lingering smell of burnt oil and braised fish. Between us, a mound of fish *mbahal* has disappeared along with eight cobs of maize and a bowl of salad doused in vinaigrette. My cousins Tunde, Ade and Olu have done their chores – the dishes are washed, wiped and put away. We have arranged ourselves in armchairs in the living room, ready for the next part of the evening. Aunt Abi, their mother, is in the kitchen, preparing a tray of tea.

Tunde flicks through the TV channels, and we pause on a football result. The commentator is interviewing a happy fan at the end of the most marvellous match of the season so far.

'Grea' innit? They are goin' righ' up there. Top of the league maiy.'

Aunt Abi comes in with her flowery tea tray.

'Just watch them talk. Who could guess they're speaking their mother tongue? They mangle the poor language every day.'

She sets the tea tray down on the low table in the middle of the room. The teapot is encased in a matching cosy.

Olu picks up his cue and goes on his knees in front of the table, ready to pour. Cups chink onto their saucers. Milk. Honey-coloured tea. Crystals of white rinsed sugar.

'Why don't you try to find us something that we can all watch together, as a family?' Aunt Abi wants to know. We settle down to a comfortable television drama.

I often work this Sunday routine into the end of my week. It's like stepping into a cocoon of comfort, where the food, the talk and the sounds are familiar: the large quantities of everything piled on the table, the undertone of fieriness in every spoonful, the gentle ribaldry at the table, the easy company, the teasing exchange in a language we all understand. There's the familiarity of the home I was rushing to leave.

My father's younger brother, Uncle Sola, lives in Richmond. He left, as many people from home do, to go abroad and study. During his brief return home, he managed to cause enough hoo-haa to scandalise my mother and her entire generation. In his wake he left an unconfirmed number of women with child.

Eventually he settled down. He'd chosen a good Krio girl from a solid family, from home. Aunt Abi was petite, with her long hair relaxed and pulled back into a chignon to accompany her tidy dress sense. Settling down, on the surface, also meant for him a well-paying job with an international agency, three healthy children, and the large house. Success was stamped all over his life.

It's an utterly random happening when a new friend from my hall of residence, Rifat, says, We're going to see a good film tonight, would you like to come? Not wishing to turn down a social event, I say yes. We go to a crowded pub in Soho, picking our way through tight streets and shops with entrances coloured with green, or blue, or red light. Light that covers the faces of the people who want to welcome their customers in. A lady calls out to Rifat, who is striding away in front, Want to see what we've got, little boy? A couple of the lads snigger.

In the bar, cloudy with smoke and hot with the pressure of beer breaths and bodies, Rifat is carried away from me towards a plasticky-looking girl with tight patent boots and lots of big hair. I find a waist-high table to lean against, grasping my beer in one hand while others in our group are clustered close by. I listen in on a shouted conversation about the results of *the* football match of the season. Some guy who briefly introduced himself earlier is commanding the debate about team performances.

A man with eyebrows that sprinkle hairs towards each other approaches. His smile lifts his eyes slightly at the corners.

'Hello, all,' he says. 'Where's Rifat?'

I nod over in Rifat's direction.

'I see. He's busy then.'

I nod again, smiling back this time. 'And you are?'

'Kamal Bensouda. And you?'

'Ayodele Roberts. Are you coming with us?'

'Aren't you?'

'Of course. I'm here to watch the film.'

With this ridiculous bit of non-conversation over, we stop, stare at each other, look away.

He smiles then, and his teeth are even, rectangular, ivory. 'Conversations are so polite over here, aren't they?'

'Well I'm not actually from here. West Africa.'

'My great-aunt and -uncle used to live in Sierra Leone.'

'When did they leave?'

'A few years after President Siaka Stevens was killed. They lost everything when the fighting broke out near the mines.'

'Really? Where are they now?'

'They run a Lebanese restaurant in London and still speak mostly Krio at home, between themselves.'

'Do you speak any?'

'I understand a bit. Not difficult is it, once you tune your ear in.'

'*Ow you do?*'

'Fine, thanks, and how about you?'

We get round to talking about what we do.

Student. What subject? Development Studies.

Teacher. What do you teach? Econometrics.

Where? Same university.

The coincidences are no longer surprising. But of course. Rifat knows everyone.

We sit next to each other during the film. We find each other after the trip to the bathroom and before the final trek to another smoky and air-heavy pub.

My eyes ring with the indignation of the illegal occupation of Lebanon. My heart sings that he knows and feels injustice.

He says, 'You know how the Irish feel about the British, too close across a tiny strip of water — well, we feel the Israelis are too close over a strip of desert.'

I watch his hands as he flings them about. I ask questions. He answers. Always with passion.

And that, essentially, is how I fall in love. Unexpectant. Side-swiped.

We drive up to Oxford. We stroll through the Pitt Rivers Museum and gawp at shrunken heads. We find a pub by a tree that weeps into the river. We hire a punt at a ridiculous price and wobble onto it. The sun isn't out but our happiness, my happiness, is not created by yellowy warmth or especially green grass. I find it while inexpertly sticking our pole into the thin cover of silt at the bottom, and moving our way upstream.

Back in my flat, after a perfect day, it does not take much to find ourselves in my bed.

'Hey, I didn't know that was your first time,' Kamal says.

'It wasn't,' I reply, my voice shaded with certainty.

He stretches the quiet with his silence for a few moments. Then he surprises me by saying, 'Are you sure?'

'I went out one night intending to be sure.'

'How long ago?'

'A year ago. With a Reuben from the sixth form.'

'Did it hurt? More or less than today?'

'Actually, it didn't hurt at all. Just a bit sore, but not as sore as today.'

As I speak, I start to feel silly.

'How many times?'

'Just the once.'

'What did he think?'

'That I'd done it with him, too.'

Kamal laughs. I cringe inside.

Reuben still phones me. His voice shines with delight when I pick up. He's studying engineering in Aberdeen and he talks about the cold and the wind. He must be lonely, to continue phoning when I give back so little.

Kamal and I try out Brighton on a Sunday morning. The dark-blue VW smells of him – the scent of his skin, fresh with citrus aftershave. It is the beginning of spring and the trees, though still empty, are bursting shoots of green. The radio is on. A raucous voice is singing rock with soul. I sing along. He seems happy to be with me.

We drive through a parade of trees, a line of plane on both sides of the road, their barks shivering. We round the bend, too fast despite the signs warning of a steep curve. In front of us, in the slow lane, is a three-wheeled beige car, putting along.

'Fuck,' he says, as he swerves across to the other lane. The speed of the turn makes the back wheels skid. He tries to correct the skid the other way. We spin again, all the way round this time, and find ourselves in the fast lane, facing the wrong way.

'Fuck, fuck, fuck,' he says again, hitting the steering wheel with his fist.

'Well, get the hell off the road then.'

He drives off to the hard shoulder, with heavily breathed sighs, full of curled-up emotion left to me to interpret.

When we arrive to park in a long line of empty road, next to a pavilioned pathway with lions and crests, the music has only lightened the talk a little.

The beach is whipped with a gusty sea breeze. The pebbles stay soaked. We get out of the car and I try to huddle close to him as we walk up to the pier. It is empty. The funfair is closed. In the huge room with gambling machines, very few heads bob above the winking lights that fakely promise cash back. We buy hot dogs with mustard and ketchup that drip onto his suede boots. The boards of the pier clunk underneath our feet.

Some things you can only see a long time afterwards. Then they are as clear as a belt of stars in an empty sky. He used to make me tremble with pride as he talked about his country. 'As if the Lebanese do not know how to govern themselves!' he'd say indignantly, his lips wet with talk, his hands flying before his face. He talked about food in open-air cafés and walks in forests of cedar. About orange streaks in the night air that would be explained in the news the next day. The thumps of bazookas and how the number of holes in buildings increase the further north you go. He even joked once about correlating distance to the border with the number of nine-inch mortar holes you could find, and how it would make a perfect example of causality. 'Justice makes no sense,' he said, 'when you look at the history of my country and all the nations that have messed about with it. They have stabbed at it, drugged it, dragged it through a gutter and now think it might be best to strangle it.'

'Hey,' I say, 'I have something to tell you.' We are in a restaurant, sitting across from each other in a badly lit Chinese-lantern corner.

My hands stretch across the imitation marble table and past the plate of white Styrofoam prawn crackers. I grab his right hand in both of mine, covering it with my oil-tipped fingers.

'What?' he says.

I blather on. 'Well, I haven't been all that regular with my little pills you know. Not intentionally, I wouldn't have meant it to be like this. It's late. My period. So, it must be.'

'How late?'

I find myself giggling. 'Two weeks. Not long really.'

'When will you know for sure?'

'I'll get a kit from a chemist on the way to college on Monday morning. Shall I pop in later to tell you the result?'

'Sure.'

There is one last round of frenzied lovemaking in his flat that night. On Monday he's gone. There is no goodbye. There are no hysterics, no slow, reasoned explanations. He simply goes. No one answers the phone in his flat. Then he sends me a postcard. He does not use my address. He sends it c/o Annette, the departmental secretary.

Teaching summer school here, let me know if you need any help.

There are certain confidences that are unshareable, even with a flatmate you've had for two years. Meena watches me and cooks me curries. Our Stockwell flat throbs with bubbles of stovetop-roasted cardamom and coriander and black mustard seeds. The heat of the curry warms my mouth, settles my stomach. My head, my heart, my fingers stay cold. Her concern and her cooking weave strands of safety around me. I go through days when my eyes smart for no obvious reason at all, just soul pain bubbling. Sometimes I manage to find those deep cloaky silences when the world goes blank, and I curl under my duvet and wait for the silence to bat the hurt away.

My body aches, every sliver of skin screeching to be touched by someone it knows. Like a crumpled can of beer once finished, my body – which had once promised pleasure – becomes empty, discarded, unwanted.

I am not pregnant. Life gets squashed flat.

*

Meena asks, 'But did you not guess anything?'

Niet. Non. Nada. Not a hint of betrayal. This time round, life chose for me, regardless of what I wanted. I had been buoyed up with the excitement of what could unexpectedly come my way, and how I could cope regardless. I considered many paths on steps sprung with air. My mind sped ahead to talking to Prof McIntyre about my status (without mentioning any other party, of course), and how I'd bravely take my exams and still try to pass honourably. I had decided that it would be important for Kamal and me to 'be together', but there was no need for marriage or anything. I'd accepted that things would have had to change. That life would be different. I'd not guessed this kind of different.

Exam time comes round. I try to retain bleak facts about world political economy. When the question comes up *In Lebanon and the West Bank, Israel is contravening international law with the connivance of the United States of America. Discuss*, I feel mocked.

While I revised for my exams, the sun streamed through my bedroom window every day. Now they are over, it hides behind damp grey clouds.

Meena agrees to get married to a description of a well-brought-up young lawyer from a good Bombay family. They plan to have a long engagement so she can finish her master's degree.

'What? When did you meet him?'

'I haven't.'

'That's ridiculous. Don't let your family force you into this.'

'They're not. I chose him.'

I go Gambian on her, screw up my lips, let the hiss of saliva escape through my mouth. My Gambian *cheepoo*, and other international expressions of disapproval – tsking, tutting, harrumphing – have no effect on her. I am interested though, because someone else's life in motion means I can move my attention away from mine.

'Don't try to sort my life out,' she says. 'I don't need it.'

'You're being silly. You didn't choose. They did.'

'Only by consulting with a matchmatcher to draw up a short-list. I'm telling you, I chose him.'

I get absurdly angry with her. Does she not realise that most men are pigs? And that the less you know of them, the more piglike they are likely to become? Was this the only thing my mother was right about? If Kamal was a pig, I had made myself a willing trough. And here was Meena, about to do the same, only in a different way.

'Why did you choose him?'

'I liked the look of him.'

'You liked the look?'

'Yes. He lives in America. I might as well go somewhere new. Further away from my family.'

'Will you meet him before the wedding?'

'Of course. But the matter will have been decided by then anyhow. We will be meeting as two people about to get married.'

She is beaming, with a quiet joy that I cannot understand, and cannot begin to fathom.

I like her. She infuriates me. She is peculiar. I am her friend. I understand only a bit of her.

On a rain-soaked autumn evening, with soggy brown leaves matting the pavement, we go food shopping. Meena pushes the trolley full of our weekly groceries towards the shortest queue in a crowded checkout area.

'Let's move over to that queue over there,' she says urgently, clutching my arm and pointing towards a queue snaking into the aisles.

'Why do you want to do that?'

She whispers back, her voice hiding among air forced low. 'Look at the guy helping to pack the things.'

'Yes, what don't you like about him?'

Her chin juts forward, her head nods impatiently as if I am the one being dim. 'Him. It's a him.'

'So?'

'I'm buying tampons.'

'Come on, Meena. Is it me being thick or you?'

'He's Indian.'

I look at the stocky, short man in dark grey trousers and a shirt buttoned up to the neck. He has a side parting, with some hair falling across his forehead. His jowls extend downwards, even though I'd have him in his twenties. I look back at Meena. She bites her lower lip. She's never met this man. But her nervousness is real.

'Indian girls, you know, we're not supposed to, I mean, be using them.'

Her eyes meet mine, but she drops hers right away, shifting her body slightly away from me, to stare at rows of butterscotch and bonbons.

I don't quite mean to, but a snigger cum snort escapes my nose, and I find myself laughing at her. Meena curls her eyebrows together in a frown. She folds her arms across her chest.

'Come on, Meena. After all this time living on your own, away from home?'

'You wouldn't like people to think badly of you, would you?'

'If I don't know them and I don't talk to them, what they think about me doesn't matter. I'm too far away from home anyway.'

I elbow her out of the way and commandeer the trolley.

We stay in the queue. I put the tampons on the carousel. Meena lurks behind me for as long as she can bear it, then she edges past to loiter behind the shopping packer, where, with his back to her, she is out of his scrutiny. I pay. We push the trolley to the exit, where we unload the carrier bags, taking one in each hand, before heading out into a wall of grey wind speckled with rain to catch the bus home.

My mother phones to ask me to buy her a hat and send it home with Uncle Sola, who is going to Banjul in a couple of weeks.

'I need a wide-brimmed one. I've already got a dark-green straw hat. This time I want a lighter colour, more like lemons than grass, with a wide ribbon and shaped silk flowers. Stylish, but simple.'

'I'll do my best, Ma.'

'Don't forget he's leaving on Tuesday night, with British Caledonian. You'll need to take it to his house in Richmond. That's not too far for you, is it?'

'Just a bit out of my way.'

'But you'll do it, won't you? And I've just thought – maybe you could add some stockings in the package. You know my colour – if you match it to the colour of your elbow skin, I think that would suit me.'

She keeps going as I interject with *Yes, Ma*s. And then she finishes with, 'Make sure you try to get a proper hat box. Uncle Sola won't mind bringing everything as hand luggage. I've asked him already.'

After our first set of goodbyes but before we put down our phones, my mother says, 'You've heard the news about that Chinese friend of yours?'

'Yuan?'

'He died in a motorcycle accident two weeks ago. His parents closed their restaurant and went off to the States to sort out his funeral.'

52

'Why didn't you tell me?' I interrupt.

'I'm telling you now, aren't I?'

The next round of goodbyes is quicker, and ends our conversation. After I put the phone down, I squeeze my ear lobes together to block out sound, try to turn off the noise of traffic, of people outside on the street. We can't die yet, we're much too young. There's so much we want to do. I hate how time and distance are breaking me up from people I once cared about. I wonder how Remi is? Amina? Moira? Death has upped the stakes. A friend has ceased to exist, and I didn't even know.

I press on the bell to the right of the dark-brown door with the number 36 in gilt bang in the middle. There is a long trembling silence after the bell rings, as if the house itself is indecisive, unsure whether to reveal itself or not. I take a few steps back, onto the pavestones that lead up to the door, and look up. There are a couple of lights on upstairs. It's the middle of the week, and I know the children will be in, doing their homework, practising their piano, life drawing . . . or whatever new project my aunt has thought up as an educating pastime.

I see a quick triangle of light, then a hurried shadow eclipses it. Soon I hear footsteps thudding down the carpeted stairs, and a few muffled steps down the corridor towards the front door. Ade opens the door with red-rimmed eyes.

'We didn't know who it was,' she says by way of explanation.

'I rang yesterday to say I'd be dropping off some stuff for your dad to take home.'

'Come in. Mum's crying.'

'What happened?'

'A woman came to the door and now mum's all upset.'

'Can I help?'

'Go up and see her if you like.'

53

'I'll leave these things on the dining room table, so your dad'll see them when he comes in,' I say, walking through the open door to the dining room, where I leave the huge green and white carrier bag declaring that 'good things cost less'.

In Aunt Abi's room, the lights are turned low. She's in bed on her side, her checked pink and green Krio scarf skew-whiff over her bright purple hair rollers. Her face is puffy as she turns to my greeting,

'Good evening, Ma.'

'Ayodele.' Her voice is wispy, swallowed thin. 'Sit down.'

I perch on the buttoned velvet stool she usually tucks in under her dressing table, and lean forward.

'Is there anything I can do to help, Ma?'

She exhales in shudders and lifts up a shoulder.

'Your uncle . . .'

I wait.

'Oh, I can't talk. Let the children tell you.'

'Can I bring up anything for you? A snack or a drink?'

'Not now. I'll sleep.'

'I'll go downstairs then, but I'll come back up before I leave.'

She nods.

Back downstairs, Ade is waiting with her chin on her palms, elbows resting on the dining table. Her brothers have joined her.

'What's going on?' I ask.

Ade starts. 'The doorbell rings, and I go and answer it.'

Olu fills me in. 'She thought it was you.'

I ask, 'What time was this?'

'About three o'clock,' replies Ade.

'And who was it?' I ask. The rest of the telling is a fast drama, with all three of them doing the explaining.

Tunde: 'We don't know – this big fat screaming woman.'

Ade: 'She just shouted at me – Do you know your father can't keep his wiggly in his trousers?'

Olu: 'Can you imagine that?'

Ade: 'I tried to shut the door, telling her she had the wrong address.'

Olu: 'I was halfway down the stairs.'

Ade: 'She put her handbag in the door and said – It's not the wrong address. I know he lives here.'

Tunde: 'Then we all started screaming, Mum, Mum.'

Ade: 'Ma came through from the kitchen, wiping her hands on a towel.'

Tunde: 'The woman at the door was really shouting now – You tell your father you want to meet the new brother or sister he's started for you all.'

Ade: 'Mum said, What's going on?'

Olu: 'The lady went berserk. She pushed at the door.'

Ade: 'She yelled at Mum – Your husband is going after school-girls and making them pregnant.'

Olu: 'Mum asked her to leave, or she'd call the police.'

Ade: 'She screamed at her – Call the police all you like, but tell your bastard husband to leave my daughter alone.'

Olu: 'And she stormed off down the path.'

'After that, I think your mum deserved a lie-down. Have you told your dad?' I ask.

Ade shakes her head, 'Not yet, he'll be home soon enough.'

Outside what used to be Kamal's door, I decide to turn right instead of retracing my steps. Each time I've done this, deliberately walked past *his* door, it's been easier. It's just an ordinary kind of corridor, with an ordinary kind of door. Solid frame painted a hopeful green, with plywooded grubby brown door inset. On the wall to the left, straying north of the door handle and at about eye height, is a signboard with a slidey thing to display laminated nameplates. It now says: *Mr Hamid Mahfouz, Lecturer, Economics and Economic Theory.*

It used to say, barely a year ago: *Dr Kamal Bensouda, Senior Lecturer, Econometrics.*

The first time I came by here after he'd gone, I stopped to trace over his name, scarcely believing he could have left, and done it so completely.

Now I find it hard to believe how dread had clutched at me, scraping away bits of skin and leaving a ribbed ridge of irritation in its wake. I was marked by an ache that started in my throat perhaps, rolling its way down past my heart, tumbling through my stomach and ending up at my leaden feet. It was as if I was stuck to the green, thin pile corridor carpeting, a bit worn where many other feet had rushed past, on their way to somewhere. I'd made up a chant:

> *A toe, one foot, one leg*
> *A finger, one hand, one arm*
> *One head, one body, and a self.*

And I willed my broken parts past that door, remembering other terrors from childhood, when a different kind of dread would dog me as we went past Berring Grun, the cemetery that slouched at the entrance to Banjul. As a child, with lips scarcely moving, I would imagine water cutting into the resting holes of the dead and carting them off, sea currents restlessly cradling human bones and rubbing them against each other and rough rocks. To try to stop the fright, I used to say – unheard, breaths uneven –

> *A bone, one face, one hole*
> *A stone, one name, one being*
> *One person, one spirit, a ghost.*

Aged eight, I could break down the hosts of phantoms into one dead person at a time, and then they seemed manageable – I knew I could confront a solitary ghost, just not too many at the same time. At twenty-one, I was overwhelmed by the ghost of a single person who'd left me.

4

Freefall

I fall into a half-hearted doze, my body accepting the weight of an arm flung onto it. My mind thrashes against sleep. I'm fighting an image of me in deep repose – slack-jawed, dribbly, and likely to murmur things out loud. Kamal used to say I wouldn't even let him go have a pee in the night without my arm tightening around him or me saying out loud clearly: *Don't leave me yet*. Kamal is gone. Someone else owns the arm now draped on me. When I can no longer bear the tension of keeping myself awake, I shake Akim and say, 'C'mon, you have to leave now.'

He lifts his arm off me, groans and mumbles, 'I'm asleep, why do I have to?'

'Just because.'

When he does not move, I jab him with my elbow and he sits up and swings his legs over the side of the bed. He stands to reach for the trousers he left on the armchair. The orange streetlamp outside my bedroom window throws in burnt light.

This is not the first time Akim and I have had an early-morning conversation like this. I've muttered reasons before, whatever I could dredge up, lies I can no longer remember.

As he leans over, his arched back is a set of planed muscles smooth to the touch, nice to hold. He is gorgeous to look at. I still want him to leave.

As he dresses he says, 'Will I see you tomorrow – I mean later today?'

'Hmm, maybe.'

'OK then, I'll find you.'

When I hear the door thud close behind him, I fall into a dreamless sleep into which the alarm peals a few hours later.

London's steel sky hides the sun. As I sit at our tiny kitchen table, I look out on chilled, defenceless gardens and laddered television aerials set at jaunty positions on slate roofs. I grimace at a day ahead filled with lectures as I spoon out the last of Meena's home-made strawberry jam onto the unwilling butt end of a French loaf.

Morning indecisiveness glues me to my seat. Shall I shower now, or in fifteen minutes after listening to the news on the radio? Shall I try to catch the bus or use the underground and give myself a spare half hour? Should I write out my Christmas cards before going in or wait for a break between lectures? Are my spare stamps in my panty drawer or in the sleeve of my manilla folder? Did I stuff my last ten-pound note into that striped cardigan or should I investigate how many coins lurk at the bottom of my handbag?

Meena shuffles in, buffing the wooden floor with her fluffy bunny slippers.

'What this country needs,' I remark, 'is a good old storm to clear the air and leave it smelling fresh. Something to shift this drabness that stays and stays.'

'Morning,' she says, stifling a yawn and heading for the fridge. 'Fixing the world, are you?'

'Kind of.'

'Where's Akim?'

'Chucked him out just after midnight.'

'Hmm.'

'What do you mean – hmm?'

'He's a nice guy.'

'And what do you want me to do about that?'

'He's rich. He likes you. A lot. Why don't you try to keep him?'

I sigh. She yawns as she extracts a carton of milk.

'I don't know why.'

I feel her look at me, but I stare out into the garden. 'It's too early to talk about this sort of thing,' I continue. 'And how are you and Hari getting on?'

'Ah, now. You're trying to change the subject.'

She lifts her heavy black hair off her shoulders, twists it into a knot at her nape, and secures it with a pink flower hairband that she slips off her wrist.

'Duh?' I reply.

'You're awful, go away.' She lifts a tea towel, scrunches it up and throws it at me.

I stuff my lazy legs into jeans, my top half into a tight ribbed cream polo neck. I add a suede knee-length coat rescued from the heap of clothes behind my bedroom door. I am going to be late for my first lecture. I only found £2.89 so I'll need to create some sympathy for me, somehow, during the course of the day.

Plan A. I could scrounge lunch off the Prof in the Senior Common Room, if I approach him about my dilemma over the future and murmur about needing to mull things over with him. I'll mention that I am thinking through possible job applications but the Careers Office is no good. Their shelves are bursting with pamphlets about rosy prospects in Shell and Price Waterhouse . . . supplemented by thin, unappetising sheets about joining fancy non-governmental organisations that will revolutionise well-building in Bangladesh. Hardworking African teachers have toiled to get me to the top of the educational heap. These choices seem a bit short of special.

They will probably have turkey (roasted) or pie (crusted) on the menu. And the Prof likes the occasional tipple at the end of the week. It being Friday today, if I get the timing right and turn up just before I need to rush off to a lecture, he will feel obliged to offer his ear, and his opinions, and that should be lunch. Guaranteed.

Plan B: I find Rifat, whose mum lives a stone's throw from college. She makes large, heartwarming casseroles with homemade bread and delivers them to his flat several times a week. I could offer to listen to his collection of David Bowie or to check out his latest game design, and the new graphics-rendering tricks he's invented.

If neither of these work, I could always end up with the no-plan option, the default. I need do nothing and Akim will take me somewhere. A complete cop-out.

The tube smells of unwashed, flu-laden warmth. A woman sits across from me with skin that drips off her face in wrinkled folds, and eyes that bulge and seem to be looking everywhere at once. Very crone-like, very *Hansel and Gretel* bad-woman type, she clutches a tapestry bag with faded colours close to her chest as if it contains a great treasure. She rubs her hand over it occasionally as she munches on toothless gums.

A couple spill into the carriage with giggles and teenage cuddles and relentless touching and kissing. One of the pair is wearing large rectangular glasses and the other is pimply. I look at the two of them cavorting on the train seats, and although I feel a twinge at the loss of innocence, I don't feel envy. I look at them with eyes that search for the hidden, the unknowable between them. One or both of them will soon find out – it's worthless. It all ends in pain.

It has been easy getting involved with Akim. I let him see the bits of me that need not be cordoned off into little secret holes of self. He has access to the bits that I can make carefree, the parts I can laugh away. I mother him a bit. I have a flat where he can hang out, even if he can't spend an entire night in it. I cook food that he's used to. He does not seem to mind me bossing him around sometimes. He has said, though, that most of the girls he's met since he's been here have only been interested in his car, his money, his ability to take them to expensive nightclubs. According to him, I have been the least resource-hungry girl he's met for a long time. I wonder how different I really am from those girls. I like the fact that he's got money. I like going to places beyond my means. The only hair split is that I refuse to let him buy me things. I've declined offers of watches, jeans, shoes. And he's never seen that in a girl he's dated. He sometimes seems Reuben-like to me, not in his clothes, but in his manner.

I get out at my stop and walk up the escalator, flashing my travelcard at the chubby-cheeked man leaning against his cubicle. I emerge from the station into the indifferent daylight I had studied from my kitchen window. Propelled by the cold and my tardiness, I run-walk down Tottenham Court Road.

I slip into the tiniest crack I can make in the door to get into Public Finance, but the door refuses to co-operate and shuts behind me with a thud. Dr Brian Brown – cords, brogues, check shirt, leather-elbowed jacket – reacts as he always does to late-comers. He pauses, closes his eyes tight, waves his right arm which is holding a stick of chalk in my direction, opens his mouth as if to speak, then closes it again as if compelled by his good nature to hold his tongue.

'Ms Roberts, in your fine opinion, what is the major burden excessive public debt imposes on a country?'

All heads swivel round to me. I sit on the rind of the swing-down seat, stuck there by the large bag balancing on my knee.

'Er, I guess it commits future generations to a lifetime of debt repayments.'

'What if, at some point in the future, a country cannot repay its debts? What then?'

'Um, well, technically, a country can never become bankrupt as there will always be someone to bail it out of trouble.'

'Unlike us as individuals, Ms Roberts. Thank you, you may take your seat.'

He turns his back to me, and his attention to the chalkboard. He scribbles: *Can a country become bankrupt?*

'One last thing, do file away, amongst your opinions about public debt, that I like *all* participants in this course to attend my lectures on time.'

He addresses the rest of the class: 'Would anyone else like to volunteer an alternative opinion on this?'

I fumble in my bag to extract a notepad and pen. I stuff the bag down past my legs and let my weight push the seat down.

Dr Brown proceeds to discuss how to deal with unrelenting inflation, when a government is so incompetent at handling its economy that the cash you thought you had at the beginning of the year is piddle-worthy at the end of it.

Prof McIntyre's door is wide open. He bellows into the phone, 'Oh no, oh no no no!!' And then slams it down, muttering, 'The fools, the damn fools.'

When I introduce myself with an 'Er . . .', he beckons me in.

'Come in, come in,' he mangles my name, 'Ayudel. How are you getting on?' He points to his visitor's chair, a leather armchair shoved up close to his corner bookshelf, and already occupied by a tottery pile of books. 'Sit down, sit down, push the books aside. Have some coffee, fresh. I need to make another call.'

I busy myself with pouring into the cleanest mug in his collection and listen in.

'Bloody fools, absolutely unacceptable.'

A pause.

'I depend on you to make them understand that some things simply must *not* be substituted. Bye.'

He turns to me. 'Administrators. Trying to cut the budget for our Christmas bash. Need someone to tell them what's what.' He pats the pockets of his jacket and then some papers on his desk. With an 'Ah, here it is,' he sticks his cherrywood pipe in his mouth, then continues searching. I hand over my lighter and he engulfs the room with tobacco-lined puffs.

'How are you?' he says.

'Sort of OK, but there are still things to decide on.'

'Hmm, I see.'

I hastily continue, 'But I've got to go for my French class in a minute, so I can't really talk to you right now, but just wondered if . . .'

'Free for lunch?'

'Sure.'

'OK, meet me there at one and we'll catch up then.'

I gather my belongings and, saying my thank-yous, leave.

I do not know how I want to be, what I want to become. Will I ever be able to go back home and live in the chunks of expectation my mother, my relatives, the whole of Fajara, expect?

*

Our French lecturer, Madame LeBlanc, is wearing some sort of negligée in green that frills around her face, accompanied by stockings of an indeterminate shade of brown. She looks decidedly un-Parisian, a *démodée* elf. Today's elvishly chosen topic is the nature of *la joie*.

'Let's start by trying to define what joy is,' she says.

'A tingle in your toes,' starts Sarah.

Other definitions pop out around the room: *A sense of wellbeing. Contentment in the world and the things around you. Inner equilibrium.*

'Is joy, ecstasy in living, a basic ambition for every human being?' Madame LeBlanc asks.

Yasmin stretches her manicured fingers under her chin, 'Yes, obviously, if we're not happy we end up killing each other.'

'Happiness is not necessarily joy, or ecstasy,' protests Carlos.

'We can play around with the definitions, being joyful always means being happy as well,' counters Sarah.

'Why do we pursue joy?' At this point, Madame LeBlanc is leaning forward, jutting at the air with her sleek Parisian pen, enjoying the role of showing us what being a Left Bank intellectual is all about.

Me: 'Scientists show that joyful people live longer, healthier lives.'

Yasmin: 'But joy isn't something that is always reflected on the surface. You cannot always see it. The Indian ascetics find their joy comes from within, and brings serenity.'

Carlos: 'I disagree. Some people in the world don't have the choice to find joy, they find it hard enough to get enough food to eat on a day-to-day basis.'

Back to Madame LeBlanc: 'Are you saying you can only look for joy if you are rich?'

'Not quite, but it's very hard to sit around debating the concept of joy if you are racked with worms,' says Carlos.

French philosophers. Colonialism. Nationalism. Freedom.

They all contribute to our discussion of how to perceive happiness, joy, serenity.

The class over, I let everyone shuffle out. I stand at the window for a moment, next to a boiling radiator, and look down on the row of cars parked in their rectangles of white paint, being drizzled on by an indifferent rain. How should I decide whether I am happy or not? It's easier to determine when I'm not *un*happy, but harder to prove any depth or texture to a happiness.

Would I have been just as happy staying home, not going to university, like my school friend Moira?

She seemed content enough when I last saw her while on holiday. She works as a secretary in the Ministry for Lands and is married to someone who trades in building materials. With a second child on the way, who's to say she's not happier than I am? Here I am, with wider, broader horizons, yet not knowing how to guarantee myself joy.

Kamal and I ate in the oak-panelled Senior Common Room sometimes, ostensibly to discuss the economics of trade. Once, we ended up playing footsie under the generous tablecloth, trying to smother snorts of mirth in the company of Engelbert Duthers, dandruffed member of the Economics Department. Memory stabs again, and I try to set it at a distance – me and this *emotion*. I walk around it in my mind, try to see the shape of it. Crumbly or smooth? Quiet ochre or intense ebony? I once wanted to claim love for myself, be intimate with it, aware of it in my eating and in my sleeping. Now, it's a stranger. I want no part of this kind of wanting that gets you dumped. I don't ever want to find myself beating a hasty retreat to the loo, to find a cubicle where I can hunch up on the seat, draw my knees up, fold them tight within my arms so I can rest my head and find some conduit for tears.

Today, although there isn't much pomp and ceremony, the

caterers have added decorative touches to the room. Poinsettia is much in evidence, to match seasonal festivities. By the time the Prof bustles across to our table, I've ironed my emotions flat and tidily folded them away.

We discuss my discomfort with Statistics (any luck with the chi-squareds and ANOVAs?), the size of the helping (rather hearty, don't you think?), the lack of snow (miserable in these parts, for the real thing you need to head for the lochs), the wine (not bad, not bad, well rounded), did I see the review of an anthropological guide to West Africa in the *Economist* (rather interesting take on your neck of the woods), thoughts on my future (have you considered journalism?), how are my personal difficulties (breezed through yet? got to keep an eye).

Sometimes you have to let the comfort of care sweep over you; he reminds me of why I would have quite liked a father.

In my last class of the day, Prof Block creates a new kind of magic in differential equations and multiple dimensions. His arms swoop, his hands swirl geometry in the empty air as he explains the shapes of forms we can only glimpse through fantastic formulae. Block sketches me into a world he's spinning with his fingers, enclosing me into the dreamiest of shapes, beyond time, past space. He dissects the reality of

$$f(x^n) = f(x^1) + f(x^2) + \text{lots of squiggles} + \Delta x^{n-1}$$

Waves and waves of knowledge whip through his excited arms. His body jerks with the energy of it all. Would it be that we could create our own worlds in our heads, worlds that are so full of wonder that they keep us alive in this other more unsatisfying, less predictable one that we do live in.

*

Akim does find me. And I have planned nothing. My evening is consumed in default.

On Saturday afternoon, Meena and I wander off to the Heath with our kites. The crisp, keen cold sharpens my skin.

'Meena,' I say, 'maybe I should look for an older man. Someone divorced or widowed. Kind, no trouble, grateful for my companionship. Leaves me alone when I want to be left alone. What do you think?'

'What's brought this on?' she wants to know.

'Well, yesterday, having a chat with Prof McIntyre about life and what I want to do and stuff, I just thought about how much easier older men are.'

'Uh, uh. Ayodele, I would have thought you'd had enough of professors.'

'Not him in the particular. I meant, what I should be looking for.'

'Sticking with older men won't necessarily protect you from hurt.'

'That way, any pain would be administered with feathers, not thorns.'

We fly our kites and then fly ourselves down the hill, our legs not quite managing to keep pace with the slope. It ends with us in untidy heaps by the footpath, kite strings miraculously untangled in our hands, giggling madly, completely winded, and laughing until we cry.

I default all through summer. Some Sundays, I visit my aunt and uncle. I let life carry me along, without wishing of it anything more. Meena starts to refer to Akim as my boyfriend. And I never have a rejoinder – as one would generally define a boyfriend, he appears to be mine.

It is summer, and I have nothing better to do. I let him be a pause, a comma in my life before I decide how to shift direction. He is fun to be with, and we go places in his open-topped BMW. He lavishes consideration on me. His mother comes to visit. He wants me to meet her. I make up an excuse about needing to see Uncle Sola, and there being an important family gathering that I have to attend. Two entire weekends in a row. I start to acknowledge I'll need to do something about Akim soon.

Rifat is in a blaze of black, Doc Marten boots sticking out scruffily on our front doormat. The sun makes a poor attempt to put a halo around his head as the last of the day's light gives up quietly to a greedy dusk.

'Hello, petal. I hope you are pleased, I'm only ten minutes late this time.'

'Phah, go on up.'

As he comes in, he complains, 'Why do you need me to arrive on time? It only leads to your getting disappointed.'

He goes up the stairs in front of me with that ridiculous gait of his, knees pointed outward, heels bouncing lightly on each step.

We're off to watch a bunch of his friends play in a post-punk band. Rifat promises it will be loud. He plans to help sell tickets at the door. I assure him the music will be incomprehensible. He says he guarantees entertainment. I accept on condition that a proportion of his earnings purchases drinks.

I've made a Gambian salad — hand-shredded lettuce leaves, slices of tomatoes, cucumber, onions, thick quarters of hard-boiled egg, halves of deboned sardines from a tin — in a version of my mother's dressing. I bought two baguette loaves and have sliced them into angled ovals. After we've joked and eaten with Meena, I make my way downstairs to pick out my boots and jacket. The doorbell rings, and I jump. When I open the door, it's Akim.

He says, 'I wanted to phone you to ask whether you're up to anything, but I decided to come round to see you in case you were not.'

'In five minutes, you wouldn't have found me in. We are on our way out.'

I hear Rifat saying goodbye to Meena as he moves towards the stairs. When they are within spitting distance the two men nod to each other in a silent male–male exchange. I say, 'Rifat, Akim.' They shake hands. Akim puts both hands in his front pockets just as a gust of wind blows up a couple of empty crisp packets around my ankles.

'We're off now,' I say, 'to see a band. I'll catch up with you some other time.'

And Akim says, 'Sure,' in a voice that matches his face. It's the first time I've seen him look at me like that.

Akim starts to phone me more often.

'Where have you been?' is often his greeting.

I start to find notes under my door:

Was hoping you might want to go out for a Chinese meal.
There's a good film on – thought you might want to see it.
Just popping by, I had nothing else that I wanted to do.

I ask him when he plans to go home. He says he might stay for the graduation ceremony and there is no particular hurry. I say I'll have to leave by mid-November as I will have run out of money by then.

I come home one day, late – around two – from a new babysitting job I've found. Akim is sitting in his blue BMW with the cover up, listening to Marvin Gaye.

'What are you doing here?'

'Needed to see you,' he mumbles. 'Can I come in?'

'Look, this isn't going to work. I'm dead tired. I need to go to bed.'

'Where have you been?'

'Babysitting.'

'It's not safe, coming back this late. You should let me pick you up.'

'I've been fine doing this for the last three weeks. They pay for my cab home.'

'Can I come in?' he asks again.

'No. Go home. It's late.'

Two months later, Akim tries to kill himself. He leaves a yellow sticky note on a table in his kitchen, with a little arrow:

TO WHOEVER
FINDS ME,
PLEASE
POST

He attaches a stamped and addressed letter to me. The police find it and a social worker brings it round to see me *and have a little chat*. Akim declares to the world that I was the one who drove him to it, that I was the cause. Isn't that the way it is in tales of romance, in which the lover gives up life to protect the beloved? One is ready to die so that the one who is loved can live? Is that the ultimate proof of love, to say 'I'd rather die than live without you' and then to go ahead and tie a rope around your neck and kick a stool away?

What I know for sure is that, as a consequence, shock and guilt rampage through my life.

*

His parents both fly over from Lagos. They arrange for a course of treatment with a psychiatrist in South Kensington, then they take him back to Nigeria.

His mother writes to me. Her letter starts: 'My dear Ayodele'. Being called a 'dear' when I feel like shit makes me cry. She says: 'I don't think you are the person my son thinks you are, but he cares about you and I thought it only courteous to let you know how he is.' She signs herself: Toyin Adebayo.

I cannot think through our summer in steps – this happened, then that happened. It's all one big jumble of emotion with near-photographic flashes of scenes. The two of us zipping along the motorway with wind in my ears, plunging into a field of oilseed rape, or sitting alongside a café by a canal and watching a boat go past with cheery folk waving to us from the deck. It had been a dizzy summer in which I screeched myself dry with the very energy of living. And I pulled him along with me, never letting him disbelieve he was my forever. I didn't know what I wanted, but I knew I wasn't ready for what he wanted.

It's taken me a while to recognise different degrees of toughness in people. After Kamal, I assumed that everyone must get – how did Aunty K put it? – a turn at the 'University of Hard Knocks', where you get a degree whether or not you realise you are enrolled. It's up to those with nous to make sure the degree's not a third-class, lacking in honours. I survived Kamal. Therefore, I assumed Akim would survive me.

Mrs Adebayo said, 'He'd written to me to say he'd met the girl he wanted to marry and that he was staying on as long as necessary so he would come home with you.' I knew he meant what he was saying with his eyes. I lied to myself and steered the conversation away whenever he tried to start the seriousness. I did not want anything said. That summer was my comma and life was going to continue after.

5

Denial

It's always easy to get work in a decrepit government, so I make my way back to The Gambia. Home. Away from tired, drizzly weather and into intense, sun-drenching heat. If I had a tail when I left four years earlier, it isn't wagging now.

I stay with my mother for the few months it takes me to find a job and a house. She does not like me thinking about moving out, planning to leave her on her own again.

She complains, 'You've come back with all these new ideas. In my day, daughters left their mother's house to get married.'

'Well, we left it to study,' I remind her.

Reuben comes to visit. I discourage a further visit by sitting on the edge of my seat, excusing myself for needing to hurry out to see my Aunt K as promised. But by the time I move out, he's become a regular visitor, and I sometimes pop in to find him ensconced in the sitting room, chatting with my mother.

I find myself incapable of expanding my social circle. I tee off rendezvous with old school friends. Amina lives in Italy and comes home on holiday. She arrives with energy and, briefly,

73

amuses me with her relentless analysis of the relationships around us, peppered with caustic comments on the nature of social pressure. Moira, I find, has descended into a mist of literal interpretations of the Bible and evaluates her friendships with a proselytising eye, pressing pamphlets on me, along with invitations to her church. The person I see most often is Remi, with whom it's easy to drift back into the ease of our early friendship. She asks me to be godmother when her daughter, Joy, is born.

My mother is pleased with our renewed friendship. She holds Remi up as an example to us, her daughters. One Saturday afternoon, Aunt K comes to visit at the time she knows the food will already be cooked, dished up into matching dishes and lounging, hot for the eating, on our dining table.

'I came to see you, Ayodele,' she says as she walks in, 'but . . .'

'. . . you wanted to see my mother's *shackpa* soup more,' I finish her sentence.

'You know me too well,' she laughs, as she settles herself into a chair. She uncovers the first dish and serves herself two large balls of cassava *fufu*, and starts to ladle out spoonfuls of the palmoil-rimmed casserole.

'Get me some water, dear child.' And I obediently trot off to the kitchen to get her a pitcher of cold water.

'Thank you. Ah. Food and good company, what more could one want in life?' she says, on my return.

My mother takes on a well-known theme. 'I would enjoy having some grandchildren.'

'Yes,' replies Aunt K, 'but wouldn't you like some sons-in-law first?'

My mother sighs, 'I only wish that *one* of my children were settled. That's all I can ask God for at this stage.'

*

I start work at a modest salary, so discreetly modest that I can only afford to rent a small house, two rooms really, in Latrikunda. I find them quite by accident, through an old teacher from school, Mrs Foon, whose parents-in-law rent out a series of rooms in their compound.

The Ministry of Finance is set in a quadrangle of old buildings with thick, fortlike walls, and deep-set windows. The courtyard and the internal covered verandah create a micro-climate – it's always cool. The pillars holding up the upper floor are darkened with the sweat of lingering palms, from the hands of people used to waiting. There are many visitors to the other departments in the quadrangle – the tax revenue office, the registrar of companies – and lines of people snake in and out of open office doors. Beyond the doors are standard-issue wooden desks, commissioned by the Department of Public Works and cut and assembled in the men's prison at Mile Two. There are often a few official heads behind the desks piled with selections of bulging files concerning government business.

The steps leading up to our office, the Department of Financial Planning, have recently been painted. In the past couple of months, as we've been trying to negotiate new lending terms for our government's debt, we've had to welcome many foreign visitors – representatives of friendly bilaterals or nosy bureaucrats from the World Bank. In the outer office, Sukai sits behind a desk, an array of phones in front of her. As always, she is perfectly made up, her eyes dark-ringed in kohl, her lips appropriately stained. Today she wears a trailing red gown with intricate patterns of lilies.

'You look lovely, Sukai,' I say as my good morning.

She smiles back, delighted. 'It's Chinese silk. Do you know who I bought it from?' She pauses to wait for my shake of the head before continuing, 'That lady who came last Friday, she gets them from Dubai. You should come and see her things next time she's here.' She stands up and moves her arms so I can see it better. Wafts of the musky *churrai* she's used to scent her clothes drift out.

'I don't think I can choose as well as you.'

She smiles again. Complimenting Sukai on a regular basis has made my working life much smoother.

'Is Babucarr in yet?' I ask.

'No, but he phoned and asked me to remind you about the speech he needs for tomorrow.'

'Thanks. I'll get started on that now.'

She returns her chewing stick to her mouth, methodically rubbing it against her teeth, its slightly sour sap acting as her toothpaste. The action merely draws attention to her fingers, which are thin, and very much part of the persona she cultivates, an elegant secretary, very marriageable. Not only is Sukai the Minister of Finance's niece, she also has ambitions to marry the head of our department, Babucarr Sanneh.

I get good at my job, really good. I can write proposals better than anyone else in the department, in my entire ministry. I write speeches for Babucarr that come to the notice of the Minister. In his turn, the Minister starts to add urgent requests for word combinations to use for an opening address to a meeting of West African finance ministers in Banjul, for a formal dinner to welcome a visiting American dignitary, or a choice paragraph that will appeal to his hosts on a tour of France. The elegant deliveries get noticed by other ministers, but I am shielded by my boss, who knows he cannot spread my skills too thinly. I am the only one for miles prepared to spend an entire Sunday tidying up words ready for the Minister on Monday morning.

The seasons pass. Storm drains carry away tumbling weights of water towards the sea. The sun burns more ebony into my skin. I let the weather do to me what it likes.

When my fame spreads to the manager of a local consulting

firm which markets management skills to non-governmental organisations and UN agencies at inflated prices, he finds in me a bargain. I gain additional employment to supplement my government income. I clean up badly written documents at high speed. I impose structure and give them contents pages, and neat headers. I add footnotes and insert diagrams when required. My income grows. I move out of the mud-and-wattle rooms. I buy a car that spends three days each month in the garage.

Taiwo comes home when she finishes her degree in accounting. I'm not surprised that she is the first to fulfil my mother's heart wish. She chooses Reuben, who has by now become a fixture in my mother's household. Reuben laps up the extra attention Taiwo turns on him.

The day Taiwo extracts a promise of marriage from him, Reuben visits my mother to formally request Taiwo's hand. My mother immediately phones me at home. 'There's some terribly exciting news to tell you. Come now, they're still here.' Her voice is sparkling. When I get to her house, her gaiety is gambolling around.

Reuben contrives a moment alone with me when I say goodnight and head for my car: 'I hope you don't mind.' His stutter is mild.

There isn't much to say in reply. 'No, not at all. After all, we are grownups now,' I reply politely and firmly.

Taiwo and my mother appear at the door. My mother gives her a delighted hug. 'Oh do go and celebrate together. I can't wait to tell everyone else the news.'

My mother's delight continues unabated through the long months planning the wedding. Only one small thing mars the day itself for her – on Taiwo's wedding day, my sister's waistline is stout.

*

Remi's mother falls ill with renal failure and is to go to Dakar for treatment. Remi asks me to move into her guest room and help look after her daughter. Everyone else she can trust is married and busy with family. She does not want to leave hubby Kojo alone in charge of Joy with the househelp as aide.

She complains to me as we work the details out, 'You employ the older women and they're no brighter than a *kirinting* lamp. You employ the younger ones and soon they're leaning over while doing the housework, showing off their pert young breasts.'

She's filling out a ruled exercise book with household details. The page is headed *Food*.

'Kojo won't eat the same kind of meat two days in a row, so I have to vary it. Here are some suggestions.' She writes: Monday – chicken curry, Tuesday – fish *benachin*, Wednesday – roast pork, Thursday – chicken *yassa*, Friday – catfish stew, Saturday – *krein krein* and okra.

Her commentary: 'But leave out cowfoot with the *Satiday soup*, Kojo cannot stand the sight of it in the kitchen so he won't let me cook it. Sunday can get a bit complicated because he likes his buffet, so I tend to get several extra things made on Saturday, and finish them off on Sunday morning.'

She sucks the end of her pen. 'So, for example, if you get Ida to make the base for the *chereh*, and to clean the fish and everything, all you'd have to do on Sunday is to heat up the sauce, steam the *chereh* and mix them together. Ida can also make some pepper soup on Saturday and wash up all the bits of lettuce you need for a salad.' Her voice trails off, 'This does seem like a lot of work to hand over to you. Maybe I should get Ida to work overtime on Sunday morning and get all the food ready.'

'I can do my best. Perhaps you could explain to Kojo that things may not be as well managed as when you are around.'

'Well . . .' She pauses. 'Kojo will be good at helping Joy with her homework, and he'll go to all her school games and stuff. But he does like his special lunch on Sundays.'

'How about this – ask him to take Joy out for lunch. She'll love that, won't she? Chicken and chips down by the beach, with orange Fantas and ice lollies?'

'I'll suggest it, but he can be a bit set in his ways sometimes.'

I move in and take charge of Remi's household. It's a novelty looking after a little girl. So I don't mind going into work a bit later and coming back earlier than usual. Remi left thinking she'd be away for a week. She rings several times to give us summaries of her mother's medical condition. I refer to Remi's exercise book often. Kojo does not seem to mind my lapses from his wife's precise instructions.

Remi sends her father home. Frederick Adams comes to visit us with news.

'The hospital won't let me stay and the damn hotels aren't cheap.' He pats the pot belly which age has embellished and takes a swig of his Julbrew beer.

'Is she better?'

'I don't know. Those bloody doctors may be lying. They say she will get better. For all I know, they're hanging on until the insurance money runs out.'

'How does she look? Can she talk?'

'Bilor does not know who I am. Remi says they need to do more tests.'

'When will you know?'

'Remi will phone if something happens.'

'Will she be able to manage on her own?'

'Remi has things under control. She sent me back so I'm not under her feet. She says looking after one is more than enough work.'

He erupts into a spasm of laughs which turn into a cough. He points to Joy, who understands what he needs and runs off to get him a glass of water.

My mother's reaction: 'What a wonderful girl that Remi is, spending so much time looking after her mother. And her husband has been so understanding, what with letting her go away and coping on his own.'

Remi returns with her mother a month later, looking thin and ashy grey around her mouth. Two days later, her mother is dead.

As the months go by, I spend more and more time with Remi. I get to understand how she's stayed the same as the girl I used to know. And how she's changed.

On the morning of my birthday, the gate creaks open, a clatter of bite-sized footsteps follows. A sober voice counsels caution and the gate bangs shut. More clatter, then a knock at the door. Joy stands a few steps behind her mother.

'We're here, whether you're going out or not,' Remi announces. I open the door wider. She staggers in with a basket full of fruit, walks to my kitchen and deposits it next to the sink.

'Goodness, that was heavy. Happy birthday, Ayodele.'

I thank her with a hug and turn to Joy, who is loitering by the door. As always, her glasses dwarf her into shyness.

'How was your half-term holiday, Joy?' She shrugs, looks at the floor and her fat, ribboned braids fly forward. I glance at Remi who rolls her eyes towards the ceiling and slides her lips apart in a rubbery grimace.

'Why don't we get some tea going? Joy, you can go through to my office and feed the fish if you like.'

Remi's pores are oozing with news. Barely has Joy scampered off does she hiss, 'I found him out. And I've got proof.'

I move to the kettle, the constant producer of tea-induced comfort.

'What proof?' I ask.

'The tickets for that dance at Hotel Manding. He didn't ask me whether I wanted to go.'

Remi and Kojo graduated through teenage love to settled marriage and are now teetering through a weary cycle of accusations and protestations. Remi tackles all her battles iron-clawed.

'He might have forgotten,' I say.

'Oh no he didn't. He bought the tickets and he used them.'

'Are you sure?'

'Oh yes. I found it on his credit card statement. And not just that – more.'

'What are you doing, checking up on him like that?'

'I found out by accident! I was looking at what he's been spending his money on, to try to convince him that if we budget better, we'll be able to afford to send Joy to a private school.'

The kettle spurts out hot water – I've overfilled it again – and clicks itself off. As I make a move towards it, Remi hastens, 'No, I'll make it for us. Here I am, spoiling your birthday with my troubles.'

'What are friends for?' I smile and let a pause settle us both. 'Remi, maybe you shouldn't be so nosy – it might work better for you and Kojo. You've got to think about Joy too.'

'Of course, I'm thinking about her. But I need to show her that women don't have to stand for every kind of nonsense. Look at all I do for Kojo. How I try to take care of him. How could he do this to me?'

Remi's face is shiny with indignation, assisted by the kettle's steam.

'He is a good father, I've seen how he dotes on Joy.'

'I can't excuse him because he's a good father!' She thumps the kettle down, keeping her hand on the handle.

'Not just that. You've been such good friends.'

'Why are you taking his side all of a sudden?' Remi abandons tea making and stands braced, arms akimbo.

'I'm trying to understand, not take sides. Are you sure he's having an affair, by the way?'

'He didn't even bother to answer my questions.'

With the sound of Joy's footsteps in the corridor, I add in my final shot, 'Give in a little. For the sake of peace.'

Remi's face is stormy and I watch her fight to stave off the stream of protests gurgling up her throat. Joy walks in through the door. I ask her, 'How is JeinJein?'

'A bit lonely,' Joy replies. 'You should get her a few more fish for company, Aunty Dele.'

Remi has the ghosts of her choices to live with. And I have mine.

Her father also drops in to Remi's more often, and I see him there once or twice a week. There isn't really a courtship. After Fred waits out the socially acceptable year of mourning, he simply turns up at my house one day and makes a little speech which includes an assessment of how his age has had minimal impact on his prowess, a brief overview of my marital prospects, and how sensible it would be of me to marry him.

'And I have always been fond of you,' he concludes.

I tell him I'll think about it.

I dismiss it as soon as he leaves.

Frederick Adams is persistent though. He mentions it to Remi as soon as he gets a chance, asking her to put in a good word for him.

Remi is unsurprised. In her assessment, 'Look, when I was growing up, there were all kinds of stories about him with women. I don't know how much he's changed. It'd be odd

having my friend as my stepmother. We'll have to work it out
as we go along. You'll have to take your chances if you're interested.'

And at first, I really am not.

Then Mrs Adebayo sends me a cutting from a Lagos society
magazine. *Cutting* does not do it justice – it is not raggedly cut out
of the magazine, but specially reprinted, stapled to a copy of the
magazine's cover which features the lead story: 'Lagos' Wedding
of the Year'.

It comes in a yellow foolscap envelope, my name written on
with a flourishy kind of handwriting, all loops and connecting
lines. It is postmarked Amsterdam, and stamped as PRINTED
MATTER. It is eight pages of glossy photographs, accompanied by
a smattering of text.

On the cover, Akim is in a white *agbada* embroidered at the
neckline. The wife is petite, in an off-the-shoulder dress made out
of the same material; a thick collar runs into a banded sleeve with
delicate swirls of embroidery similar to the main pattern on
Akim's outfit. This co-ordinated look is commented on in the text.
The outfits were designed by Bishola Adeyinke, an in-demand
who clothes the president's daughter.

The church is a cathedral. It has ripples in the dressed
stone and the doorway meets in a sharp arch above the rows of
people standing in their plumage, surrounding the pair in white.
There are close-ups of the bride's bouquet, white lilies against
petal-tight roses, and sprigs of fresh green palm leaves cradling
them.

The photos of the reception show identikit little bridesmaids in
fluffy ivory-and-yellow-pastel dresses, and reams of smiling relatives holding plates of food. There are pictures of couples standing
with drinks in hand and smiling towards the camera, crowned

with names like Hon. Chief Omolabi Adekunle with Mrs (Dr) Jumoke Oyintola. Most captions are followed by a short CV: Deputy Minister of Justice, Chief Executive Officer of the National Petroleum Corporation, Head of O TV network, Finance Director of Northern Airlines.

In one of the pictures on the last page, the caption describes Akim as having a successful career in reinsurance, and as currently the Risk Analysis Director of Nipon Re. In the photo, he sits behind a huge desk, almost bare of papers, an expanse of smooth dark wood with a flat screen settled at the side, three telephone sets clustered on the other side. A huge old-fashioned blotter pad is in the middle, with fresh paper tucked into its flaps.

It's as if I'm on a large empty plain, and I've run full tilt into the only baobab tree for miles. Bang, face on. That I've winded myself and am now lying sprawled across its roots. I look up through sparse empty branches, some with the odd furry green fruit pod, straight through to a sky without a cloud in it. Flat on my back, unsure of how I've navigated myself into this position. Unsure of how I came to be like this: alone.

Did I know what I meant when I said no? Who says I couldn't have spun my own happiness in a life aligned with his?

I didn't kill him. The therapist sorted him out with time enough to rebuild a life. Mrs Adebayo had included a thick sheet of cream paper stapled to the front: *I thought you might be interested in knowing this. With best wishes, TA.* She had found me after all these years – just to tell me.

A temple-throbbing headache beats a refrain in my head:

and you said no
AND YOU SAID NO
and you said no

Each beat of the rhythm tramples my choice into my history.

The next time Frederick Adams helps me get a mechanic to fix my car and asks again, 'Why don't you, eh, marry me?' I say yes. He isn't perfect. I do not expect him to be. I've heard the rumours. As I tell Amina later, I am weary. I do not want to shoulder love at an intensity I cannot bear. I want respectability and some sex.

My mother sniffs when I tell her: 'Well, at least everything I trained you for won't go to waste. You'll have a household of your own to run at last.'

Other comments and advice come thick and heavy, laced with humour or spite.

Moira: I guess by this time of your life, you've got to take what you get.

Kainde: Why don't you try someone younger?

Amina: Sample the goods beforehand.

Aunt K: The world changes as you watch it.

Moira: Marriage is a trial but God can get you through it.

Taiwo: At last!

Reuben: I hear congratulations are in order.

Amina (by phone): Not to worry sweetie, my sharp ears tell me he's been around town and some.

Meena (by email): As long as your family is with you, it'll be all right.

My mother buys me a new Magimix that can chop *peppeh en yabbas*, cream butter and sugar, grind fluffy *akara* batter. She raids

85

her cupboards and digs up an inheritance of her household treasures: tablecloths and napkins, embroidered sheets and pillowcases, tea towels with pictures of Buckingham Palace, Arcoroc glasses printed with butterflies, teapots with painted-on sunflowers, sharp kitchen knives.

She says as she hands them over, 'I saved these for many years. I've given Taiwo hers and these are yours. Kainde's are still waiting for when she's ready.'

At our wedding, my mother's magnificent hat shadows my face as we stand in the sunlight on the steps of the registry office.

6

Rejection

'Boy, I'm telling you, I saw this with my own eyes. Grown-up men like me and you, rubbing their noses in that man's shit for a post in government.'

Frederick Adams is expressing his views on our verandah, lit by two kerosene lamps stuck on hooks on the pillars. There is no electricity tonight.

'And look at this. Even if we'd been fighting a war, there'd be nothing worth bombing. We're sitting in all their vomit. Ten years and still the same floating dustbin we had with the old guy.'

His friend, Musa Kinteh, replies, 'They call it progress. Did you see the Celebration of Liberation Day headlines yesterday? We came to power to give "Justice to the Poor".'

'You said it, also Water for Wasters. Farts for Farmers. All idiots, that's what we've got.'

'What makes it worse is that they are *young* idiots. At least the old guy knew how to do it with style.'

'These young ones threaten, then bang! bang! Six foot deep.'

The two of them are playing *damiyeh*, loudly slapping round wooden pieces on a homemade board cut slightly out of its square by the gardener, and then painted black and white on an uncertain grid.

'And then they go after your family.'

'You're right. We can talk and complain. But we have family responsibilities and you never know when they'll go after them to get at you.'

'*Tai. Tai.*' With each bang of a black-painted counter onto the board, Fred skips over Musa's white ones, embellishing the noise with his own sound of victory before settling to a final '*Tai*. You were getting a bit overconfident there, weren't you?'

'Watch your back. One little game does not mean you've won the match. Tell that to our government.' Musa stretches his arms out over his back; his chin, speckled with white beard, juts out.

'What do you say, Dele, look, I've whapped him again. He thought my mind was on politics but it's all tactics.'

I bring out two more lamps and a tray of snacks for the men. Another two of Fred's friends, Suni and Alhaji, are bent over a charcoal brazier, one holding a small teapot aloft while the other pokes at the coals.

It's game night. The men will play *damiyeh* on two boards in their own mini-league, well into the start of Sunday morning. A fresh pack of green tea waits on the small table on the verandah. The tea will be mixed with water and brought to the boil. Someone will add sugar. The first round will be light and sweet, with no depth. They will simply pour this away into the flower-bed where those stubby succulents with boat-shaped flowers grow. There's no one younger to give it to, no one who cannot as yet take the bitter tang of subsequent brews, the hit that drives away sleep. Their *ataya* will be thick and strong, but with a sweet undercurrent. There's a little metal plate that holds four cups. Suni will point the spout downwards and pull his hand upwards, making the tea froth into the tiny glass cups. He will pour it all back into the teapot and make it boil, thicker, blacker, sucking the tannin out of the leaves. When he's satisfied that it's almost ready, he will pour little tasters for the group to confirm his analysis. Heads will nod, or they will rudely tell him to continue his work, to deepen the flavour, to not lighten his hand or they'll choose someone else.

I go to bed early and leave them to it. Despite the threat of mosquitoes easing their way through holes in the netting, I open my bedroom window.

I can hear them.

'Ayodele? Yes, she's good to me, good for me. Right age too. Young ones want to go discoing every night. Older ones lose elasticity and only talk about who's died and who's born. She's in the middle. I think she'll do me right.'

'Your first wife was a fine woman too. Gave you three good-looking, well-brought-up children.'

'I'm not saying I haven't been lucky. But Bilor stopped delivering the goods soon after our third child was born. She couldn't see the point.'

Hearty laughter, one note brays out a nasal honk – Musa's laugh. Fred's laugh is mixed in too – heh heh heh. Then Musa's voice: 'That's why you went sampling.'

'Man, you can't blame me. I had needs that had to be met. We all do.'

A back is slapped. The night carries the hollowed thump.

'Boy, we know you well. Which of us has not been tempted? We've all been there. At least you didn't leave her.'

'Not that I didn't think about it. Bilor did many things well. She kept the house clean, she held on to the dalasis I gave her. She didn't seem to hear the gossip. So, it worked for all of us.'

'Say it again! Don't we all like the good women in our houses and the bad ones in our trousers.'

More laughs which rumble, almost seem to stop, then catch again and carry on.

When they come to pick him up, they come early in the morning. Even the loudspeakers on the mosque in Latrikunda have not been turned on. They come in a quiet white Peugeot 405, and back up its duck-behind in our driveway, blocking Fred's navy Honda with its crumpled back door. I am awake anyway. I often am, letting the sounds carried on the mixed air of early morning keep me company. Most of the footsteps are quiet treads of boots with thick plastic soles. Then there is the scratchier sound of a smooth-soled pair, wiping grit out from under it on the first step of our verandah.

The knocks on the glass pane are smart, sharp. Three times. Three knocks.

As I feel my way out of bed, Fred turns and grunts in his sleep. I misjudge the opening of the bedroom door and the edge sears into my big toe and wrings an *aah* of intense pain from my lungs. I wait to find myself and then limp out. My feet meet the rough softness of our sitting room rug and I hobble along to the front door, not quite ready to put a light on inside the house.

The bulb on the verandah reflects off the shorn shiny head of a young man in dark sunglasses. He stands with his legs slightly apart in a pair of khaki trousers. His short-sleeved shirt is made of a printed leopard fabric and cropped just above the hip. When he sees my face peering out at him through the curtains, he lets his right hand swivel back so I can see he has a holster on.

'Special Investigations. We're looking for Frederick Adams. He lives here.'

I cannot find any questions to ask. No time to think. No place to consider hiding him in. My head nods itself and I pull away from the door. Back to our bedroom where I try to shake Fred up.

'Men at the door. They want you.'

He turns over onto his back and blinks up at me. A plank of light falls into the room from the corridor. He's never easy to wake.

The knocking is repeated at the door. I shout out, 'He's coming,' but the noise continues.

I shake him again. 'You need to wake up and talk to these people. Shall I ring Musa?'

I walk back to them and say, 'He was sleeping.'

'If he doesn't hurry, we'll come and wake him up ourselves.'

I go back to get him. Fred's sitting up on the bed now, hands on knees, still fast asleep.

'You'll have to go in your pyjamas.' I'm shaking his shoulders as I tell him. 'We can't make them crosser than they already are.'

More sharp raps on the front door. Fred gets up and shuffles along, only just waking up enough to say, 'But what do they want with me?'

At the door, the young man says, as I open up, 'Old man, you took your time. We want to ask you some questions. You're coming with us.'

I notice the young man's shoes. They are black leather, buffed, with the tips of the toes curled slightly upwards. As he turns away, I can see the laces, threaded through in a classic crossover pattern. When I was six, I was taught to do mine just like that.

Two of the three men who'd been standing behind him all this while, dressed in army fatigues and berets, step forward, each taking one of Fred's arms. They propel him so it seems like he's being carried.

I shout out, 'Where are you taking him?'

'We'll bring him back when we're done.'

My toe hurts. I look down. The door lifted a flap of skin off. Underneath, blood is slowly oozing out. I need to sit down. I need to clean it.

*

91

I ring Musa as soon as light breaks. It takes him three days to find Fred. He's being held in a cell at the main police station. Fred's been heard saying things about the government. Now they want to know where he's getting his opinions from.

He comes home five days after Musa finds him. There's a darkly lined inch of healing skin high on his right cheek. His eyelid is twice its normal size, and has forced his eye half closed. His voice is slurred as if his tongue has swollen to fill up his mouth and left no space for words.

It takes three weeks of fiery soups, fish, oxtail, and pig's trotters to get him to stay out of bed longer and longer, until he stays up after breakfast, goes in for a nap after lunch and sits up in the evening to listen to the radio. He says little. Whenever I ask 'How are you feeling today?' he looks at me, steadily, then says, 'Just fine.'

Musa, Suni and Alhaji drop in to see him sometimes. They phone at other times. It's not until early November, when the sun has started to bake the moisture out of the ground, that they decide its time to have another *ataya* session, as they used to.

When I look at him next to his friends, with a picture of how they used to be barely three months ago, I see how Fred has lost his jaunt. His skin is stretchier, his body has shrunk in it – his jowls, rough with several days' worth of stubble, fold over like a new definition of landscape. Air can puff in under his shirt to take up space freed by his shrinking paunch.

Their renewed *ataya* sessions are like a two-day-old balloon, not quite full, and with a skin that gives a tired *thwap* rather than a high-pitched *thwop*. You see it if you look closely, but otherwise you won't realise that the skin looks more like crêpe than smooth enamel, that light no longer glints off it, that its bounce is a little lower.

Musa beats Fred in a straight run of three games.

'Boy, I'm seeing better than you tonight.' I can hear their conversation, fluttering in with the billows of the curtain by the door, and there is a ring of delight in Musa's voice.

Musa's lead increases to a run of six games. I hear Alhaji's high voice: 'Six, man, what *are* you doing?'

I drop a splodge of thick dough into a pool of hot oil. I am frying some pancakes for their snack. In the sizzle, I don't catch what happens next.

There's a babble of four men's voices, all of them speaking at once. Fred comes through the front door, clawing at the curtains that refuse to part before him.

'Something's broken. We need a broom and the metal dustpan,' he says.

'Cupboard beside the back door,' I reply.

His shoulders slope down as he takes small steps towards the kitchen door. He is in no hurry to finish his errand, or to return to the verandah, to his friends.

When I go out later with a bowl of hot fat *beignets*, Fred is playing with Suni, who is letting Fred win. But the jollity is no longer in the air. Musa is helping Alhaji with the *ataya*. There's a scatter of charcoal shoved towards a corner, and there's a patch of wet to the left of the draughtsboard.

I come home one day from visiting Aunt K. As I walk into the kitchen, I ask the househelp, '*Ainge na?*' Has he eaten?

'He's at the table, right now.'

It's like a switch goes off in his head, sparked by my voice.

'Where's the salt? How can you cook food without taste?' He bellows with rage that confuses the ear.

In the small silence that follows, I offer, 'I'll bring some for you.'

'What kind of house do I live in? Call this food? It tastes like boiled water.'

He's shouting at me as I round the corner into the dining room. I'm holding out the salt cellar. He pushes back his chair with a fierce scrape. He puts his hands under the table and pulls. For one moment I think he won't pull high enough. But he does. He gives one final angry shove upwards and the table topples. The blue jug full of water that was furthest from him is what I hear breaking first, then there's a clang of Chinese enamel bowl and lid clashing onto thinly vinyled floor. His plate and his glass send their shards right over to my feet. The apologetic tablecloth tries to mop up the puddle of tomato-stained water, the clump of rice, the tiny bowl of *ranha* upended and lending a splodge of green.

Of course, there have always been times during our five-year marriage when I have not known where he is, or could be. It takes him a while before he starts to go out at night again. At first, I am worried whenever he leaves. I try to ask.

'Where are you going?'

'Out with the boys,' he'd say.

'When will you be back?'

And he'd stretch an eyebrow upward and reply, 'I'll be back when we are through.'

To begin with, I try to explain, 'I'm only asking because . . .'

Sometimes I say something about 'you never know with these people', or 'roads are not safe at night with all the guns about', or 'I heard they've put up a new roadblock on Pipeline Road'. Anything.

He never picks up on my word baits. Apart from the one time when I tried to dress a welt on his back after he came home from the police station, and the Savlon bit into his skin, and he jumped up with the pain, shut his eyes and muttered 'those bastards'. He never said anything else about his eight days in a police cell. Instead he poured release into himself in golden liquid from a

Johnny Walker bottle; he blew out the pain in drafts of smoke that eventually steadied his fingers.

He used to spend one or two days a week out with his friends, but quite often would have them round at our house, to chat, watch the news on television, and loudly declaim about events in the world. Now, he's at home maybe once a week, and mostly silent when in front of the television, sated with news, bulging with opinions, but keeping them to himself. The rest of the time he's 'out for a quick drink'. This continues, until around Christmas I'm hardly seeing him at all.

The four of them form a tight lattice of evasive answers when contacted for information about the whereabouts of any one of them.

'Ring Musa and check – he might know.'

'Last saw him playing billiards.'

'Dr Faal had mentioned Rotary.'

'Are you sure he hasn't rung?'

Circular enquiries with no answer except that provided by his key in the lock in the early morning, fumbling. Then followed by uneven breathing, uncertain footsteps. And, always, a shower and the smell of Colgate toothpaste before he comes to find me.

I never expected him to be perfect.

I am making some pastry: a measure of flour, half a measure of groundnut oil, plus a bit of water to make it all stick together. My filling, minced beef with fried onions and a hint of chopped-up green chillies, has been cooling. I roll the beige pastry out thin. When I hold it up to the window, I can see light through it as it bathes itself in borrowed sunshine. I use a large plastic cup, green with stripes of white, to cut out rounds for filling. I have put on a saucepan with deep oil, to heat through. As I work, I hear the oil start to kick up sputters and I see little tunnels of bubbles skipping off the bottom of the pan. I fill the pastry and smooth some water onto a semi-circle of its edge. I clamp the ends together and use a fork to press down, leaving welts. I drop the first one in to check the temperature. It immediately sinks to the bottom, the oil isn't quite hot enough yet. I continue making some more rounds while I wait. When the frying pie starts to float and gently bob with the currents of bubbles, I know I'm ready to start doing big batches. I pick up a towel to hold on to one side of the saucepan and spoon out the pie that is now ready. I concentrate so hard that I leave a tail of towel hanging into the open blue tongues of the gas fire. I look down when I feel the heat licking my palm. With one throw I fling the towel off in an arc of hungry flame. My other hand clatters the frying spatula into a pool of its oil at the foot of the stove. I stand and watch the line of black burnt cloth spread, arc, advance and smoulder.

My househelp comes running in.

'*Woiye. Lu hewh?*' What's happening?

She's out of breath. Her chest heaves as she wipes her hands on her *malan*.

'*Du dara.*' Nothing. Nothing much.

She takes in the hunk of blue cloth charred black and grey, the tiny steams of smoke still coming from it. She smells the charring. She looks over at me, standing by a lit stove with a blackened meat pie in a slick of oil. She walks to the sink and fills a cup with water. She pours it over the towel.

I turn off the gas.

7

Age

Age sweeps across my husband, leaving his mind intact and his body decrepit. His right leg is arthritic. He uses a cane stick carved of ebony smuggled from Cameroon. The trunk of the elephant-headed top winds around the cane. On either side of the trunk, two slides of scoured wood mark the ivory. Two years ago, his prostate was removed. Age shouted and descended with a pension. All that was left youthful in him ran away for good. The gift left by his fear is a new desperation to live.

We now have a cook who can create what Fred wants for breakfast – porridge oats or coos pap, with slices of orange-pink papaya or mangoes cut and turned out to sit like crowns on his plate. The meal I learnt to cook best from my ma, *krein krein*, is no longer on his list of acceptable foods. The palm oil in it has too much cholesterol. 'But it's packed with vitamin A,' I protested. In its place is steamed fish with a side salad for lunch. Supper is vegetable soup, with a small round of bread. No chilli peppers, bad for the gut. No cheese, much much too much fat.

*

My mother, on the other hand, looks fit and healthy, but memory has been grated from her mind. When I tell Taiwo that I cannot devote my life to two invalids, she screeches back, 'Why can't that Remi help to look after her father? It's left to us two to look after Ma. Now that Kainde's decided her life is in America, she's never going to come home to do her share.'

'Kainde's working hard. She's got an important job with lots of responsibility.'

'I've got responsibilities too. There's Reuben. He's been promoted and he's also working all hours.'

In the end, we work out a rag-tag arrangement. Some of the nurses at the Fajara Clinic write out a roster that lets them check on Ma on their way to and from work. Nimsatu no longer does my cooking but looks after Ma during the day, getting a relative of hers to cover weekends. The final step is paying a Sierra Leonean woman, a refugee, to live in Ma's house and keep an eye on her at night. Kainde sends over some money – much, much more than her share.

As I am driving into work past a clutch of yellow-striped taxis, one of them swirls into a fast U-turn and aims straight for my left headlight. The driver looks at me as if it's my fault.

We both stop. We have to.

We get out of our cars and move towards our engaged bumpers.

'Mama, you were not looking where you were going.'

'Look here, young man, I am no more past this white line than you are.'

'If you hadn't swung out.'

'What do you mean, me?'

Before either of us knows it, the conversation starts to involve index fingers being wagged, hands set on hips, long teeth sucking *tcheepoos*, and faces twisted into knots of anger.

Cars start to honk in both directions. There's no space for them to go around.

In the red Mitsubishi behind me someone shouts, 'Just move your cars and give us some room to get by.'

I shout back, 'We're waiting for the police. Find some other way.'

'How? Look at all the cars behind me.'

I shrug, 'Well it's not my fault this nincompoop takes out my light on my way to work.'

Eventually, a beret-topped man in a dark blue uniform comes up to tell us we're going to have to move one of our cars to clear the road. The police will use the other to measure where the accident occurred.

He organises several of the able-bodied men in the now sizeable crowd of stall-holders and casual passers-by lacking excitement in their morning. Together, they wrench my car free of the taxi and, with me in it steering in neutral gear, perch it on the side of a large open stormwater drain.

I ring the Graceland Garage. 'What did you say is wrong this time?'

I explain.

'We'll send out our Land Rover rescue truck.'

In the next few months, I call out Graceland Garage at least four times.

Remi comes to visit her father sometimes. She brings Joy. When Fred complains that Joy cannot keep still and has to play outside, Remi gets cross and storms off, saying that if he can't appreciate having his granddaughter around, then he'll just have to go through old age on his own. The cold lasts until the next time she feels guilty.

The day my mother dies, I am in a mini jam near Latrikunda, in traffic that is so sluggish a tortoise could outrun it. We move forward one painful inch at a time. At the corner where a man sells some *tara* benches and beds, I notice there is a tiny dirt road, swirling red murram dust around the wheels of the minibuses as they turn into it. What I miss is the end of the storm drain, which has no marking, the bricks once built to guide traffic having been knocked off soon after. I edge the car out of the main line of traffic and turn right. The back wheel does not make it onto the bridge. I hear an ominous thunk and then the grinding of the wheel against the concrete. The car settles onto its back axle and refuses to budge when I press down to inject petrol into its engine. Everything stops.

It's getting dark by the time my car is back on four wheels and a mechanic is checking underneath.

Taiwo phones. 'Mum died ten minutes ago. The hospital just called.'

My mother's timing is impeccable.

'What! I'm stuck in a ditch in traffic.'

'Reuben says he'll leave work early and come pick me up to go to the hospital. Get there when you can.'

The mechanic pronounces the car ready. I rummage around my bag but cannot find small money, just a fifty-dalasi note.

'This is for everyone. I have no change,' I say.

There's a mad scramble as all those who profess to have been involved in the car rescue move forward to claim their portion.

Lights are coming on in the little shops around. Those that are legal, on marked land designated for the purpose, have bare bulbs powered from the electric grid. Others that are perched on the road verge, with makeshift covers over the stormdrain for their customers to stand on, have kerosene lamps looped over nails, offering weak, dimmed light in the dusk. The mechanic waves his hand around. 'I think you will all agree that I must first take my fees for being a mechanic. The rest, I will divide up for everyone else.'

There are a few murmurs of disagreement, but I turn the car round, edge back into the traffic and head for the hospital.

I guess it must happen to many people, that when you are unhappy to the degree that I am at the time my mother dies, all kindnesses become nests of comfort. Foday Sillah, the priest at my mother's church, comes round on the Sunday after she dies, doing his rounds of spreading goodwill in his parish. He seems prepared to chat and I drink it up. I kneel like a deer at a waterhole, support my body with lowered front limbs, put my head down to the water and drink my fill.

The comfort is in the little things.

It is in someone who is prepared to sit through silence. When I serve him tea, he sips it slowly as the light in my mother's living room plays with his face. I sit opposite with tiredness pulling at my eyeballs, and my shoulders frightened into tightness.

Kainde flies over for the funeral. We meet as siblings to plan, with Taiwo extending an invitation to Reuben for advice from a male point of view.

The week shudders along and the places where I can find quiet are less and less. My mother is gone. Yet the breaths of my mother's house swirl around me.

At the supermarket, I stand in the queue with my basket. In it are my calcium tablets and a tub of ice-cream. I'm behind a girl in a black leotard top with a deep V-neck and a skirt that swirls around her ankles. She is able to keep still with one knee bent, balancing on the other and not appearing at all stiff. She turns around as if she's felt my stare, and smiles. I smile back and strike up small talk.

'I used to have a skirt like that once,' I tell her. 'Yours looks good on you.'

'Thanks,' she says, 'what colour was yours?'

'Red,' I reply. 'Red – and it had two layers of froufrou at the bottom and was made of silk, and I used to wear it with one of those wraparound tops, long-sleeved. White.'

'That sounds lovely,' she says.

'Yes, it was. In it, I was too. It was one of those outfits that raise your mood to its level – my skirt was vibrant. Do you dance?'

The cashier extends a hand with a receipt and coinage as change, the girl in the black skirt stretches out long fingers to take it, and she half replies: 'Yes, modern. Bye then.'

She walks off, her body tightly tucked into itself, wearing a piece of my past.

The cashier's mouth curves into a smile that only lifts up at the very edges of her mouth, and she starts to put my stuff through the till. I come here several times a week to pick up things, always small items that I can fit into my tote, but she never throws me a look of recognition.

When I was a girl I used to think all cashiers brimmed with poise. I wanted to become one. They always looked perky in buttoned uniforms a bit tight up top, slightly open, and had finger-nails that used to take my breath away. The ones that impressed me were long talons, bright with pink lustre or geranium red, holding each item from the basket as if it were a treasure. The hands to which they belonged would turn an item over to locate the price, tap the number in, and then slide it to the packer waiting behind.

I see the cashier turn a wide-toothed grin, with a hint of a glisten of gold, on the customer behind me – a sharp-suited young man. I gather up my bag and leave.

I opt for a brisk walk on the beach, as brisk as I can make it. I stop at the golf course. The cut grass is freshly green, neatly sloping down the bank towards the sea. The park keepers have planted jasmine against the low wooden benches, so when I sit down for a rest, I prick off some of the tiny white flowers and let their crushed sweetness melt over me. The water plays with the breeze. I have a snack with me: neatly wrapped tuna sandwiches, a pack of crisps and a tiny flask of hot sweet tea.

While I eat, I notice a family on the beach with children. Their voices carry. They are shrieking at each other about sweets.

'She won't share. She's being greedy!'

'Calm down, you two. At once. Or I'll take the Skittles away. Now.'

A wail follows.

'She hit me,' screams one.

'She did it first. She scratched me,' screams the other.

'That's it! I'm taking that,' yells the mother.

Double wails.

'Pleeeeeease NOOOOOO!! Muuum!'

It's not that I *mind* children. My mother always expected me to become a mother in my turn, and a lot else besides.

I must have chosen this path in little steps, I have been so afraid of the harm I could do to a single other person. Harm was done to me too. Is that how it goes? The hurt yo-yoing from person to person until it loses its bounce and then stays in that last person – still and immovable. With all the Akims in the world, this is what I chose.

My mother – towards the end – when her memory played tricks on her would hold me one day and ask me never to grow up; another day she would scream at me for taking her favourite child away. She asked me once, almost playfully, 'And what do you think of childbirth, eh? Does it hurt, jab at you and make you yell like there is no tomorrow?' A contented smile appeared on her face. 'I bore twin girls, beautiful girls. Not everyone gets to have twins, you know. A blessing, a balm for my heart they were.' I barely knew her then. My Ma as I remembered her, acid of tongue, unreliable in praise, was gone. And instead was someone who wandered between different tenses: when her past became future and her present was never remembered. In odd moments, she seemed to glimpse that she had somehow lost herself, but mostly she hardly knew what she was. She became scared of the dark, and always needed a light on in her room. Faces from long ago she treated as old friends and her ever-present daughters were forgotten.

A young couple come ambling past sharing jean pockets, jumping the little steps to the beach together.

Fred is at home, possibly sitting in his wooden chair on the verandah, with a blanket covering his knees. The radio is probably on, very loud, as his ears have gone, and he needs new batteries in his hearing aid. I have ordered some from England which should arrive next week.

I go down the steps to the beach, not walking in the middle, where they are worn and the tread has an uneven edge. I walk with my body tilted sideways, making my right leg take the next step and carry all my weight before I bring the left to join it. Then the next. Halfway down, I stop to take my breath and let my eyes catch the sea. The waves are frothing busily in whisked white. There's a huddle of boys kicking a ball around on the beach, skimming splashes of wet sand.

We used to come down here sometimes when I was a girl, and I would skip down the steps to a beach empty of people and hotels, my flipflops flapping, my braid ends wrapped in red ribbon and bouncing. I'd wait at the bottom, watching my mother and Aunt K come down with a picnic bag each, packed with things from home – hard-fried tiny dough pieces, freshly warmed roasted cashew nuts, *wonjor* juice, and maybe if we were lucky a teardrop-shaped bottle of imported orange squash. 'I've beat you again,' I'd shout to my sisters. 'You're bigger,' my mum would shout back for them. 'You're still slowcoaches,' I'd yell back. Sometimes, the wind would whip the words away and we would keep shouting at each other until they came closer, when Aunt K would put down her bag, park her hands on her hip and let out an aah of accomplishment and pleasure.

'Can I choose today? Can I choose?' Taiwo might say as I ran off to find a good sitting spot. 'Pleaaaasse,' she'd beg. When I refused, she'd appeal to our mother. 'Ma, Ayodele won't let me choose where to sit. I *never* get to choose.'

I have taken to going to my mother's house in the evenings to rummage amongst the things she kept in my old bedroom. I find the old jewellery box that played a tune. When I open it, the ballerina in her pink tulle is still there. But her leg is broken. She is lying mixed in with heavy braids of gold chain and a tangle of silver brooches and earrings. I twist the key and the clockwork judders, as if to prise itself out of a bump of metal rust. The mechanism still works and the tinkle begins, slower than I remember. The stump of the ballerina's leg begins to twirl.

I look for some photographs, anything that will bring back the faces, that will slice the time between now and then. I show some to Fred. There are pictures of Remi and me, dressed to go out on my eighteenth birthday. She has on a slinky silver dress. I am wearing trousers and a see-through top. Fred doesn't remember.

I find a grey-toned picture of me sitting on my father's lap, both of us dressed in Sunday finery and smiling widely. My ear is resting against a cloth-wrapped button on his safari suit. When I peer closely at his face in the picture, I can see what seems like a worry on his brow.

There are pictures of my sisters, just after they were born, their tiny heads together in identical pink babygros. There are more pictures of them as toddlers, with fat cheeks. Then as the pictures go on, Taiwo gets plumper and Kainde rangier. I am there too, on my first day at school, with two new upper teeth bursting free, and my knees freshly slicked with Vaseline.

School pictures. Home pictures. Party pictures. As I leave, I glance up at the ceiling. I see that it was painted with only one thin coat. I can make out fuzzy edges of faded brown underneath the paint. Not enough to dream a whole future, but enough to imagine how the past could have been. The time that has passed between me lying on my bed, making my choices, and the now, with hardly any choices left to make. My life is more than half over. I am next in line to go now, now that Ma has gone.

STORY TWO

Yuan

8

Libido

Remi and I approach the disco in celebratory mood, my arm tucked into hers. The door swings open to a blast of dark and thudding. It is our invitation to pull on our party faces. As we wait to pay and be checked out by the bouncer at the door, I glance back at the row of lights dotting the narrow footpath along which we have walked. The disco is right next to the ocean, and doubles as a restaurant, with outside seating in thatched alcoves with flowers creeping up their sides.

The door swings open again to let us in. We move into the strobes and the promise of a good time. We sweep right up to the dance floor, and the song rhythms into my toes. I spot Yuan leaning on an elbow against the bar, a beer in one hand. I wave as I take my space in the mass of bobbing heads and bodies. I slip into the pulse and shake some wildness out.

We dance until a slow song plays. There is a general exchange of bodies as the freestyle dancers like us move off towards the bar and another batch of bodies, previously in clutches around the disco, disentangles itself only to re-entangle on the dance floor.

'What would you like to drink?' bellows Yuan.

'A Coke please, with a bit of rum,' I holler back. Remi asks for a Cinzano.

I watch as a tiny bird of a girl, on sturdy platform sandals, is swept up by a pair of greedy hands that move down to touch her bum as if they owned it. I turn my eyes away and instead fix them on a line of high-legged flamingo stools next to the bar.

There are a few girl-only groups dotted around, clumped in the pods that come off the circular space in the middle of the disco. One girl bends forward to say something into the ear of her friend. The friend's eyes swivel across to us, taking in Yuan's black jeans, his thick belt with a chunky brass buckle. They notice the stretch of muscle underneath the T-shirt as he leans over to pay the barman. Then they stop at me, assessing my ability to compete. First the cursory check: body shape, boob size, evenness of face; then the detailed look: not bad hair, good makeup, hmm dress, shoes will do.

I recognise Amina in the centre of a tight-dress-with-heels group; Moira is on the fringes, in a floral dress and sensible shoes. I shout into Yuan's ear, 'Saying. Hello. Amina. Stay. Here. Coming. Back.'

'Hello,' Amina says as I come close. 'You're looking good.'

I grin back my thanks, smooth my velvet trousers over my thigh and feel my courage building up. I am confident enough to rearrange my list – remove two names and leave two others on – Yuan Chen and Frederick Adams. It should be possible to make the choice and stick to my plan – somehow.

We dance some more and move around, holding onto elbows of friends, shouting bland intimacies into people's ears. Remi's boyfriend Kojo has arrived and the two of them are dancing together, laughing into each other's face. The darkness will make things seem easier. I find Yuan and ask him to dance with me. I allow the bold me to elbow the shyness away. I say, 'I want to talk to you,' then lead him away by the hand.

It's still early, partywise. Most people are eyeing each other up inside so there are only a few stragglers outside. It is easy to walk out with Yuan, steer him towards a bunch of rocks under a baobab tree by the cliff edge and say 'Hey, listen,' before turning to practise my first real kiss.

Once he understands what I am after, he asks, 'Are you sure?' He smiles at me and brushes my cheek with the back of his hand.

'Of course,' I say.

'Did you have somewhere in mind?' he says.

I shrug, not sure I can show I did plan ahead.

'How about my house?' he says. 'My parents will still be at the restaurant, clearing up.'

I nod. We head for the car park. The lights on the pathway seem brighter than before, the music behind us incredibly loud. My toes kick up a spray of gravel. The breeze is bringing wet air ashore. I rub my arms up and down as Yuan unlocks the car door on my side. I let myself in and wait for him to go round to the driver's seat.

I notice a question in his look. Before he can frame it in words, I lean over to kiss him again, so he knows. I am sure, I really am going to do this.

The road is busy with cars following each other nose to tail. I let Yuan concentrate on his driving. The doors close us in, we've left the windows wound up; the air in the car is thick with the thoughts of things we cannot tell or ask of each other. It's not far. As he predicted, his parents' car isn't there. The house is wrapped in its own quiet. A lone bulb shines on the verandah, dangling from an unshaded socket, with a thick strand of wire feeding into the ceiling. A gecko flicks away from the keyhole in the metal-framed door, its creamy body letting some light soak into its skin.

The key clicks. Yuan reaches round the door to turn on a light, then invites me to 'Come on in.'

He locks the door behind him and holds my hand, leading me towards a corridor that starts at the right-hand corner of the room. I've been in here before, but the light-coloured Chinese carpet seems swirlier than I remember, and the scroll-like paintings of mountain scenes and bamboo on the wall seem doubly alien.

But it's fine in the end. My fingers discover his skin, his fingers mine. Our breaths mingle. My ears feel hot. Us two lying on his bed, squashed, with me squeezing his hand. I repeat in my head over and over, 'I've done it.' It's strangely wonderful.

We hear a car door slam.

'Quick, bathroom. Parents back early.' He hops back into his jeans, grabbing my dress off the back of the chair by his desk. He shoves a pack of tissues into my hands, pushes me into the corridor, points to the next door and repeats, 'Bathroom.'

I hear the exchange of two male voices, and Yuan mentioning my name.

Yuan's voice is addressed to me, in English. 'It's my dad. Are you almost done?'

'Almost ready. My stuff fell out of my bag. I'll be out in a moment.'

I hear the front door open again and the metal frames clang. His father's footsteps are short and quick. A car engine starts.

When I emerge, I find Yuan in the sitting room with his legs stretched out in front of him, head back, hands linked together on his forehead, palms outward. He stands up to explain.

'Sorry about that. The watchman at the restaurant saw a light on in the house, went to tell my dad and he came to investigate.' He smiles. 'You OK?'

'My heart will stop hammering soon,' I say. 'How did you explain me being here?'

'I told him we have two parties to go to and we were en route to the second when you thought you might like to redo your makeup. So I brought you here.'

'He won't mind, will he?'

'Much less so than my mum. When my dad and I had our "you're now a man" chat, he did say that as there were no Chinese girls my age around, I could "get some experience with the girls at school". Not, of course, that I have done this before, I mean, at home, you know.' His voice trails off.

Nothing's changed in my body. Yet at the same time everything must have changed. As I walk towards the road in the morning, intending to take a taxi to Banjul, I can feel the wind at my elbows, the sun playing with my cheeks. I consider ways in which today is different from yesterday. It's happened, what next? Do I quietly enjoy it? Noisily celebrate it?

The taxi drops me off in front of the post office and I walk to the open-air section with the postboxes. The numbers 111 on our box, painted in white on a green background, remind me of stretching myself out alongside Yuan, being straight, almost touching but not quite, unsure. Was it mere accident that our bodies eventually found out what to do with each other?

When I open the box, I find a postcard from one of Kainde's many penfriends, this one from Calgary, Canada. There is a slight brown envelope under it, addressed to me, with a 31-butut stamp and a smudged date: 3 July. I slip my little finger under the fold at the side and roughly tear it open, leaving ragged flaps on one side and matching indentations on the other. The letter is on stiff paper with the crest of the British High Commission.

Dear Miss Roberts, it begins, RE: YOUR APPLICATION TO THE WALPOLE FOUNDATION.

My mouth dries and my tummy whines with tension. I unfold the bottom part of the letter.

I am pleased to inform you that . . . it continues, and the typescript starts to swim. I lean against the grid of postboxes for support.

. . . *you have been granted a scholarship to a British university of your choice to follow a course of study that will further the economic development of your country.*

Life seems to be rushing at me, handing out bars of chocolate with layers of marshmallow inside. A car door slams far away. A woman comes past me, her quick footsteps tapping staccato on the hard concrete floor. She walks to the opposite end of the line of postboxes. The letter is still in my hand when she comes back towards me to her car. It's Aunt Kiki. Her head wrap has slipped and her hairline is showing. She dabs at her face with a handkerchief edged with blue flowers.

'Ayodele, my dear, I didn't see you. Good news?' she asks.

I nod a yes, unable to make much of a sound. She quickly reads through the letter I hold out to her.

'Well done.' She holds out her arms and squashes me into a halo of Yardley's Lily of the Valley powder. 'I'll make sure I phone your mother later to offer her my congratulations. Must rush now, need to get to the market before the morning's fish is sold out.'

I manage to squeak out 'Bye.'

I walk to the groundnut seller to buy a scoopful of roasted nuts wrapped in a cone of white paper and then walk slowly to the Amet shop to buy a cold drink. I sit on the rough wobbly bench outside the shop, holding the bottle between my knees as I rub the skin off the nuts and pop them into my mouth. A part of my life will soon draw to a close and a new one has started.

*

When I arrive home, my mother's acknowledgement is sharp, high.

'Ayodele!'

'Yes, Ma.'

'*Bo*, where's your respect?' She emerges from the kitchen cradling a calabash full of wet rice. Smells of stewing tomatoes follow her into the corridor. 'Why do I have to hear news like this from outside?'

It does not take long for the rest of the story to emerge.

'Uncle Wole just came by to offer congratulations, having heard from Kiki that you got a scholarship. And there I was, mouth open like a fool, not knowing my daughter's news.'

I take out the letter from my bag and try to explain. 'I met Aunt K at the post office.'

'It doesn't matter where you met her. There are certain things that have to be said first within your family before you go mouthing them everywhere else.'

'I was holding the letter in my hand. I'd just opened it.'

'Even so! To be told my own news in this way. You might as well have broadcast it to the whole world.'

I stand and stare beyond my mother's face to the curtains breathing in the breeze beyond her, blowing away from the window to let a slab of sunlight paint the lino tiles on the kitchen floor. I watch as a gust of wind makes the curtains billow out, rounded, full, expectant. Then my eyes come back to my mother's face. I mutter, 'Here it is,' as I push the letter into her hands. 'I'm still getting used to it, Ma.'

'And so am I,' she replies, talking to my back as I walk towards my room. 'You have to remember I am your *mother*.' Her parting shot is all I need for the edge of my tears to come spilling past my cheeks onto my T-shirt.

*

That evening, Yuan calls. 'Hey, I hear some letters are coming out and that you've got one.'

'Yes,' and even as I say it I know my voice is drained dry of joy.

'What's up?'

'Can't talk about it now, really.'

'Want to come out?'

We find some tree trunks to sit on at Pa Tembo's restaurant. The coconut fronds shout at the wind and jiggle in anger. The wind growls back. I explain my misery: 'Certainly not because of yesterday.'

We end up back at his parents. And I stretch myself out, flat, straight, next to him and wash myself in his comfort. It's a warm kind of dark, with the lights outside throwing slanted lines which wrinkle across us and onto the floor.

'I'll be pleased to go away,' I say.

'But what about me?'

'You're a new thing. You hardly matter.'

'Ouch.'

'Well, you know what I mean.'

'I was thinking that . . . perhaps I could also come to London, if you don't mind, that is.'

'Us as boyfriend/girlfriend?' I ask in the wooziness of an evening that wraps itself around me, like a cloak. 'I don't want to be like Remi and Kojo – all over each other all the time. I can't do that.'

'That's OK. I can stay a friendly face if you want.'

At home much later that night, our watchman Osman shines his torch at the front door, so I can see the keyhole.

'Your friend was here earlier.'

'Who?'

'Remi. She was with her father.'

'Thank you. I'll talk to her in the morning.'

The door needs persuading even after the lock is undone. I press down the handle and shove the door upwards in its frame. I force it free of the sag in its loose hinge. Wood drags on wood. I let myself in, trying to deaden the sound as I manoeuvre it closed.

As we prepare to leave for university, I start meeting classmates of mine whose plans are also coming together.

At the taxi park, a bright blue Peugeot 504 estate with a we-know-Africa spring in its rear chassis waits to fill up with passengers. Amina is in the front seat, next to the driver. A large lady behind her, in a pink lacy grand boubou and matching headscarf, converses with a friend who leans in at the window.

I stop next to Amina, 'I'm going to Banjul too. Come and sit in the back with me.'

'Ooooo yes. I'm hearing things about you around town,' she says, gathering up a bag lying at her feet and opening the door.

We both clamber into the third row with its smaller, elevated seats sheltered by sloping panes of clear glass. In the open boot is a sack of rice in a brown sack stamped with Chinese lettering. A woven basket with a mix of vegetables – pale-skinned onions, earthy potatoes and a smattering of red chillies – is next to it. A chicken lies there with its wings outstretched and its legs tied. It flaps its wings, resigned to its fate.

'What's this I hear about you and Yuan?' Amina pats my thigh, us two conspirators in the art of dissecting our known experience.

'It's all true, but we're leaving for university soon. Anything can happen. He *is* easy to have around.'

'Have you . . . ?'

I incline my head towards the pink lady, crunching the skin between my eyebrows and rolling my eyes.

Amina shrugs. 'Sex isn't anything to be secretive about. She's' –

117

Amina nods towards the pink lady – 'probably found that out by now, anyhow.'

I mouth my 'Yes' in answer, not quite willing to discuss it in full, not just yet, and certainly not with the ears of strangers close by.

I am rescued by the arrival of two lean Mauritanians swathed in hues of indigo-dyed *mbaseng*. As they settle in next to the pink lady, a sharply tanged musk wiggles out of their clothes. One of them pulls out a handkerchief from the folds of vest and boubou and blows his nose. The pink lady shifts herself left. She interrupts her conversation to layer a look on the men, commanding them to behave in her presence.

A final passenger saunters up and the driver starts the engine and turns the car's nose towards Banjul.

We take the beach road, and whiz past mangrove swamps with their roots abandoned in thick, part-dry mud. As we wait by a one-lane bridge over a tidal inlet, I catch glimpses of crabs scuttling out of holes with neat piles of sand alongside.

Amina tells me how she intends to choose a college. '*Everyone* seems to be going to Dakar or England. I want to go somewhere else, even if I need to learn a new language first.'

We arrive at a bustling taxi terminal outside the main market. We say our goodbyes and I head towards the Standard Bank on Leman Street as Amina sets off for the Italian consulate on Jawara Avenue.

Time whistles by. Soon I am packing up a suitcase, stuffing in the best clothes from my wardrobe, selecting four pairs of shoes that will help me cope with the beginnings of winter. I am to leave on the early-evening flight for London. Yuan left a week ago and has rung to say he'll be meeting me at the airport tomorrow morning.

The house is full of the charred smell of chicken barbecuing. People have been dropping in all day. My school friends come to chat and leave cards wishing me well. Aunts and uncles, by blood or by friendship, visit with little envelopes of money – *dohlies* – 'just a little something, to help while you are settling in'.

Aunt K comes to say goodbye.

'She's leaving you now,' she says to my mother.

'Yes, *walai*, after all these years, they do grow up. Aren't they lucky to be going off by themselves? She can do anything now, no matter what I think,' my mother replies.

'I'm going to take her to her bedroom, for a little talk.'

We sit on the bed, me cross-legged with my back to the wall, Aunt K sidesaddle on the bed's edge. I start first. 'I'm leaving all this, Aunt K.' I look again at my room, through my soon-to-be-gone eyes, at the yellow walls, the fake velvet prayer mat I use as my bedside rug, my wardrobe with its doors that never quite shut. My desk that was littered with Letts revision notes only a few months ago.

'I wanted to talk to you, woman to woman. Your mother's mentioned this Chinese boy that you have been seeing. He's going to England too, isn't he?'

I look up at the brown stains on the ceiling, diluted in the middle and sharply defined at their edges. They are making me promises about life, showing me how to allow the future to be. I start to reply, 'But Aunt K, you don't have to worry . . .'

'Listen to me, child. I have seen you grow up. I know you are sensible enough. But this is the first time I won't be around to see or hear what you do. You'll be going to a big city and you can live however you like without busybodies like me to spy on you.' She pats the bed, creating two soft puffs of air. Her dress has stitching around the neckline in a network of sweeping curves that arch towards each other but never quite meet.

'My advice to you is to get your priorities right. Remember, you are going to study. Do that first, do it well. I hope you will get married one day, and a boyfriend is nice to have. But they can take your mind off what you are there for, and they can also get the most sensible of girls pregnant.

'I need you to think,' she continues, tapping her temple with her right index finger. 'Make sure you get a piece of paper that you can use to decide your life, so that you can get work that pays well regardless of whether you have a man or not. Only then should you allow babies into your life, or, if you want, marriage.'

'I'll try not to let you down.'

'Another thing. I know your mother can be difficult. I've known her a long time, and seen her suffer the man she chose. She's done what she could; being grown up does not mean we are completely without fear.'

'She's always telling me off, treating me like a little girl who can't do anything right.'

'She only wants the best for you.'

'I don't see that often, Aunt K, just her complaints about the way I am, or the way I do things.'

'I'll talk to her.'

She reaches into her neckline and tugs at her bra. A bundle of purple crêpe paper follows her fingers.

'Look. I've got you something of mine I'd like you to have.'

She unfolds the crêpe paper; inside are two diamond-shaped filigreed silver earrings. She holds my left hand and places each one carefully on my palm. Then she forces my fingers to close over them, pats my fist and says, 'Every time you wear them, remember your old Aunt K.'

England offers a poor welcome to visitors from warmer climates. It looks pretty enough from the air. There are tidy patches of

120

green as soon as the plane strikes the south coast. I see little clusters of stone within thickly wooded villages and small towns. The plane flies lower, over a sprawl of red brick and television aerials and busy roads with Matchbox cars. When I step out of the plane and my ears try to get unused to the dull throb of engines, they are greeted instead with a shushed silence. The carpet absorbs the footsteps of tired air travellers. The trapped air cuts off sound from the outside. There is a cloak of politeness and watchfulness in the staff welcoming us off the arrival tunnel. Outside I see careful rain that chooses not to convulse out of the clouds, but instead comes down in droplets of mist.

Nevertheless I find adventure rising in me, waiting to explode like a huge firework hidden under a plastic bucket. It has nothing to do with my surroundings or the climate. As I move towards the immigration desks, obediently following the track for non-European Community nationals, it feels like there is a giant curtain in front of me, made up of large patchwork squares. Some are indigo-dyed patches of *mbaseng*, others are marked with batiked shapes of crocodiles in kola nut dye, there are eye-deceiving patches of black velvet reflecting silver, and bright floral patterns strong with sunflowers, strips of sturdy corduroy, bits of plain white calico. And it seems that the curtains are about to part and I am going to move into a life that is spanking new, to which I can add bits that come only from me, unmodified by my mother.

In answer to the questions posed by the unsmiling male officer, I demonstrate proof of funding through my scholarship, I extract a piece of paper with my hall of residence address and am eventually allowed to push myself past the sentinel-like desks into a hallway where a signboard announces where I should pick up my baggage.

As promised, Yuan is waiting beyond the barriers. He pokes his head way out of the line of people, waving his arms into huge arcs in the air.

I'm relieved I have someone to hug, even through a midriff swollen by layers of thick jumper.

'I brought you something for the cold.'

He holds out a leather jacket for me to slip into. It smells of him – a fresh accent of soap, which used to be a pinky-orange bar of Lifebuoy, but is now something I don't recognise.

'You've changed your soap,' I say.

'One of the joys of doing my own shopping.'

He commandeers my trolley and ushers me towards the underground, to the entrance of the dark blue train line that will swirl us into the city.

The train is noisy and it's hard to talk. We touch each other's hands when we need to exchange information.

'Give me your address so I can look it up in the *A–Z*.'

'When do we need to change to the other line?'

'It's getting close to rush hour so the train will start to fill up as we get closer in.'

These little snippets of exchanged information start to warm, melt, ease, fill the air between us, building familiarity again with each other's spaces.

We spot a spike-gelled couple in greeny-black clothes, studded noses and eyebrows.

'Fancy a safety pin in your ear?'

'Or a few spikes of purple?'

'All is possible now.'

'There's no one to see!'

The train trundles upwards out of the tunnel. When the doors slide open, a blast of fridge-coated air hustles in with the passengers. The wind creeps under my trouser leg to wrap itself around my sock-covered ankles.

'Has it been cold?'

'A couple of days of weak sunshine. According to my mother, we see this kind of weather whenever seasons change their faces.'

'Thank goodness for your coat.' I hug it closer, bringing the collar ends together.

In between stations the train blasts out a forceful stream of hot air, but chills whenever the doors open. I am grateful when we descend once again into a tunnel that shudders with compressed air, yet offers more consistent temperatures.

Yuan and I phone each other when we can. We visit each other at weekends, when I try out my mother's *benachin* recipe and he tries out a stir-fry. We both settle into our own peculiar rounds of lectures and the rhythms of our universities. We start to meet other people and a few grains of friendship settle. Nowhere offers much privacy, and in any case, there is so much of the new around us that the bond of having had sex cannot compete. The memory creates a mist of knowingness, and keeps itself alive because of home. Home – a different kind of place, with its unstructured streets and weather of strong passions – sticky heat, pelting rain, cloudy dust.

Distances in London surprise. As does the amount of work we have to do. I start to go out enmeshed in groups that form within my hall of residence, my lectures and the clubs I join. So does he. As the term deepens, Yuan and I phone each other less frequently, we don't see each other every weekend. Yet I find times when I do not wish to see my new friends. I force myself to be with them, to enjoy aspects of the new, to embrace all that has been offered me beyond my patchwork curtain.

The cold hardens, rain melds into iced droplets, and another kind of greyness starts to envelop my days. It is not until close to Christmas that I realise I am homesick. My hall of residence allows foreign students to stay over the holidays in self-catering apartments – Yuan's doesn't. He moves out to stay in a student sublet. Without the rhythm of lectures, we find time to spend with each other once again.

It's two weeks before Christmas, and I have bought presents for my sisters, mother and Aunt K. When Yuan comes I am wrapping them up, for posting the next day. The heating is on high and all the windows are closed. He puts the kettle on for tea and says, 'It's a bit warm in here, shall I open one of the windows?'

I am still on the floor, surrounded by bits of wrapping paper, Sellotape and scissors. I have avoided jolly Father Christmases and red-cheeked angels. Instead my paper has wreaths of green holly with spots of red berries, or silver stars on a background of purple sky. I find that the cold stream of air, which refreshes the room and my overheated nose, makes me catch my breath. I squeeze my eyes tight.

'What's up?' He's come back into the room with two mugs of tea.

I try to explain. 'It's the rain being icy and the apartment so hot. And how it gets dark so quickly in the afternoons yet the mornings are slow to wake up. The pavements are full of people, the shops are full of cheery music but I am shopping alone. I like being able to decide what to do by myself but I miss my bedroom at home. I've made a few new friends, but they've all gone off on holiday. Here's you, my old friend, and I hardly ever see you.'

With the tears come hugs. With our hugs comes the fever of longing. Away from home and the familiarity of things around, I can know an old friend again. I will my mind to let go, I allow my body its space. I sink myself into him.

9

Grief

This is all I remember of his last morning with me in our London flat. He's clattering away with bathroom stuff: the shaving foam and razor that he hardly needs to use, the manly shower gel that has replaced bars of soap, the dental tape with which he religiously flosses his teeth at night, his special-action triple-layered toothbrush and associated paraphernalia. I am sitting at our breakfast table with a jar of strawberry jam and the remnants of a croissant-dominated breakfast. The leaves of the plane tree outside dapple the window.

He shouts across to me. 'You know what, despite your nitpicking tidiness, I think you're cute, and one day I might ask you to marry me.'

I reply, 'You know what, despite your tendency to pick your nose, I like your lips, and one day I might even say yes.'

There's a snort from the bathroom as he walks out carrying his bag of toiletries, which he shoves into the suitcase propped open in the doorway.

'I like planning life with you,' he says.

'And do not forget the practicalities. Find us a fantastic flat.

Make sure it's got two large desks and a great big shelf for all our books,' I say.

'Hey, you're not going to be much richer as a master's student, even in America.'

The doorbell rings and we kiss and hug. He says at the door, 'See you in a couple of months. I'll phone as soon as I get there.'

And he's gone.

Life does not necessarily warn you, so you can't take precautions. You don't try to delay the moment, you simply let him go. And later, when he phones, practically every day, you go on about other stuff. The girl at the National Audit Office with brass hair and green lips. The supervisor at the temping firm who insists you can only type at 30 words per minute, when you know jolly well you rattle along much faster than that. And you ask about the stickiness of Boston in the summer, and laugh about how houses have central air conditioning. And then it comes – the silence. Three days without a phone call. He'd said not to bother to call him, as calls were so cheap from the States. 'But just in case you get lost or something on your way over, I've written my cousin's number in the little address book by the door.'

When I ring, I start with, 'Hello, Chang. This is Ayodele, phoning from London. Yuan gave me your number when he left, but as he hasn't called for a few days, I just wondered how he is. Can I speak to him, please?'

'This isn't Chang. He is at the hospital.'

'Then can I speak to Yuan please?'

'Chang is with him at the hospital.'

'I hope it's nothing serious. When do you think Yuan will be back?'

'Well it's serious enough that his parents are flying over tonight.'

'What do you think is a good time for me to ring back? When am I likely to find him in?'

'Try again in about three hours.'

I ring back and again ask for Yuan. This time Chang answers. 'My brother told me you called earlier. You're Ayodele, right?'

'Yes, but I thought you were in hospital, are you all right now?'

Silence can have many layers, and it traps air bubbles between them. Chang's silence sears the moment in my memory. I get a spasm in my gut, where they used to imagine the centre of a person was. My lips are leaden, unable to form any more questions. My fingers, gripping the phone, seem greasy. I clutch harder on the handset, holding on to the silence, the last few seconds between my chattering and my knowing.

'I left the hospital only when Yuan's parents arrived. They are there now.'

I've been saving money while I work, so paying for my ticket over is easy. I take a single piece of hand luggage. I convert some pounds into a handful of green notes. On the plane I squeeze the ends of my lips upwards to offers of food or drink: 'No, thanks, I don't need anything.' I get off the flight with dread in my ears and a twitch under my right eye. My shoulders are frozen into a position that helps me carry myself out of the airport, get into a taxi, ask for the Mount Auburn Hospital. Roads soar over other roads and a bridge crosses a slate-coloured river. There are boats and rowers on the water. There are people riding bicycles. The world is careless with my pain. I cannot respond to the taxi driver asking me where I am from. I hear him OK, but my brain is reluctant to string words together. I reject several combinations and after a lengthy pause, can only mutter 'England.' The truth would require many more syllables and would doubtless prompt a stream of other questions. He interprets my one-word answer for what it is – a reluctance to talk, possibly an inability to communicate. When he drops me off, I tell him to keep the change.

This is what the hospital record says:

July 3. Male, early twenties, head injury. Result of motorcycle accident. Brought in by ambulance 19.20. Broken ribs. Lung punctured. Cardiac failure in emergency room. Resuscitated. Put on life support.

Much later, when I've left the weeks to creak by, after I've wondered about life's flick at a dice, about chance and how hope can be whisked away in the slice of a single day, I ask Chang to describe to me what happened.

This is what he says:

We were both on my KTM, and Yuan was my passenger. It was a Sunday so the roads were relatively quiet. We were roaring up to an intersection. A delivery truck was backing up to park. The driver did not see me. I crashed into the truck, but held on as the motorcycle skidded. My leg got trapped under the front wheel. Yuan spun off with the impact. He would have been fine if there hadn't been another car coming up fast on the other side of the road. I . . . He . . . It . . .

Chang cannot finish his story, four weeks after the accident, and three weeks after the life support machine was turned off.

Grief gets itself stamped on faces. Puffed-up faces, blanked-out faces, underlined eyes. I watch Yuan's parents and it's as if I am watching myself. Chang's apartment becomes a place of refuge, for Chinese tea, and for sitting around talking in half-whispers. Yuan's uncle flies over from San Francisco to sort out the funeral arrangements. Yuan's parents decide on cremation and plan to take him home and bury his ashes in their garden.

I can't go back to England. I can't go home. When awake, I get flashes of Yuan saying something, doing something. When I sleep, I imagine how the crash was, I imagine him saying to himself, 'This looks pretty bad.' And then the impact with the second car plays with decided slowness – pausing so I can hear his ribs crack, his mouth open in a scream. Then I see the ambulances rush in, and the stretcher, and a course ploughed through black-tarred streets by screeching, urgent lights.

I phone my sister Kainde, now a student in Newcastle, to talk about everyday things like flats that need to be cleared – refrigerators that need to be emptied of milk, rental documents that need to be found, spare keys to be picked up from the property agent, Yuan's books, my things.

'I can't go back to England,' I blurt out.

'I know,' she says.

'I need you to help me.'

'I'm going to London the day after tomorrow. I'll get the keys, sort out the flat and hand everything over to the agent.'

'Thanks.'

'And what about you, how are you coping?' she asks.

I allow the silence to fall, and let it speak for me: *I'm not*.

'I can come over to the States if you want. I asked Ma to ring Aunt Yadi and ask if we can stay with her in Connecticut. She says we can, as long as we need to.'

Little by little, I let other people make plans for me and help me glue my life together. Kainde finds her way from the airport to the cheap hotel I've been staying at. With one look at me, she starts to cry.

'Oh Ayodele, I am so sorry.' We hug but I can't cry. I am relieved she's here.

'Thanks for coming.'

I am packed and ready to leave. We take a taxi to the train station where she buys us our tickets and we wait.

The grief comes in tiny little ways. This morning I woke up smiling from a memory of Yuan, but as soon as my eyes flickered open to morning, my insides got knotted. The emptiness flooded in and I knew, yet again, that he is gone.

Kainde buys us both coffee and croissants. She picks up a *Boston Globe*. I add in three spoonfuls of sugar and sip carefully, glad to have something to do with my hands. A man walks fast along the forecourt of the station towards a gate, moving towards a train that is about to leave. I get shivery all over as I watch the back of his head, which is about Yuan's height, with hair and a neckline just like his. My eyes tell me what my mind knows cannot be true. I follow him along seeking the one thing that would confirm him as someone else. The man turns his head slightly to talk to a train official. I can see his nose in profile. My eyes sting.

Our aunt is waiting to meet us at the station. Once again I get the condolences.

'Ayodele, I'm so so sorry.' I also get a hug.

Kainde hands me a pile of letters she brought from the London flat. I look at them with distaste. I know already that they will force me to deal with things I do not want to acknowledge.

'Leave them for a while, you don't need to look at them now.' She gives me the excuse I need.

A week later, she says, 'Shall I open them for you? I might be able to help.'

I decline. If I look at them now, I will end up having to know. I will need to decide.

Another week passes before she insists, 'Look, there might be some really important stuff in there. You've got to open them.'

I say, 'I'll go and sit outside and try.'

It's a sunny day. I sit under the canvas shade protruding over the deck and watch some birds hop and twitter a few feet away from me. I have the letters on my lap and a glass of iced tea on the side table next to my seat. I rifle through the letters, trying to guess the contents of each. I pick up mail from Reader's Digest, the Reliable Patio Company, and ornamental conservatory builders. There are offers for garden furniture and book clubs. There are our bank statements.

A postcard has a smiling Rajastani woman in a red and yellow outfit. A brightly coloured scarf sprinkles her forehead with tiny silver balls. It's from Richard, a friend who's gone off to spend his summer in India.

Hello you two. Hot and sweaty here most days but loving every minute. Am in Jaipur with two other travellers I met in Delhi. We try to avoid the standard tourist locations, so are holding off on the Taj. In my adventures, I have found little temples on river banks, spice markets, fantastic dhosas and many friendly people. Don't want to come home . . .

I turn to two envelopes. The one addressed to me is a slim beige letter. It's a confirmation of acceptance for a two-year master's degree in international development and includes a form for me to sign. Yuan's envelope is massive, brochure-sized and white. The business school is sending all the information he needs for his MBA. Life could have moved on just as we'd planned.

I cannot ring the university to tell them about Yuan. I don't feel either Kainde or Aunt Yadi is eligible for the task. I call Chang, saying, 'I'm not even related. They're going to want to know who I am. I won't be able to tell them.'

'That's fine. I'll ring them.'

That's how it begins, my way of keeping a link to Yuan through his family. Later, once I've made up my mind, I ring Chang to tell him I intend to take up my place at university.

Kainde and Aunt Yadi try to talk me out of it. Kainde has gained a gaunt look in this past month of looking after me. Aunt Yadi has been quietly taking time off work so she can be around. Aunt Yadi says, 'Perhaps it might be wise to wait a while, Dele, and only go back to university when you are feeling much better.'

But I insist. 'I have to do this. I need to stay here because I can't go back to the memories in London. Here at least I'll be closer to where we'd thought we'd both be at this time. It will help me keep some part of him alive.'

I leave the safety and comfort of my aunt's house and head for a tiny room on campus. My new comfort is in being invisible in the common student uniform of jeans, sweater and sneakers. I need not attend any social events or orientation evenings. I find the lectures I need. I note where the classes take place. I buy the books and know how to cocoon myself in the library. I work on my essays and hand them in on time. I read everything I am supposed to. I nearly make it through to the end of the semester.

I start to feel brave enough to sit in cafés on Sundays and watch the world go by. I choose places that are not very close to the university. I relish the sense of feeling warm in a steamed-up room full of people I don't know, who chatter but don't need to be talked to. Then a couple walk in. They look nothing like me and Yuan. He is well built, broad-shouldered with a deep brown mahogany tone to his skin. He has on a woollen hat pulled low over his forehead, almost reaching his eyes. He is holding the hand of a petite Indian girl with a single long braid down her back and a red dot on her forehead, under the shadow of a soft-brimmed velvet hat. He ushers her to a table and after they settle down with coats and bags, he walks towards the display case and the cashier. He checks his step and goes back to whisper in her ear. She puts her head back and laughs, a clear single note which encircles the room. Several heads at nearby tables lift to look, but not stare.

The laugh stays in my head, it enlarges in my eardrum and starts to boom. I can see her mouth is shut. I can see him make his way back to the cashier. Suddenly I cannot bear to be in the same room as them. My fingers are shaky as I push the table forward, making my little jug of milk spill. Such is my urgency that I cannot do up my coat, can only hug its edges together with my hands shoved deep in my pockets, my shoulders hunched. The wind adds to the cacophony of sound as I step out. It bites at my ears and pokes shards of ice into my bare head. I start to shuffle-run in my sturdy heavy boots. I hit the elbow of a black-coated man who drops his briefcase and utters a curse: 'Fuck! Why the hell don't you watch where you are going?'

He grabs at me, but lets go when he sees my face streaked with tears.

'Hey, just be careful, right?'

I nod and walk on. When I get back to my room, the laughter is still there, not as loud as I remember it, but the consistency of an echo. My head is empty, my face is only a sheet masking a huge hole. I stay in my coat, with my boots on, sprawled on my bed. I doze in and out of sleep that night, and each time I wake up I hear the laughter. It changes shape, sometimes it comes towards me like ocean waves, hurling itself at me; at other times, it swirls around like a tornado. Once in the night, it felt like sleet, driving sleet, each thud of icy chill holding a beat of the laughter.

In the morning, I find it easy to get ready. All I need to do is find my hat and gloves somewhere in my coat pockets before I make my way to Student Services. I am referred to the Talk Unit. In a hushed, carpeted room, I meet a green-jacketed lady seated on a three-person sofa.

'My name is Dora. How can I help you?'

'My boyfriend is dead. I am here. And she's laughing.'

Somehow, I explain some of myself to her. Someone gives me a glass of water and some tablets to take. I wake up to find my boots off and my feet resting on the sofa with a cushion under my head. Everything hurts. My eyes ache. My toes throb. There are sharp stabbing pains in my chest, my tummy, my guts. I am alone.

Aunt Yadi is called. She drives up from Connecticut overnight to pick me up. When she comes into the room where I have been left, mostly asleep, I wake up in a daze.

'What time is it?' My tongue feels coated with tar and mucus. It also feels too large for my mouth.

I sit up too quickly and my head begins to pound so intensely I fall back onto the sofa with a groan. Aunt Yadi rushes over to my side.

'Take it easy, Ayodele. You need to rest up. I'm here to take you home.'

'What day is it? Lecture . . .'

'The nurse here thinks you need a break from studying. The important thing is to come with me now. You're not well today. When you're a bit more sorted out, we'll work out how to get you back to your lectures.'

I try to shake my head, but that only feels as if I've left a piece of ultra-heavy rock inside which I am moving slowly from side to side as I incline one way then the other. There is no point in arguing.

'What about my room, my clothes?'

'I was there this morning and I've packed most of the things you'll need. The Student Service will send in a volunteer to clear out your room later.'

We leave together. I am escorted like an invalid – I shuffle along, and lean on Aunt Yadi as we make our way along the corridor. I have to concentrate hard on where I am putting my feet, and I aim to put each footstep as close as possible to the next wine-coloured triangle in the carpet.

The journey is soothing. The first time I wake up, we're still in Boston, and on a raised roadway with most of the high-rise buildings on our right glinting back reflections from the sky too bright for my eyes. The next time, we're on the three-lane highway, moving quite fast, with the wheels of the car tracking the joins separating sections of the road. When I next open my eyes, I can keep them open for longer and I stretch my legs and move my head a bit.

Aunt Yadi asks, 'Water?' and nods towards the drink holder set into the space between us. The water tastes funny – as if it has grit in it, chalky grit. I drink some anyway as my throat is dry and I haven't eaten anything.

'Where are we?'

'Almost there, we're coming up to the last big town before I turn off the road towards my house.'

The road narrows and trees, mostly bereft of leaves, edge closer to it. Some plucky evergreens jut their sharp angles across the skyline. Everything else looks lifeless, and tinged with chill.

In contrast, the house feels warm and smells faintly of *churrai*, incense that Aunt Yadi burns to flavour the air.

'You can go through to your room to rest if you like. Or stay in the sitting room with the television on. Either way, I'll make you some hot strong tea and bring it in to you. Let me take your coat.'

The weeks pass, with Aunt Yadi nursing me by telling me what to do: when to eat, shower, go to bed. She returns to her job, as a lecturer in a small state college nearby, leaving me to occupy myself during the day. I cannot read, so she gets out books on tape or CD. I put them on for the comfort of a human voice, but the stories are usually too long for my mind to concentrate on for more than a few minutes at a time. I play them over and over again.

Winter morphs into a soggy spring, when the blossom comes out briefly before being blown away by gusts of wet wind. I borrow boots, a long slicker with a hood and start to venture outside for walks. The tears which spring unbidden, seeping out of scratched, clawed eyeballs, seem less conspicuous in the rain. With a wet face, I am able to cry whenever I want and for whatever reason. When I am able to look around me for longer periods, I start to notice other people, buildings, plants trying to stuff life into unwilling branches and twigs. Soon, staying at home all day listening to books on tape is no longer enough.

A neighbour of Aunt Yadi's pops in to borrow some wood polish, and mentions in passing, 'I don't know why I bother to pay her. I honestly cannot see a difference beyond my desk looking a bit tidier.'

I offer to do her cleaning.

She looks startled, her eyes fly to Aunt Yadi's face. 'Have a chat with your aunt about it first, and let me know.'

After the neighbour leaves, I explain, 'It'll give me something else to do. At least I'll have a reason for going out.'

My first cleaning job, for three hours a week, pays $10 per hour. My fame soon spreads, and I am busy every day of the week, going from one house to the next in the neighbourhood.

I always tackle the kitchen first, it's the messiest room in the house. I load the dishwasher, scrub the top of the stove clean, scour the sink. Then I finish off by sweeping and mopping the floor.

Each movement is rhythmic, the dipping into the bucket, the squeezing of the mop, the backward-and-forward swishing over the floor until my shoulders ache.

Bathrooms are places where it's hard to hide slovenliness. I pick clothes off the floor, dump cleanser into toilet bowls, squirt it into sinks to remove spat-out toothpaste, drench baths to dislodge rings of dirt left around the rims.

I go through bedrooms and shake bed linen free. I load up washing machines and take out fresh linen from airing cupboards. I open windows to let the air free, vacuum carpets and polish floors. A necessary job. My arm muscles start to gain tone and I look less like an invalid. I brush my hair before I go out, and always change out of my pyjamas before I leave the house.

While I clean, my entire purpose in life is to restore order. There's the detritus of daily living all around me. I put things away and leave with rooms tidy, clean, with everything in its place.

10

Altruism

Mali doesn't have many tarmac roads. This one is a memory of what it used to be – the tarmac crumbled a while ago leaving little hummocks of gravelled tar tipped with laterite dust. I left America and came here for distance, so I can be miles away from dashed hope, from home, from ambition. I am in my six-year-old Citroën Deux Chevaux, bought new when I first arrived with my generous relocation allowance. Its motorcycle-sized engine hums away, sounding like the self-satisfied purr of a very fat cat. It is interrupted by the kind of frequent burps a small government official would make after eating a huge mound of crispy fried fish. Market stalls displaying fruit line both sides of the road. Apples imported from France, tinged with an almost golden green, sit in specially moulded rough cardboard dividers that separate layers of fruit. Spiky-topped pineapples in their brisk orange skins squat alongside. Whole bunches of green bananas are propped up against the supports of the stalls, with their squat black-tailed ends curving upwards.

My observations are cut short when the car simply stops. I am on a slight rise in the road and start to slide backwards. I twist and turn the handbrake back. The fruit seller at the stall opposite mouths something I cannot make out.

I shout back, 'Pardon?'

He walks out from behind his stall and crosses the road over to my window, with its bottom half swung open and held up by a flimsy metal clasp.

He bends down. '*Des difficultés?*'

'I think so, yes,' I reply, as I eye the fuel indicator.

Empty. If only I'd made it to the top of the rise, I would have been able to coast down to the petrol station.

'Do you need help?' he asks.

By now, my car is attracting other people. A boy bends down to grin at himself in my right-hand wing mirror. A bandy-legged toddler waddles over to view the headlights. A woman with a sleeping baby tied to her back and a sun-yellow scarf on her head pokes the man who's just asked me the question. He turns away and they start a conversation, of which I understand little. Other stallholders abandon their wares and drag their feet into flipflops to come and check out what's happening.

I make my decision. 'No. I don't need any help. Thank you.'

I try to close my window as a prelude to executing my plan.

'Excuse me,' I say to the man who has one arm stretched out on my car, seeming not to have heard a thing I've said.

I prod the arm and point. 'I want to close the window.'

He stands up straighter but continues talking to the yellow-scarfed woman. Someone else, with her loosely slung baby suckling at one elongated breast, joins their discussion. I slam the window down and the three of them glance at me, temporarily pausing their extended discussion of my situation.

I pick up my handbag from the passenger seat and slide the little lock on my door to Open.

'Excuse me,' I repeat, pushing the door an inch. The suckling-baby woman shifts her feet slightly. No one else moves. I holler again through the crack. 'Excuse me.'

It does not seem to please them.

'*Madame*, wait a minute.'

I don't want to wait, so I jerk the door outwards, forcing the woman to take a further two steps away from the car. My exit isn't wide enough for me to get out but I put my left foot outside, to add emphasis to my declared motive.

The man at the centre of the throng of people tugs at her arm and pulls her closer to him. He seems to be in charge.

'We can help you.'

I cannot face the repercussions of how much I might have to pay for the help, even for a tiny push up the hill, given the number of people for whom I have provided a diversion from fruit selling. I want to walk. At the petrol station, I will ask someone to lend me a jerrycan and fill it up with petrol. Then I will walk back to the car and pour it in.

'No. I will get some petrol.' I point up the hill, and ease myself through the crush of bodies.

The older children detach themselves from the group and start to follow me. A few sharp admonitions from mothers make some turn back: Ibrahim! Fatima! Mohammed! Miriam!

The rest giggle and run about. A couple of them try to match my stride and my walking style, waving their arms about and bending forward slightly with looks of intent concentration on their faces. Their bare feet stir up little dust clouds and we soon crest the hill. They run down the hill, with arms in the air, screaming for the sheer joy of it.

At the petrol station, it's not quite as straightforward as I expected. There are no jerrycans on loan. I can rent one for half an hour, but first I'd have to pay a deposit for the jerrycan equal to twice its sale value.

'How much is a new one?' I ask.

'We are actually out of stock, madame, and the only one I have available is a used one of my own. I could sell that to you at half-price.'

I accept and ask for petrol to be pumped into it. I should know how trade works – a needy buyer and a willing seller. I am the one-person international trade department for the regional economic community, based in Mali.

By the time I get to the office, it's mid-morning and the secretaries have begun their tea break. The cleaner, Seydou Sankara, is delivering the last of the enamelled tin cups filled with hot tea. The tray he proffers to the receptionist has a large spoon stuck in an enormous plastic jar full of sugar and three large cans of La Vache Qui Rit evaporated milk, each with two holes pierced for pouring.

At my desk, I find a new pile of documents, most with a black plastic spiral binding and thick cellophane covers, which clearly indicate their source: internally produced reports. On top of the pile is a blue sheet of paper, headed: *From the desk of Musa Faal.* My boss has scribbled something:

> *Prepare summaries of all documents, and a position paper on West African cotton by Thursday. Attending fisheries meeting in Ouagadougou. I shall also want your decision by the time I get back.*

Musa travels to any meeting he can. The per diems are good, and he often traces a route to and from Mali that goes through Dakar. In this way, he gets to see his wife and children, for whom Bamako exists only as an edge on their geographical boundary of sensible places to live. From what I can tell, the map extends around Dakar then out to sea, and briefly comes back inland to circle St Louis in the north of Senegal. Then it scoots past the Mauritanian coast and zooms up to France and encloses the French half of Switzerland, up to Geneva. It follows the French border up to the Channel, cuts a choppy way across while ensuring all of the United Kingdom is missed out. Then there's a hasty trip across the Atlantic to catch the northeastern coast of the US, with a small enclave around Montreal. To access a chunk of America's western coast, it has to take in a snippet of Panama before a final dive for a funky slice of California.

I've never met his wife, but his teenage children have been to visit. I asked Lamine, lanky and be-jeaned, how his holiday was going.

'*Il y a rien à faire ici*,' he replied.

I knew what he meant, but felt it would be a betrayal of Bamako not to acknowledge its simplicity in its dustiness. The river, wide, lazy, with its huddles of unwanted sand, deserves better. The orange light that blankets the brown buildings at sunset should count for something.

By the time Lamine's father returns, I need to decide whether I can live here for another two years.

It takes the rest of the day for me to speed-read the documents. Around eight, with sooty darkness as company, I get into my car. Life closes early in Bamako; a few people go winking by with their blue metal kerosene lamps – but apart from that, the roads are pretty deserted. Only two cars pass me, their headlights nodding as they negotiate the dips and bumps of the road.

My watchman, Ndiarra, scrambles to my gate, which is simply metal tubes shaped into two rectangles, with a flimsy grid welded on top. My house is box-shaped with a covered verandah jutting out in the middle and darkened windows on either side – on the left, the kitchen and dining room, and on the right, my bedroom and study. The house is painted cream, but this can only be seen where the external lights carve arcs out of the inky black shadows. The garden is hardy brown, with nothing growing in it except for dust-covered, scraggy hedge plants. There are also two unwilling mango trees that flower expectantly with the rain, and then deliver tiny fruit that are mostly stone and never ripen.

I have too many things to carry in, and Ndiarra walks up to help. He waits and watches me search my handbag, my briefcase, and finally head back to the car to extract my keys from the ignition. We dump the piles of paper inside the living room, which leads directly off the verandah. I switch the lights on as I walk through the house into the kitchen. There are two saucepans on the gas cooker. My househelp has grilled some lemon chicken and made some flavoured rice for my supper. Both are lukewarm, so I light the rings and watch the blue flames lick the thick aluminium bases. I fill a small milkpan with water and put that on a third ring, for tea.

I return to my living room and plump up cushions before settling back. The phone wakes me up, and at the same time I smell charred rice. I answer the phone with a 'It's Ayodele, hold on,' then dash into the kitchen into a hearty melody of burnt smells and sizzling saucepans. I turn off all the rings. There is no water in the milkpan, I can see brown-tinged circles in the rice, and all the chicken pieces are stuck to the bottom of the saucepan.

Dealing with centimetre-thick bits of charred food would have been a lot more pleasant than a phone call from Frederick Adams, who I discover is on the other end of the phone.

'Ah, Ayodele, we are just passing through, on our way to the conference in Ouagadougou.'

'Fisheries, isn't it? But aren't you late?'

'Yes, but you know, I only need to go these days to help with the wrap-up, heh heh heh.'

His laugh is a cross between loud donkey braying and self-satisfied chicken clucking.

'I see.'

'Your mother gave me a letter for you, you know how these old ladies hate to waste money on stamps, heh heh heh.'

'Oh, how nice of you to bring it.'

'But we leave tomorrow. We can bring it to your house now, as we've just finished dinner, but we'll need instructions. These dusty streets are not easy without proper street signs, are they? Next minute, we'll be well on our way to Timbuktu, heh heh heh.'

'It'll probably be easier if I come to you then, to pick it up.'

'We're at the Hotel Dogon.'

'I'm a very lucky man to have such a dedicated secretary,' he says as he pats the knee of the slender lady sharing a two-seater couch in the hotel bar.

She simpers back and says, 'I am luckee too, to 'ave zuch a nice boss.' She pats him back on his green-suiting-covered knee.

He is wearing a full Kaunda suit, in the old style. The jacket has a series of fabric-covered buttons extending from his neck downwards to an enlarged midriff. His beard, now peppered with grey, covers a slightly slackened jaw.

She is his Guinean secretary and right-hand person. Without her, he could not operate in his very busy job.

'A busy man needs a busy secretary, heh heh heh.'

She smiles again, her even teeth glaring past her burgundy-red lipstick. She has a smooth dark complexion and a thin face, the regular features that define a certain kind of beauty. Her head is fringed on either side with a mop of brown-tinged curls falling to her shoulders – a wig. Her long black skirt has slits all the way past her knees; with one leg swinging over the knee of her other leg, she displays a strappy sandal with several inches to its heel.

I am having a beer, so is Mr Adams. Yolande has opted for a pink Martini.

'Remi sends her greetings,' says Frederick Adams. 'Life as a married woman is busy, heh heh heh. That husband of hers will keep her on her toes.'

I stretch my mouth into a smile.

'Now, where's that letter from your mother?'

He pats his top left pocket, and then his tummy as if the letter might have slid down while he wasn't looking.

'Yolande, my dear, could you go up to the room and see if you can find it? It's a white envelope and I am sure I had it in my hand earlier.'

Her first step suffers from the Martini-and-heels effect. She sways. 'Oh la la,' she says, and Mr Adams laughs heartily along with her.

'You take it easy as you go up the stairs,' he says, sending her on her way, in tiny little steps, towards the stairwell. 'She's a marvel. I really don't know how I could travel without her.'

Back home, I find my reheated rice and chicken cold and congealed. I need to eat something so I take the only clean frying pan, spoon out brown-speckled rice and a piece of chicken with a black crust. I cover it up with a lid and stand there to watch over it while it warms.

I sit down at my dining table and start to eat, taking out my mother's letter to read as I do so.

My knees are very painful at times, and if it weren't for the fact that I have a bit more padding than most, I am sure they would be much worse. A doctor was visiting from Germany, and he

said he wanted to see my case specially, as I sounded so unusual.
He suggested that I get some special fluid injected into my knee
joints. He comes here every six months or so, as a volunteer
with the hospital, to help train our young doctors.

The letter repeats some of the news I've gleaned from Frederick
Adams. As to be expected, she has added her own interpretations.

That Kojo Joiner, he's such a nice and stable boy. He's finished
his master's in business studies and come back to manage a
bank. There are so few well-trained people that he's bound to
go far. Just the kind of boy Remi needed. Hope you are starting
to get over things by now. It's sad when you lose someone, look
at me and your dad. But life moves on. I hope you will find
someone nice, like Remi has, soon.

Any sympathy I might have felt is burnt up by the rage building up in me. How dare she? How could she even dare start to
compare what Yuan and I had with what she had with my father?
He *deserted* her.

I push the plate away. The anger cannot sit for long beside a
surge of grief that comes to gnaw at my insides, that convulses my
stomach and eventually has me half running, half crouching,
clutching my midriff on my way to the bathroom. I throw up in
the corridor.

At work the next day, I plod through my reading. I have a go at
writing an outline of my report, and slot in quotes and figures, jot
down notes for my main points in each section, and a few recom-
mendations. Sometimes it's easy to rail against a world where the
prices are set to make the African cotton farmer unable to compete. Today though, the concepts of agricultural subsidies,

redressing trade imbalances, and reducing protectionism all seem too grand, too opaque, too removed from me. I leave early, piling the documents back into the car, hoping to use the evening to gather my thoughts together and say something sensible.

I stop at the river on my way home, needing to feel a sunset. I park the car under a tree and get out. The water is brown with little circles of still right out towards the middle, where the wind and the current are in such perfect balance that they create holes of quiet in the water. Mostly the water's surface is the consistency of light pancake batter being churned through an egg beater, with movements in all directions. A few dugout canoes are pulled up at the edge and I notice two teenage boys tying them up, looping rope through a metal hook driven into the bark of the nearest tree.

The day is losing its heat as the sky is dyed red by a disappearing sun. The clouds are high, wispy fronds playing out a stately, slow dance. I find a damp coconut trunk to sit on near the dark river sand and stare out, watching the water move. I do not notice someone else has been watching me, until I feel a tug at the handbag I put down by my feet.

The two boys from the boat come dashing up when they hear me shout. They run after the thief and manage to trip him up. The boys find it hard to hold him down and snatch my bag back. When they finally succeed, he scrambles up and runs off. As the boys walk back towards me, they slap their palms together in a high five. One of them holds my bag out to me. 'Here, *m'selle.*'

'*Merci,*' I say.

To which they reply, in unison, 'You're welcome,' and go back to their boat rope looping.

My boss Musa returns on Thursday with a lilt to his chubby step. His infectious chuckle wafts through to my desk as he does his 'bonjour' tour around the office, starting with the receptionist. His aftershave precedes him into my office. His cheeks are gleaming and his eyes are alive with merriment.

'First of all, my dear, *bonjour*,' he starts, bending to touch cheeks. Pulling up one trouser leg for ease, he perches on the edge of the table. He wants to hear how my report is going. When I'm done, he rises, rubbing his hands together. 'Excellent. You must leave that on my desk by lunchtime so I can have a look. There's the other matter, too. Will you be ready to discuss it tomorrow?'

The boys who rescued me are at the river when I get there today. This time I leave my bag at home. I walk down to where they are working on the pirogues. They are sorting through fishing lines and nets, disentangling them from the bits of hard packing foam that fishermen use as buoys.

We exchange greetings.

'*Kaira be.*'

'*Kaira dorong.*'

My accent mangles Mandingo words I picked up in my childhood; they use Malinke, a variant; to that, we add a smattering of French words, enough to make ourselves understood.

'And your family?'

'They are well, thank you.'

'Are you catching many fish today?'

'A few.' One of them indicates the catch of Nile perch lying on the other side of the boat, further up the bank. 'They'll sell well tonight.'

We break for a little silence while I watch them work.

'I've wanted a ride in a pirogue ever since I got here,' I say next. 'Can you take me?'

They nod. One of them points an index finger. 'Get in that one over there.'

I climb in, but there is nowhere obvious to sit. I start to sit in the middle.

'No, move up a little, nearer the front. You can sit on this.' He throws a pile of fishnet, still damp, into the inch of water lying on the bottom of the boat.

He lifts up a long pole which he tucks into the pirogue. The boys exchange a few words as they push the boat into the water. The back dips lower once it is free of the mud, and a bit of brown river water sloshes in.

My navigator clambers in and the boat tries to right itself. My arms lift of their own accord, trying to balance me. The boys laugh.

'A short ride only. Maybe to that tree over there?'

I point to where I can see a gnarled neem tree further up the river bank, where the river starts a gentle loop.

He sticks the pole into the mud, pushing hard. His ebony-covered muscles strain with the effort.

'We live quite close to here.' He nods in the general direction of the river as it flows down from Ségou. 'What about you?'

'That way.' I point in the opposite direction, as the river flows towards Kayes and the border with Senegal. 'My office is near there – I work to help governments sell the things we grow in West Africa at a good price abroad.'

'Like cotton?'

'Yes.'

'You should have come when my father was alive.'

We both pause to watch a fish eagle swoop low and pluck a piece of wriggling silver from the river.

'What did you do after he died?' I ask.

'We came here, to our aunt in Bamako, after we used up all our maize. This was in the drought.'

'Did your mother come with you?'

149

'No, she stayed to look after the land.'

'And after the drought was over . . .?'

He pauses. We are now where the river flows strong. He lays the pole down and picks up two paddles.

'She harvests enough millet now to eat. We send her money to help look after our younger sisters. She manages.'

'Is fishing good work around here?'

'We are lucky, our aunt helps us sell the fish. We make a bit more than we need.'

He picks up a rhythm with the paddles, and with each stretch of arm the pirogue rocks to the side the paddle was dipped in. We are both quiet. Apart from a few shards of scattered conversation that float over in the wind, all I can hear are the sounds of the paddles slapping into the water and pushing it back, against the busy twitter of weaver birds flitting around, still gathering bits of grass to complete their nests.

When we reach the tree, we turn back. Nearer the bank he switches again to the pole as he guides us into shallower water.

I hug my knees close in to my chest. My decision is already filtering into my mind, and it concerns cotton, scratched out of the hard, unforgiving crust that smothers this country, planted with hope once a year by people who have few alternative ways of earning a living.

Back on solid ground, I give him some money.

'For the boat ride,' I say. 'I'm Ayodele, what's your name?'

'Alasane. My brother is Salif.'

My boat guide walks over to their catch of fish. He picks up two medium-sized fish and says, 'A gift for you.'

'*A baraka.*' Thank you.

It *is* worth it. To stay here to work, and continue to forget.

11

Childbearing

'Just look at her. Bursting with bloody happiness.' Kainde sits next to me. The two of us are in the family *ashoibi* – yellow lightweight damask embossed with a peacock design. The tailor has embellished the hems of our skirts as well as the necklines of our matching tops with embroidered swirls of gold and brown threads. Our sister, Taiwo, chose the fabric for all close members of her family to wear. She also chose a different *ashoibi* for her friends and our more distant relatives, and we see several of them dotted around the hall in various outfits made from bright green and yellow Dutch wax fabric.

Kainde's comment is understandable in the context of the who-to and why of our being here. Taiwo is getting married today and has been twittering all week about the arrangements. Busier than a weaver bird. More fluttery than a sunbird. Our irritation has been griping at us all week. 'Especially,' as Kainde had earlier put it, 'considering *who* she's marrying.' We should be excited and supportive. We should be sisterly and blanket her with love and concern. But do consider the groom – Reuben.

The church part is over. As expected, the Old Testament reading was not from a raunchy part of the Song of Solomon, as
Kainde had proposed, but instead from the rib creation passage of
Genesis. The New Testament reading was pure Pauline – the par-
allels of head of household with the head of the Church, and the
necessity of the head being male. Kainde and I have further roles
to play today, and neither promises much joy. We have found it
hard to be enthusiastic in today's celebration. Kainde is Taiwo's
official flower girl. 'But of course we can't call you that,' Taiwo
had twittered to her twin sister, 'you'll be my maid of honour.' I
am to give the vote of thanks to the guests at the end of the
speeches. Taiwo had said to us, 'But you have to, otherwise what
will people think?'

'Honestly, who would imagine we were brought up in the same
household. In fact, who would believe I shared a womb with her
and let her come out first.' Kainde has her chin in her hand and
her eyes stare out of the hall, through one of the doors thrown
wide open to the garden.

Our mother makes her way through the tables, heading in our
direction. Her arms are halfway raised, ready to lightly land a
hand on the nearest guest who stops to congratulate her. She has
expanded into her role of Mother of the Bride, clearly demon-
strated by the beams of joy radiating from her face, her
gold-loaded neckline, her recently painted nails, her carefully
done-up hair underneath the large headscarf, and the wine-
coloured lipstick applied by the girl commissioned to 'make us
look our best'.

She gets closer. I give Kainde a quick pinch on her midriff to
jolt her out of her morose daydreaming.

'Ow,' she starts, turning to glare at me. As she swivels round,
she catches a glimpse of Ma on the move. 'Ohh,' she says. Ma is
within ten metres of our table.

'And what are you up to, you two? Shouldn't you be greeting the guests?' She flutters a hand towards the entrance. 'Or checking on food?' The other hand trembles the air between us and the efficient-looking caterers behind a line of white-clothed tables that will hold the buffet. 'Or maybe just mingling with the crowd?' This time her hand sweeps across to include the whole room.

'We've done quite a lot of that already, Ma,' mutters Kainde. 'We're having a quiet moment before Taiwo gets here.' The bride has gone home to freshen up before the wedding reception.

'We'll have lots of time to socialise later,' I add.

'Hmm,' Ma says, her eyes scanning our faces in turn, 'do remember this is a big day for me. I don't know when I'll be mother of the bride again.'

I take a breath, but clamp my mouth down again. Aunt K is clumping her way towards us in her heels, her bust parting the way ahead of her, and her rear halves happily complying with the course set for them. She's spotted potential trouble and is en route to clear the air, and separate the likely combatants.

'Millie,' she says to Ma, 'I think you'd better come and talk to the people who are setting up the microphones. I am not sure they know where to put them.'

As she puts her hand through Ma's elbow and guides her towards the front of the hall, she turns round to give us both a warning look, with the edge of a frown between her eyebrows.

'I suppose we'd better do our best to behave,' I say to Kainde.

And we do try, not making faces at each other even when our mother ends her speech with this: 'I am proud to welcome the first of my daughters into this wonderful stage of life – married life.'

My vote of thanks includes a joke about a spider in a colony of ants. Even though she deftly avoids the bouquet Taiwo throws at her, Kainde's confetti throwing is noticeably energetic.

Once the stressful part of the day is over, we can sit around and socialise at the evening do. We cluster with Amina and Remi around a low square table on which we rest our drinks.

Talk starts with the usual familiarisation. What we have been up to. New shops we have discovered this time round. A new seamstress in Serrekunda.

My mother's voice carries from over by the drinks tent. 'The *okor* has just phoned to say they will be late.'

Kainde puts her hand to her forehead and moans. 'Oh, and what an *okor*. How on earth are we going to cope with the years ahead of calling him our brother-in-law?'

Amina perks up in a supporting role. 'We're not gossiping are we, if we discuss something I find spicily important – would you say Reuben has changed over time, or has he always had this in him?'

Kainde mutters, 'This stuff is inbred, if you pinch him, it gathers under his skin; if you slice him, I'm sure it will come out with his blood.'

Remi offers, 'I guess to his credit, he has a strong sense of social justice. I heard him the other day lament about how the "lack of courtesy is at the root of decay in modern African society".'

'I'm sure somewhere, if we search very deep, we could discover the motivations for his pomposity. The problem is when he says something, you want to disagree on principle because it's come from him, even when he's probably right,' I add.

Kainde continues, 'That's exactly the point. When you think about all the problems in our society, only Reuben would pinpoint courtesy. *Courtesy*, I ask you.'

Amina again: 'Well, your sister seems to be very taken up with him, anyway.'

Kainde groans. 'Oh my God, you should have heard her. "We're just going off to buy our bedsheets. Reuben says the ones from

Elhaj are the best value." "Reuben thinks . . .", "As Reuben was saying just the other day . . ." It was so horrible to listen to, I forgot to puke.'

I smile at the memory of painful days spent listening to my sister. 'It really was Taiwo's reverse version of Simon Says, wasn't it? If she said anything that did not include a reference to Reuben, we looked up and listened. Otherwise, I for one just imagined my ears were sponges, through which her words were passing.'

'Aren't we being a bit harsh? Surely anything's better than being alone, isn't it,' says Remi.

'Huh? I would much prefer to stay unmarried than to be hitched to that kind of man,' says Kainde.

A girl wanders up with a tray of crescent-shaped deep-fried meat pies. Kainde pauses in her potential tirade to scoop a few handfuls onto the snack plates we are sharing.

'Honestly. Just as well there are good things to look forward to in life, such as delicious meat pies,' Kainde concludes.

Kainde and I came back for the wedding. Amina happened to be here for the Christmas holidays. Remi lives here. We're together for a short while, from different places and different lives. Anyone taking a snapshot of our group of women, first bound by attending the same school and later by friendship, would see what on the surface is a pretty conventional group.

Kainde is wearing our family evening *ashoibi*, in a cream-and-black weave shot through with silver, made from machine-embroidered cotton strips. Her huge head wrap is perched on her head but has slipped slightly to the right. Look closer and you'll see a nose ring. Should the head wrap fall off, you'd see a shaved head with a sprig of ponytail dreadlocks stuck in the middle. She has silver rings on every finger.

There's Remi, on the other side of childbirth. Her frame is still small, but her stomach is no longer held in by active muscles and it pushes against the Yoruba-style wrapper round her middle. Her hair, braided into chunky rows with extensions, peeks from underneath her headscarf.

Amina meanwhile is all manicured nails and zippy lipstick. Her interpretation of traditionally styled clothes is in the form of a tight-fitting panelled long skirt, with a halterneck top. She has dispensed with head covering and shows off hair that she has had blow-dried, wrapped, tonged and combed out with precision. Long sparkly earrings scrape her shoulders.

I'm in between the frump and the glam.

Conversation steers towards topics that do not heat up tempers or demonstrate our complete lack of sisterly pride in the wedding we are celebrating.

I spy Moira out of the corner of my eye. Her glasses cling to a nose much too small for them, crowding out her face and leaving only a bit of tightly drawn lips to define her personality. We can't all shrink into our seats, she's seen us and walks towards us.

'Lord have mercy,' from Kainde.

'*Ow oona do?*'

Smatterings of 'We are well, how about you?' from us.

'Praise God, without Him, I wouldn't be able to say I am fine.' Her attention is focused on Amina. 'I'm Moira, I've been saved for eight years. Who are you?'

'Amina, of course. I remember you from school.'

'Oh sorry, I didn't see you properly. Perhaps it's the shadows. Or maybe it's just that I am getting blinder the older I get.' She roars at her own joke, pushing her head back, revealing her unbraced teeth. Her glasses glint muted reflections of the lights strung out around the garden.

We suffer a few more minutes of Moira. She invites us to the New Year's Eve prayer meeting at the church. 'There's communion of course, but reserved for those who commune regularly in the congregation.' She giggles again, her chest heaving with hilarity.

When she leaves, Amina says, 'Oh. My. God,' and staggers off to get some more beers.

'She clung to the church when that no-gooder left her with three children.' Remi tries to find an excuse for an old friend.

'Why oh why did she not simply ask him for his sperm and then get on with it by herself? Look at the end result of trying to make a marriage work. Ends up with a screwed head,' is Kainde's judgement.

Moira, who investigations can show is a second cousin thrice removed, is involved in the late-night dispensing of marital advice before Taiwo is sent away from her mother's household into her husband's. My mother wisely holds back, and her sole contribution is brief: 'Taiwo I am very happy for you. My only advice is to say this – marriage needs work.' It is Aunt K who takes up her advisory role with an even-handed, practical approach. 'My dear, it is up to you to define how you want your marriage to be right from the start. If you want to work alongside your husband to build your family together, then that should colour every aspect of your life. Talk to him. Tell him your views. But above all, listen.'

Moira, taking advantage of a slight pause in the proceedings, grabs the verbal space and volunteers to pray. 'We see around us today many barren women, women who cannot produce children in answer to God's command to go forth and multiply. So today, before our dear sister Taiwo leaves this room, I want to command the devil to leave her womb alone. Instead, we claim it for Christ and pray that it will be fruitful, that she will have many children who will be the crowning glory of her marriage.'

Kainde smothers a sound from her throat, halfway between a

snort and a giggle. Moira continues, undented. 'And so, Lord, we pray that you will reign in their home, that you will be held high, that you will dine each day with them at their table.' In the micro-second that it takes for Moira's oratorical breath, Aunt K breaks in with, 'Thank you, Moira. We all hope God will indeed bless their marriage. Now, we must let Taiwo go and start her married life.'

The days burn bright, and my eyes ache in cloudless noons. Three days after the wedding, it is New Year's Eve. Taiwo and Reuben have gone to Zinguinchor for their honeymoon, God speed them. There are a bunch of relatives and old friends still around. I get invitations to lunches, beach trips, river cruises, *ataya* tea drinking sessions, nightclubs. But the buzz of thoughts inside me makes it impossible to accept. Wherever I look, emotions seep out of my skin, coating it in a thin layer of memory-drenched sweat.

The nights bring swift sea-chilled breezes off the Atlantic, and indigo darkness. Whatever I manage to fob off during the day slinks back semi-crouching with tail down and belly skirting the ground. I remember. In the jumble between sleep and wakefulness, Yuan talks to me. He laughs. He makes promises.

I will leave in two days' time. I have put off visiting Yuan's parents. I decide to walk to their restaurant, avoiding murderous taxis on the tarmac. I hope the trudge through sand-infested roads will calm me. I arrive to find two waiters outside setting the tables. There are carefully rolled napkins on which chopsticks are nestling. Little flowery bowls are upturned on plates. Several tables are still naked brown wood, waiting to be decorated.

My face feels dry, drawn. My head is heavy and my legs unwilling. I force the words out, feeling my heart drum out a loud irregular beat. I ask for Mrs Chen.

'She's in the kitchen.'

I don't know either of these waiters – they're new, they're young. Neither of them looks in the slightest bit curious.

I pause, uncertain what to do next.

'Do you want us to tell her you are here?'

'Yes please.'

'What's your name?'

Mrs Chen comes out wearing a red apron, wiping her hands on a towel looped through the front.

Her arms stretch out and as we meet, she enfolds me into the apron smells of burnt rice and soy sauce.

'Ayodele. How lovely to see you.'

'I wanted to visit before I leave.'

'We didn't know you were here. Let's sit down for some tea.' She flutters her hands. One of the waiters goes off in search of freshly brewed green tea and rice-grained cups to drink from.

When the tea arrives, we are talking about my life in Mali.

She pours. 'Did you know I have a new granddaughter?'

'No, when was she born?'

'Last December, she's a year old now. She's called Ivy. I'll show you a photo. Dawda,' and she turns to one of the waiters, 'can you please get me the photo album from the reception?'

'Whose daughter is it, Lee's or Wu's?'

'Lee's. He's living in California now. Married an American.'

The album arrives. Mrs Chen selects one of the loose photos inside the cover. In it is a chubby-cheeked baby with strands of dark hair sticking past her hairline. Behind her is a brown-haired woman, kneeling and looking down at the baby. She's smiling. I detect many things in that smile – pride, contentment, pleasure, assurance. The baby has something in her mouth, a plastic chewing toy with a hole in the middle. She is staring at the camera with a slightly surprised look, holding out her left hand.

'This picture was taken when we were visiting them in San Francisco. Look, here is another one.'

And there are more: Mr and Mrs Chen with a pushchair outside a purple-painted wrought iron gate. Lee lying on a picnic blanket with a polkadot-hatted Ivy sitting on his stomach, looking at him. In a streetcar. On a bridge. Eating at a Chinese restaurant.

I sit in the front row of the economy-class cabin on a Ghana Airways flight home, to Bamako. Next to me is a Bohora woman in a two-layered blue gown; the top layer is tied around the neck in a neat little bow. Her matching headscarf lets out a fringe of black hair onto her forehead and allows wisps to poke out of the side. She has a chubby-cheeked boy next to her, and is bouncing a chunky six-month-old baby on her lap.

She smiles at me when the flight takes off, revealing tiny rabbitlike teeth with gaps between them. We snack on packets of Ritz crackers and fizzy drinks. Her son is now kicking his legs up in the air, thumping against the cabin wall while lying back on his seat with his head crooked.

'He needs to go to the bathroom. Can you hold her please?'

I nod a surprised yes, confirming it with 'Sure' then reaching out to take the baby onto my lap. She's got dimples in her fingers and smells of Johnson's baby powder. I breathe in baby essence. When they come back, I don't want to hand her over.

'As long as she's happy, I can hold her.'

'Thanks for your help. It's a bit hard because I am travelling without my husband.'

She's going home to visit family in Kenya. Her son is two. When the plane touches down, I pass over the scented bundle of talc back to her mother.

*

The fisherman, Alasane, and his brother have become my friends. Alasane has left a message with my watchman: I am to call him as soon as I get back to Bamako.

'Is everything all right?' I ask.

'Very much so,' Alasane replies. Then he pauses. 'I want to tell you my news. My daughter was born on Wednesday, while you were away.'

'Fantastic. How are they?'

'Sidibe and the baby are both well. The christening is tomorrow and we want to name her after you.'

'I'd be honoured.'

'I do have to tell you, though, that some of the relatives think I should name my first child after someone in the Prophet's family.'

'In that case, don't worry about me, do what they say.'

'These are relatives who only come out for celebrations. My mother and sisters, who know how much you've helped us – they think differently. Now, because I moved back to the village, my uncles think my life is theirs to play with.'

'I guess that's how village life is.'

'They have kept on and on at me. I will bring bad luck on my baby, my family, the entire village. They called in the imam and the village chief to talk to me. So much pressure over such a little thing!'

'Will it not be simpler to use an approved name?'

'Yes, but we won't give in completely. Sidibe and I have decided that we'll call her what we like at home – after you. But we shall christen her Fatuma Ayodele Coulibaly.'

As Alasane instructed, a skinny boy in a light blue kaftan much too short for him is waiting by the mosque. He detaches himself from the shaded wall he's been resting on and walks towards me.

'I'm Mohammed. My cousin asked me to meet you and take you to the compound.'

My hands are weighed down with two bags full of presents.

'Is it far to Alasane's house?'

'Not very.'

He leads me through lanes with hard-packed earth and walled compounds. We squeeze by a few donkey carts and are nearly clipped by a hasty cyclist on a black Gunpowder bicycle.

'It's here.'

He pushes open a door made of corrugated iron sheeting, its aluminium sheen corroded by the wear of many hands that have gone in before us. The door grumbles under the clunky weight of its automatic closing mechanism – an old tin of tomato puree with a metal hook stuck into its cement fill. A rope connects this hook to another in the back of the door frame, recessed into the mud archway.

The festivities have started. Three groups of women sit on woven mats outside huts clustered around an open space. In a shadow-cooled corner, men sit on benches. They accept drinks from a tray held by a chubby girl in a cream-coloured dress made out of woven cotton strips. Alasane comes over to greet me.

'I am happy you are here. Come and meet my daughter.'

He leads me towards a square hut in the corner of the compound, ducking to get into the darkened interior. My eyes take a few minutes to adjust. I see a woman on a bed cradling a baby's head in her arm while it breast-feeds. I murmur my greetings and sit next to Sidibe. She hands me the baby. The crocheted wool hat on her head leaves little to see of her face. Her white bootees peek out of an acrylic blanket with patches of yellow, pink and white. Asleep, her eyes seem puffy in a wrinkled-up face. Her fingers are tightly rolled into balls.

When she opens her eyes and looks at me, I know she cannot

really distinguish me from the shadows of the walls and the slats of light that come through cracks in the wooden windows, which are shut. But I hold out my little finger anyway and coax her fist to wrap tight around it. In the split second before she yells, I understand something new, a flash – *Yuan dies, she lives.*

Her cries are strands of sound full of compressed hunger or a need for arms that she knows. I leave the hut. I sit outside on the mat with the women. We watch the drummers. The baby is named. Some people get up to dance. And all the while, as dust is kicked up from unwilling, hard-packed earth, I can feel the grip of tiny new fingers.

That night, I dream that Yuan is on a boat in the river. I am standing on the river bank and he is shouting something out at me. Every time I cry out *What?*, the wind whisks the sound away and scatters it into trees bare of leaves. Then he moves away from me, one rower in a team of four, and I keep shouting *What?* until finally he throws out a rope with words in glow paint: *Would you like to make a baby?*

With the scratch of light and sound that starts a new day, I know we can't. Not a baby like Mrs Chen's granddaughter. Not a baby like the one gurgling on the plane. Not one like Alasane's.

I work through the rest of the desert's harmattan dust storms until the winds change and the air dries as the sun drenches cloudless days. Ponds begin to present cracked cakes of mud alongside insistent bunches of bulrushes which are sucking the last bit of moisture caged in the ground. The light scours the eyes and slices the head. Then merciful clouds begin to float across the sky and smother the sun's rays.

Alasane and Sidibe visit sometimes with little Ayodele.

'And look, she can smile now.'

'She can lift her head while lying down on her stomach.'

'She can sit up if you support her with cushions.'

The memory of the little fingers doesn't fade as I watch her grow. And the desire to know how to give comfort, the wanting to be needed gnaws.

On a day when the clouds sheet rain, when the sound clatters on the roof like a thousand tin kettles banging, when the line of white fungus has crept down to greet the tops of my window frames, I phone Kainde, having made my decision.

'I'm having a tough time with this baby business. An opening has come up as a senior lecturer at my old university and I could do it. The main thing I'm thinking is that I could try a sperm bank and get one by myself.'

'Bloody hell.'

'I knew you'd say that, so what do you think?'

'Fine if you've thought it through. But what about not knowing who the father is, and what to tell the child?'

'It won't matter for a few years . . .'

'Yes, but it will matter one day. What will you say?'

'I can't figure it all out yet. I'm sure I can ask what other people do, there must be someone offering advice somewhere.'

'Oh, mum will have a field day if you tell her all this. What will you say?'

'That I've had an immaculate conception, of course.'

We burst out laughing simultaneously.

By saying it out loud to someone, I make the desire real. The wanting had built up without me seeing it. It had shredded my hope into little pieces – rough and torn at the edges. After Yuan died, someone else's laughter had torn all of me apart. Now, my sister helps me laugh a new kind of laughter, which heaves my shoulders and stutters my breaths – a laughter that stitches me back together.

My choice need not be about missed chances, about life skipping away with all my luck. I gulp down balmy air and soothe my lungs, and I laugh some more. My shoulders shake and the shakes rumble my head. Tiny hands gripping my finger. I don't need to have a baby of my own. I have a girl called after me, here in Bamako, where I live.

The laughter eases the want away and turns the future the right way up.

12

Senility

Ma looks the same as she's always done. I find her sitting in an upright wooden chair by the window, staring outside at the pomegranate bush, with its red bulbs and shivering stamens. I say hello. She looks up, turns back towards the small tree, and says, 'All my children have abandoned me. Daughters who should have known better. God denied me sons. No friends visit. But there are always red flowers. Beautiful flowers.'

Taiwo had not explained properly. Ma is worse than I expected. I kneel next to her chair and pat her busy hands. She's got one of the living-room cushions on her lap, a geometric pattern resembling one of Escher's designs – this one a staircase that never ends. Her fingers are restlessly picking at the piping on the edge. Her veins rise through her skin as she tenses and relaxes her muscles. Age's gravity has stretched her face, added lines around her eyes, and a bit more jowl to her cheeks. Yet she looks much younger than her sixty-five years. I remember her mouth looking more pinched than it does today. Her face has mellowed with her mind.

'Ma, it's Ayodele.'

'Ayodele, where have you been? Get up, child. Go make your-self busy in the kitchen. Get some drinks for the guests. There should be some *wonjor* in the freezer. Why are you looking at me like that? Go, go, go.'

I get up and move towards the kitchen. I have only been home twice in the last ten years, both times to attend christenings of Taiwo's children. She'd stopped after the second child, and there had been no other reason to come.

I stayed at my posting in Mali, unable to make much headway with beef exports, but enjoying moderate success in bringing cotton to the fore of trade talks. Home brought back too many memories each time, and too much tension was cloaked in the hugs and hellos from my mother, Taiwo and Reuben. I preferred to go to other places. Rome, to see Amina. Toronto, to see Kainde. I rushed around Africa, from conference to conference, or one familiarisation tour to another – Ethiopia, Egypt, Eritrea, Equatorial Guinea. Then I went further afield whenever I could, the more foreign-sounding the destination the better, especially if I could not locate it using a ten-year-old map – Tajikistan, Turkmenistan, Kyrgyz-stan. There wasn't much reason to my travelling except to stay on the move. I accumulated lots of air miles, per diems, lots of reports and business cards.

Then Taiwo wrote a long email to both Kainde and me:

I thought she was being stubborn about her diabetes medicine. I used to get really cross that I'd measured out all she needed to take every day for a week and put it in little labelled plastic containers . She would not take them. Her blood sugar would rise and I'd have to take her round to the doctor's yet again. I actually thought she was being dopey when she looked blank as I yelled at her about wasting my time and risking her life. At the doctor's surgery, we mostly saw the nurse, who measured her blood pressure and took a blood sample. But last month, we saw the doctor and he had a quiet word with me afterwards about a further appointment so he could do more tests. I thought it was all to do with the diabetes. But no – it turns out Mum has got Alzheimer's. I am at my wits' end with it all. She needs constant looking after. There's the maid of course, but I think mother needs <u>medical</u> attention, a nurse or someone living with her at home. Reuben thought I should ask you to help me sort this out. If either of you have leave coming up soon, could you please come home and see for yourselves. I did it all because I've been here. With the kids at school now, my family needs a lot of attention. I don't see how I can handle this new angle of Ma's illness on my own.

I spoke to Kainde first. She offered to go home for a while. This I related to Taiwo when I phoned her later.

'And you, Ayodele, what about you? Can you come home too?'

At first, I said I'd have to see how a visit fitted in with work. I didn't want to see my mother. I didn't want to come home at all. Home was where the past was, and I preferred the past to stay where it was – far away. Physical distance meant emotional separation and, gradually, the selective forgetfulness of voluntary exile.

That simple question had grated – can I go home? Not, will I go home? The will did not want to go, although it had every means at its disposal to do so. I'd been at my posting for fifteen years – there was nothing new about the job any more. I would get a full pension if I left now, particularly for a compassionate reason, a sick parent.

Human Resources at head office swung into action at my tentative request for information. They sent me photocopied brochures, links to the website on pension options, and a helpful little reminder that the organisational president was encouraging early retirement.

I began to feel unnaturally optimistic about home and started to make plans. I could buy some land. Build a house. Settle some-where along the river. Graft mango trees. It seemed feasible, and I gradually evolved an entirely unproven wish to return and help my mother through her twilight years. I wouldn't have to live in her house, but could find a place to rent close by and visit once or twice a day. I could help supervise the nursing care. And for once, I would be home without my mother interfering in my day-to-day living.

We have a family meeting later that day. A taxi drops me off at their side gate, and I find Reuben in a low-slung wooden arm-chair with cushions. He is reading *Newsweek*.

'Have a seat. Taiwo's gone to the market to get some fresh *bonga* for you. She's going to cook some *chereh* this evening, saying she wants to welcome you back with your favourite dish.'

I settle into the armchair next to his; a low table with his pint glass of Julbrew separates us.

'Something to drink?'

'Yes, a beer would be great.'

'Modupeh,' he bellows into the open door of the sitting room, 'come and say hello to your aunt and bring her a beer.'

It's quiet on the murram road past their house. By the low verandah walls, some perky succulents are offering nectar-filled triangles to hovering sunbirds.

'Look,' I say, 'those pink flowers are the ones we used to open and lick for nectar when we were children.'

He is surprised. 'These ones? Isn't the sap poisonous?'

'The three of us are living proof that you can lick them and survive.' I know Reuben was a child when I was, but somehow it's impossible to imagine him as anything other than himself, as if he'd only ever been a miniature version of the person I am sitting next to now.

Modupeh emerges with a bottle of Julbrew already beaded with moisture. He clutches a glass in his other hand. Before he can open his mouth, his father says, 'Come on, greet your aunt.'

He does. A polite how are you. His big clear eyes explore my face. I have only seen him twice in his seven years. He puts the bottle and glass on the table and darts off as quickly as he can, his mud-brown legs looking as if they can barely hold up his body.

Taiwo soon comes home, slapping the door of her white Toyota estate shut and coming towards me with a smile and her arms wide open.

At supper, Taiwo fusses around the table, getting up to shout instructions through a hatch between us in the dining room and her househelp in the kitchen.

'You know Pa Reuben likes us to use the big glass serving dishes when we have visitors, why did you put it in this one?' She is holding one of their everyday serving dishes, yellow-painted enamel ovals with curved handles.

'You can never get them to do exactly what you say, even if you repeat yourself fourteen times a day,' she complains as she swings round to the table. She settles the dish on the cork-backed, floral-pattern trivets in the middle of the table.

Reuben offers grace while the children sit with their hands held together in front of their faces, their eyes tight shut.

We talk generalities while the children are with us. About schools and teachers and the cost of uniforms and books.

After dinner, Modupeh is encouraged to recite a poem from school.

'"The sunbird", by Wilson Obote,' he begins.

> *'Quick of wing, rainbow feathered*
> *A trembly jewel pecks at my window*
> *The flash of light, the red of sun*
> *Only the sister of the flower*
> *Opposite.'*

'He's doing very well at school,' Reuben declares. 'We do all we can at home. What about you, Iyamide? Can you play your star song on the piano now?'

Iyamide jumps to her feet to pick out her tune on the piano.

'Now children, you can go and have showers and get into your night clothes.' And off they go, tiny backs down the corridor with crystals of light bouncing off the oil-painted beige walls.

The grownups can talk now. I represent the concerns of Kainde and me. Reuben represents himself and Taiwo. We move to the sitting room chairs, which are copies of the low-slung armchairs outside, but covered with a brown velvet fabric.

'Quite frankly, Taiwo here has done a lot for your mother while you and Kainde have been away. It would be good if she had more time to concentrate on the children for a change,' Reuben starts.

'Yes, but of course I will still help in some ways, especially at weekends when the children are at home. I can make lunch on Saturdays and Sundays, and Reuben or I will drop it off,' offers Taiwo.

And so we agree. I shall take on main responsibilities during the week. Two nurses will be hired to sleep in Ma's house at night, in rotation, making sure she takes her diabetes medicines.

At the beginning, I'm reminded of the way you get used to life at sea, retching during the first few days with the movement of water under foot. Ma is impossible. I am sure she has devised some inner game which she deliberately uses to irritate me. One minute she is lucid and willing to chat about Aunt K's antics when they were young. The next minute, she wrinkles her forehead and laments that all her daughters have deserted her.

I get used to the swaying and the lapping sounds against the boat. It starts to feel normal, and the memory of a ground that used to feel solid, that never once moved, fades. She becomes familiar. Lots of things annoy her. Like how the nurse moves her plastic flipflops whenever she's not looking,

'I put them under that chair, there. And now, she's moved them. What are they doing in the sink?'

My irritation sometimes becomes anger; at other times, I am flooded with pity, in an odd unsatisfactory surge of tenderness. I feel sorry that my mother is vulnerable. I always imagined her strong, imperious, commanding – right till the very end. That she was capable of fighting disease, and of pushing off death I had been in no doubt. Now, as her mind disintegrates, I sense bewilderment.

'You see, when you take the *krein krein*, you have to wash it well before you put it into the, that thing that you cook things in.'

Words drop out of her vocabulary. Sometimes she finds the names for things, even objects that might seem complicated, like 'toilet flush', but at other times she does not know what to call a pot, or a door.

When Aunt K visits, Ma always knows who she is. They find memories in the long ago to talk about, which make Ma laugh. Her whole body moves, her shoulders shake. She cannot explain what is funny. I laugh mostly with relief at the sound coming from her mouth. She giggles, she stutters, she points with her index finger. She squeaks with merriment, bending over with the pleasure of her laughter, clutching her side. Her face looks alive, with crinkled eyes, flashing teeth, uplifted cheeks. The laughter can stay for five minutes or be slashed away in a few seconds. Aunt K and I learn to sit and laugh with her, laugh at the joke of life, the inconsistency of memory, the cruelty of language. We laugh.

She likes to have some noise. The radio stays on and she mutters along to the news in Fula, Jola and Serahuli. The light always needs to stay on.

One evening, when I am sitting outside on the verandah with her nurse to discuss my mother's care, the power goes out. Ma is in bed, asleep. Haddy, the nurse, goes inside to get a candle. We hear a loud crash, then an almighty thump. Then a scream: 'I cannot seeeeeee. Alone in the world. All alone. I cannot seeeeeee.'

My mother's scream is a lament, a screech to rail against the holes in her mind that she can see reflected in the world around her. Dimmed, with hulking shadows that hide memories that might leap out and consume her.

Haddy comes from the kitchen with a lit candle and we meet at the door of my mother's room.

When we open the door she is not in the bed or on the floor by the bed. My eyes find her in the corner where we installed the sink. Ma must have walked over to where the glint of moonshine shows through the curtains. Her foot snagged under the stool we leave by the sink, she lost her balance. As she fell, she caught hold of the sink with her right arm. It did not hold her weight. She's pulled it halfway off its metal struts and is now half lying under it, with her red Colgate toothbrush on her chest, the toothbrush holder by her head and the tube of toothpaste flung halfway across the room.

Haddy pushes the candle into my hand. 'Hold that please.' She kneels next to my mother and holds her thumb against Ma's wrist. 'A bit irregular. Leave the candle on the sill. Get some more.'

Time freezes. The skin around my eyes is tight. I cannot see

173

through the corridor dark and stretch both arms out to feel my way along the walls to the kitchen. Here, the light is better because the windows have no curtains. The moon shines in, casting huge swirls of shadow from the metal grille-work on the windows. The cupboard where we keep the candles is open. I crunch on something. It's a box of matches on the floor. I light two more candles and take them back into the room.

'Come closer,' Haddy says. 'We need to get her to a hospital. Go and make the phone call. I will try to settle her down.'

I do as I am told.

'The ambulance from the hospital in Serrekunda will be here in about twenty minutes,' I tell Haddy a few minutes later.

My mother is now on her back, supported by a pillow at her side. Haddy has more news. 'Her arm is broken.'

She dies with her arm still in a cast. In the six weeks she is in hospital, the bone never sets. She dies in a web of tubes that balance her breathing with oxygen, feed her insulin and glucose, and take urine from her bladder. She dies alone, after I leave her room to go home for a shower, after being reassured by the duty sister that her condition is stable. The sun has set, drowning the air in orange light, keeping the world still, slowing us all down as the taxi takes me home.

Moira had taken to my mother's condition as part of her prayer portfolio. She inveigles her way into family discussions and seems to be consistently around my mother's house. She's usually here by mid-morning, after I've had my breakfast. I often make coos pap, from air-dried balls of millet flour rolled in a calabash with sprinklings of water.

Moira sticks as closely to us as sap from the frangipani. With nightfall, she clatters about, finds her shoes and says to either one of us, 'I am going . . . until tomorrow.' Kainde and I get used to leaving her in the sitting room and going off to a bedroom to make plans. We choose the Methodist church at the top of the hill for the funeral because it's not large, and will be less ostentatious than a cathedral ceremony.

Moira is banging around in the kitchen the day the priest comes to see us.

'My housekeeper gave me your message about the funeral. I thought it would be wise to pop in and see you, because although I did know your mother, I have not met all her daughters.'

He is Foday Sillah, and has been installed as priest for three years. I introduce myself.

'Where have you been?'

'I gave up Christianity early,' I say.

'Well,' he laughs, 'I took to religion late. I was a Muslim before and did not take any of it seriously.'

'Oh, what made you convert?'

'Rather like Paul, on the road from Farafenni.'

'How?'

'You really want to know?'

I nod.

'We came upon a car accident that had just happened. The car was crushed, and there was a sheet of windscreen across the road. The driver was folded into his seat with the steering wheel stuffed into his stomach and the front-seat passenger had flown out of the glassless windscreen, over the bonnet. In the back, on the floor between the seats, was a little boy, wrapped in layers of blanket. He must have rolled off onto the floor before the accident and got wedged in. He was crying when we arrived, but completely unharmed.'

'In Africa, fate plays with our lives every day.'

'For whatever reason, on this particular day this little boy made

175

me see life differently. More like a mystery gift that needs to be looked at closely.'

'What happened to the boy?'

'We took him into our car and fed him biscuits and water. He would quieten for a bit and then bawl out, *Mama*. We waited around, sent a message for the police with the next car that came along. The orphanage eventually traced his family. What I kept seeing in my head was a repeat of the last moments of his parents' lives. The consequences of death. The appointments that were not met. The clothes left in the wardrobe.' He pauses. 'Do you believe in God?'

'Did a long time ago. Perhaps when I was about ten?'

'And now? What is our purpose as human beings?'

'We're lucky enough to be animals who can think. Sometimes, occasionally, infrequently, when I notice people helping others for no obvious reason, I feel a glimmer of hope.'

'Helping others in what way?'

'Well, the kind when a bus driver waits for a pregnant woman, that kind of helpful.'

'But isn't that his job – to ferry people around? Isn't he looking after himself, doing what he is paid for, making sure he'll keep his job?'

'Think about it, lots of people get paid to sit in stuffy old offices with piles of paper who don't do what they're paid to do. They don't supply phone lines, malaria tablets, passports, title deeds, or whatever. It's never only a job.'

'You'll only believe in God, then, if you think it will make you help others better?'

'If you want to put it like that, yes.'

I am feeling cosy with all the thought attention I've been given. I detect in his look a promise that more of what has happened can be delivered. Then Moira walks in.

'Oh, Father Sillah, how lovely to see you. I hope you have been trying to talk Dele out of her unchristian ideas.'

'Which ones, exactly?' he replies.

'Hasn't she told you she's going to hold a funeral *charity* for her mother?'

'Me? Not just me, we. I am doing it with my sisters,' I chip in.

'But they only agreed because of her,' says Moira.

'True, but it was because I had persuasive arguments,' I counter.

'Which were?'

'That we are losing our traditions and replacing them with things not from the heart. I remember my body tingling when I was told that the dead float around in spirit for a while before they toddle off to the never-never. It felt mysterious, but it also felt right.'

Out of the corner of my eye, I see him smiling. Moira's face is a picture of attentive disagreement. But I plough on.

'Right because the memory of someone lingers after they die. Not only do I remember how my mother's face looked, I also remember her little habits. How she always sat on the tipping edge of the floral-pattern chair, first rearranging the supporting cushions to take her back just so. There are physical things – her old pink gown, green flipflops, toothbrush, a comb with her hair in it – cluttered around. It hardly feels that she has left.'

'Yes, but we don't have to celebrate a pagan ritual that is completely unchristian,' says Moira.

'Of course, Moira has a right to her views,' says Foday.

I am pleased about his answer.

'Think of it as a celebration of a finished life, Moira. Lots of food, lots of people who knew her, eating together.'

'Anyway,' I continue, 'we celebrated this tradition before the Bible arrived. The missionaries who brought it here scrubbed it clean of Palestinian life. This Christianity you talk about is lifeless without culture.'

'But no one seriously believes her spirit needs to come and sit at a table and eat food,' Moira says, her mouth set, her body tense.

'Yes, but many do believe that a saviour can die with cruel wounds and rise three days later. And that is entirely consistent,' I say.

'These beliefs are not the same. You cannot look at both of these events in the same way, it's blasphemy to talk about them in the same breath.'

The conversation ends with all of us secure in the way we see and understand the world.

We hold Ma's *charity* the day she is buried. More people come than any of us had expected. We run out to the supermarket to buy more drinks, and phone Mama Cobola to fry emergency dough-nuts and deliver them to the house by taxi. My head swings between a sense of loss and cynicism – in the end, we all die. Ma's gone, and her brand of self has disappeared for ever.

13

Stepmothering

The day starts crisp, the crispest kind of morning you get this close to the equator. The sky is baby blue, freshly gelled with combed-through clouds spreading thinned lines of vapour against it. Inside I stay calm, but I know bad stuff can still happen, even when there's only three hours left. There is no need to spell it out to myself: 'Stuff happens.'

I slip into my outfit made from white lace in twelve-inch strips. The fabric has been transformed into a two-piece. My top's scalloped edges face each other in a trail across my tummy. My breasts are cupped in a ruched spread of more scallop, joined in their shadow. A great deal of skin is exposed from breastline to neckline. The sleeves puff out to strips of lace that extend down from my shoulder blades. My back is solidly covered, with a long zip to enfold me into its shape. The skirt falls simply to my ankles, in horizontal strips stitched on top of a greyish poplin that peeks through the holes in the lace. Two side slits allow me to walk.

My shoes were handmade by Sierra Leonean refugees. They

are tapestried in silver-streaked wool into an intricate floral design. The wool design slashes across each foot, and my heels are raised at least an inch by sturdy stumps of shaped wood.

After a series of quick taps on my door, Kainde bursts in. 'Come *on*, how much thinking time do you need as you get ready? The car is downstairs, and I've got to check you're put together properly.'

'See,' I reply, 'my makeup is where it should be. The eyeliner is mostly around my eyes, and look, the lipstick line is on my lips.' I turn my face from side to side. 'Powder. No shine. I told you I could get ready by myself.'

'Well never mind that. Stand up and turn around. Slowly. Let me have a good look.'

I do as I'm told. Her critical eyes make her unbelieving hands touch my head wrap to check it will not unwind, touch the hair slides that secure it in hidden places. My chin is tipped upwards to verify that there is no visible foundation line. Her hands adjust imaginary seams and straying threads, and, finally, she pronounces me ready.

I choose to walk into a church and meet Foday Sillah arrayed in a white embroidered *agbada* with long-sleeved shirt, *chaya* underneath, and white leather slippers with slightly upturned tips. I agree to marry him in sight of an assortment of friends and family in a little building atop a cliff. As we move deeper into the ceremony, little dribbles of happiness trickle inside me. By the time we have made it through the reception, the trickles have joined to form a rivulet of joy that finds and fills tiny crevices everywhere in me. I touch my cheeks against those of well-wishers and have my hand pumped for luck. I dance unencumbered by heels and shift clouds of dust onto my skirt's hem.

We spend a week in St Louis, mostly in a second-floor room of a weathered house on the quayside. The yellow paint on the room's door-sized wooden shutters is crumbling; they shudder in salty sea breezes and open onto a tiny little balcony.

Then it's over. The commitment has been made. I move into Foday's house and settle into the skin of a stepmother, inheriting three teenage children who hardly know me. I also try to wriggle into the mould of a priest's wife.

On our return, Foday's first sermon is on 'Joy, the undefinable feeling of wellbeing, that all is right with the world, despite an inner knowledge that people are sick, being tortured to the point of death, hungry and beggarly all over. And yet, we all need to learn how to slice moments of wellbeing from our daily lives, in the midst of humdrum everyday things, to claim for ourselves an existence of joy.'

He looks over at me.

At the end of the service, I cannot decide where to stand. Next to Foday at the door would mean shaking hands with everyone, in the spirit of preacher's wife. Staying seated in the church would be rude. Running out to the shade of the flat-topped flame tree outside would be verging on imbecilic. I stash away the thought and label it: *to be discussed further, and at length*. And skulk towards the organist to chat about music.

'How do you choose what tune to play with each hymn? You played some unusual ones today.'

He turns towards me, his eyes watery through large, brown-framed glasses that generously cover a third of his face. 'I do that to keep everyone on their toes. But I always make sure I test it out with the choir first.'

Foday comes to rescue me when all the pews are empty and there are bubbles of conversation outside intermingled with doors slamming and car engines starting.

'Come on out – why are you hiding?'

181

I let him lead me outside, and we head slam bang into Mrs Acheampong, whose heels eagerly scrape the concreted floor in her hurry to reach us with an outstretched hand.

'The new Mrs Sillah. How lovely to meet you at last.'

She tilts her face to clear space for her eyes to make contact with mine underneath the brim of her hat. There's a certain angle to her chin.

I mumble a hello.

'We'll have to come over to have a chat. The Mothers' Union in this church is very active, you know. We would like you to get involved as soon as you've settled in.'

I smile and murmur, 'We'll have to see. Thank you for thinking about me.'

There is a muffled bang as the fly door on the back verandah swings shut. A few thumps and shuffles follow, and low murmurings. I believe I hear someone say, 'You go first.' A moment later Foday's eldest daughter, Sira, comes into the dining room, where I am sitting at the scrubbed Formica-topped table, with a rusting metal reading lamp perched on my makeshift desk.

'Watch ou—' I start to say, but Sira walks straight into the loose arc of white wire linking the lamp with the old-fashioned plug. The lamp topples, and I try to grab at it. My fingers shriek at the heated metal shade and I immediately let go, twisting its trajectory. I watch it swipe at my washed marmalade jar filled with an assortment of pens and pencils plus eraser, sharpener and six-inch ruler. The split second before the noise is dead silent, as if Sira, me, the house, the sea in the background, have all stopped breathing, waiting for gravity to have its moment.

The metal curve of the lamp's base clangs against the polished red floor, and the bulb tinkles into shards of glass. They are joined by the splinters of heavy glass as the jar is smithereened, an arched firework burping out writing paraphernalia.

'Oops,' she says, and edges forward, crunching glass under her German orthopaedic sandals.

'Stay where you are,' I order, as two more pairs of shuffling feet come into the room.

'Wazup?' says one.

'You can see wazup,' I snap in answer. 'Get us a dustpan and broom if you want to be helpful.'

Sira doesn't say sorry. I don't realise it now, but she will never say sorry. She may try to explain herself, or the circumstance, but that single word that was murmured to me throughout my childhood, and that I learnt in my turn to say to soothe the feelings of others, is something I will never hear her say.

'I wanted to say hello,' she says, but her mouth curls up slightly at one corner. One braid, long and thick with extensions, has slunk out of her hairband and is lying across her eye. She is enjoying my bad behaviour, my snappiness, my lack of warmth towards my new stepchildren, on their first day back in their father's house after our wedding. They have been staying at an aunt's for a fortnight so that 'the newlyweds can have some space'.

I keep my head down; my irritation dampens into shame. I look up at Debba when she hands me a brush, and mutter, 'Thank you. I was trying to sort out your father's accounts.'

'And look where that's landed you,' Sira murmurs.

Embarrassment streaks my face. I am sure she can read me. I deal with it the only way I know how.

'I guess we'd better make some tea. Would you mind putting the kettle on?' I say this to Ebrima, who is now leaning on the door jamb leading to the kitchen. 'Clearing up this mess is a one-woman job. Perhaps you two can help him?'

The soles of Sira's shoes carry some remnants of glass and they scrape and crunch as she walks past me. Her bare legs lead up to hot pants, a strip of jean cradling the small of her back and stopping at the very top of her thighs.

At supper that evening, we sit together at the table that caused so much ruckus earlier.

'I hope you'll be coming to the church service tomorrow,' starts Foday.

'What for?' says Sira.

'A show of support. A good family trait sometimes, no?'

'I'll come, Dad,' says Ebrima, 'and I'll wake up the sisters too in good time.' He looks at his sisters. Sira's lips turn down, and lines lock her eyebrows together.

We chew on morsels of chicken *yassa*, which I seasoned in lemon and a sprinkling of chilli powder with a crumbled cube of Maggi stock.

'Did you enjoy St Louis?' says Debba.

I look at her gratefully and nod. 'Yes, it was absolutely fantastic. It's in a time warp and more leisurely, less hassly than Dakar.'

'Did you go on a pirogue?' Debba asks.

'I wanted to go out fishing but Dele wouldn't let me. No life jackets, wasn't it dear?' says Foday.

'Have you seen those boats, they sink so low in the water, there's nothing between the boat's edge and the ocean. I told him to go paddling in the harbour instead.'

Both Ebrima and Debba laugh out loud at this.

'I'm surprised you had any time to paddle outside your honeymoon bedroom,' says Sira.

She pushes back her chair against the floor and stands up. I watch her part her lips to let a *tchah* escape them. She's sneering at me. Us. Our marriage. Foday's and my attempt to start living together as a family. All our breaths are caught into a transparent balloon of suspense floating above the centre of the table. She pushes at her chair harder, back, away from herself. The chair hits the floor with an angry thwack.

'Now, look here, young lady,' says Foday, 'pick that chair up and sit back down.'

Sira strides out. In the heaviness of her departure, the slam of her bedroom door declares a final exclamation mark to our paragraph of an evening.

'Reverend! Reverend!'A loud, throaty voice vibrates the skin of silence over the house late on Sunday morning. The service is over, lunch is in the oven. Foday and I sit out in uncertain shade cast by a frangipani tree in a halo of pink scent. The kitchen door does not have a bell or anything obvious to attract attention with; most visitors shout to announce their arrival or need for attention.

Foday walks round the side of the house to the front, and there's a grumble of voices: the throaty one at the high end of the vocal scale, and Foday's – lower, steadier, deeper. The voices drift closer, with the wind blowing away most of what they are saying to each other. Little counter-gusts shower confetti fragments of their conversation: Sure / Surprised / Fried / Dare.

Foday and the visitor come closer. The owner of the throaty voice should have been obvious to me earlier, but my ears have been blurred by other noises: the sea, the chirps of unidentifiable brown birds hopping from frond to frond in the palm trees beyond the frangipani. Mrs Acheampong breathes heavily as she plants a heeled black patent shoe on the patio, its full shine clouded by dust. A volcano of emotion shakes under her heaving chest.

'It's the collection. I popped out of the vestry to check on a loud bang.' She clasps a black patent bag underneath her bosom. She twists apart two knobs of gold-coloured metal to snap it open and extract an embroidered handkerchief. She wipes her forehead free of busy droplets of sweat.

Foday offers her a seat. 'Do sit down. Can I pour you some tea, or would you prefer water?'

'Some water. Cold please. The shock of it all!'

While Foday is inside, Mrs Acheampong divests more droplets of information. 'It happened while I was counting. Just completely gone.'

As well as supervising the Mothers' Union, Mrs Acheampong is also on the rota for recording amounts given during the Sunday offering. Two wooden bowls come out of her accommodating bag, one lying within the other. 'I brought them with me. Look, this is what I usually do.' She plonks one bowl on the table. It has a large stone in it, the kind we pick up from the beach to scrub hardened heels with.

'The stone keeps the notes down while I count.' The other bowl is thunked down onto what is now a crowded side table, still cluttered with our mugs, teaspoons and a jar of sugar.

'Usually, I sort it out into piles of notes. I'd finished counting the twenty-fives and the tens. The total was five hundred dalasi. There were ten twenty-fives and twenty-five tens. I remember thinking how unusual this was.'

She has been clutching her patent bag hard, and now as she moves to put it down on the ground by her feet, I see her palm prints, foggy imprints of sweat on the shine.

'Five hundred dalasis. That's what's gone missing. I was sure I'd locked the front door of the church so I walked up to check it was closed. By the time I got back to the vestry, the counted pile of notes had disappeared. Now, who would do such a thing? Whatever is the world coming to, when someone—' and here she pauses mid-sentence, as Foday makes his way down the steps, holding a tall glass from our wedding gift collection, beaded with ice sweat.

'Oh thank you. And God save us all. What will the Bishop say?' Mrs Acheampong concludes, after draining the glass.

'Like I said, we'll discuss it here first, among ourselves. We should avoid getting the Bishop involved, until necessary. If we agree on how to count the collection from now on, I think we can make sure this doesn't happen again.' Foday tries to bring the impromptu visit to a close: 'You can leave the rest of the collection here today. Do you know how much of it is left now?'

'Yes, oh, yes. Before I came round I counted it over and over again to check that I hadn't gone wrong. The five-dalasi notes come to a total of three hundred and eighty, and the coins add up to thirty-three dalasi and fifty bututs. Nine hundred and thirteen dalasi – that would have been the collection announcement in church next week.'

'Never mind, it wasn't your fault. Let me walk you to your car. We can discuss this in the week.'

What I start to suspect becomes a band of anxiety, tight against my chest. My bra digs into my ribs and starts to rub off skin.

'It's all my fault,' I begin, when Foday comes back. 'I think we got off to a bad start yesterday. I have no idea how to be a step-mother.'

'I doubt it's you, Dele. As far as Sira's concerned, she wants to teach me a lesson. I asked her to go to church this morning, and she behaved as if it was an order.' Foday stares away from me, looking out to where the Atlantic is unconcernedly blinking its blue, tossing its froth, sliding its water. 'She did it to show me she does not conform with grace. And the thing is, she's old enough to know how to live life the way she wants to. I don't see how I could have done it different. It's not you.'

'How can I hel—' I start, but he doesn't let me finish. He shakes his head, willing me to stop, asking me to leave him alone.

During the night, a dust storm blows, heaving fine particles all the way from the Sahara, and depositing them in a layer on our dining room table.

As the week progresses, seismic undercurrents shift our emotions this way and that. Rumours reach my ears, via Radio CanCan, as Aunt Kiki used to say.

Mothers' Union meets on Tuesdays, so the first hint I have is when Beti Bright comes to say hello. She'd found Mrs Acheampong and two of her closest allies in hot consultation in the vestry. She waited outside the door for a few minutes and heard parts of the conversation. She hadn't quite dared to go in and display the crocheted table mats she'd made for next week's bring-and-buy sale.

'Look, I'll show you them,' Beti offers.

She puts a crumpled blue plastic bag on the dining table. She's made five mats from white cotton circles, and added on bubbly crocheted stitches for edging.

'Look,' she says, 'I'm on the last one. I was aiming for a set of six.'

'They are lovely.' I pause, just long enough to signal a change of topic. 'And you were saying? About what happened in the vestry?'

'Oh, well, I didn't go in. You're the first person I'm showing the mats. They weren't whispering, you know. The door wasn't closed. But they did not see me.'

I know what's coming even before I hear it. Not the specifics of course, but the intent, the purpose, the gossip.

'Mrs Acheampong's voice was especially loud, but her friends also had things to say.'

As she catches sight of my head, stiffly inclined towards her, she shifts the chair, which eeks a screech on the concrete. My eyes hardly blink.

'Oh, none of the things they said were especially bad,' she soothes. 'But I know you are new here, and these things can worry.'

'Hmm.'

'They were saying things like: "Those poor children", "Of course she doesn't know how to handle them." I mean, they meant you don't know how to handle them. They said Foday's children are "going wild". And that you have said you're not sure you're a Christian. One of them said "not even believing in God" yct "daring to be a preacher's wife".'

She stops to catch her breath. 'I also heard something about your trouser suit – they didn't like you wearing one to church on a communion Sunday.'

The next day, Wednesday, Sira is supposed to be in school. When I pop my head round her bedroom door, the backpack she carries with her is not there. I assume she's left with her brother or sister. It's not until much later in the morning, when I go into the back garden to pick some chillies, that I notice the drift of a sharp-sweet, singed-oil smell. Thinking it odd, I gather a handful of finger-thick chillis and return to the kitchen to drop them into the catfish and onion casserole.

I start to worry when Debba comes in, late afternoon, without her sister in tow.

'Where is Sira?'

'I don't know. I didn't see her at school and she was still in bed when I left this morning. I had to go in early to check a chemistry experiment.'

'Where could she . . .'

The memory of the tangy air. I know exactly where she is and what she's been doing all day. Skiving off school to sit in the tree-house their father built for them. Smoking *jamba*. Unspeakable cheek.

'Come with me,' I say, with a knot of anger in me, sprinkled with granules of apprehension.

Back in the garden, we make our way towards the mango tree. Looking up, I notice a leg hanging over one edge of the wooden platform. There is no ladder. I have to climb. My rage has doubled in volume. I grasp the tree's rough bark and angle a foothold into the Y formed by the branches. I heave myself up and look for the next foothold.

'Please, Aunt Dele,' begins Debba. 'Let me go up, let me speak to her.'

I concede my place, and when I get back to the ground, I find my hands are trembling. I hear the murmur of Debba's voice when she reaches the platform: 'Sira, Sira, wake up.'

I make my way back into the house. I cannot wait to hear more.

'I'm sorry, it's harder than I thought. I don't know how to talk to you about her. Or how to be with them. I'm not sure why I ever thought I'd fit into a readymade family.'

Foday and I are in our bedroom. I've been crying while Sira has been sitting sullenly in the sitting room, defiance wiring her eyes, curling her toes under the chair cushion, setting her shoulders in utter lack of shame.

'Well, you've never had children to care for so it's not surprising it's hard.'

'I've been a child. I've grown through it all. I remember how it feels – surely that should be enough.'

'But being a parent . . .' he starts.

'Goddammit,' I say, not letting him finish. 'I'm *trying*.'

'You cannot take God's name in vain while you are living under his roof,' Foday's voice is loud, with a grumble and a roar in it.

I tut. 'My, my, getting all Moses-like are we?'

This stops him in his rage, and his mouth opens but no words come out. He closes it and swallows, and his Adam's apple moves slowly up and down as if a mole is trying to poke its head through his throat.

His eyes meet mine, and then immediately flicker to the window.

A wind puffs out the striped curtain I put up a month ago. Beyond I can see the edge of the day's sun slipping below a line the ocean has slashed against the sky. The water reflects streaks of orange light, holding broken bits of the last of the sunlight as it fades away.

'I am sorry,' I say. And the curtain slowly flutters down.

STORY THREE

The Un-named

14

Birth

In a way it works the way I wanted it to. He picks us up from the disco and I insist I need to collect my sports kit from her house. So she stays and we are alone. I know it's time to go home, I say, but I'm not really tired. He says, do you want to go for a drive along the beach road. Good idea, I reply. A few beers to take with us, he says. He stops by a roadside bar, carefully parking the car in the deepest of shadows. And then, with windows down, we drive way past the last of the hotels, where the cliffs dampen down to a sandy beach and the sound of the sea becomes a slush rather than a crash.

I have one extra beer. It is cramped in the back seat. He's as eager as a teenage boy and very sweaty. I can no longer dictate what he does with me. No time to take the condom out. He grunts and moves my legs this way and that. After, a bit of silence in which we rearrange our clothes and he clears his throat. It's late, I should take you home, he says.

I lean my head against the door jamb and pretend to fall asleep while all of me screams: *Is that it?* At our gate I say goodnight and he says take care.

Our watchman lets me in. I could walk straight into the house. Or maybe I could continue in the vein of what I've started tonight. Target. Entice. And see what happens, eh?

The next few months pass in mute. Most of us get ready to go away. I'm allocated a Senegalese scholarship to Dakar, not the British one I'd wanted. My induction year attempts to teach me enough French to understand the lectures for my degree in African and Development Studies. Living in Dakar feels like living in a proper city, large enough so no one knows me. But all around me there are signs of home – the indignation of street beggars at being forced off the pavement, boiled groundnuts and roasted maize with frozen tubes of baobab juice for sale at stalls outside the university. It's a strange familiarity, but one step removed. No Remi or Amina or even Moira. We've been scattered to start our new lives.

Soon it's time to go home for Christmas. My clothes start to feel tight around the waist.

Five o'clock arrives with that smothering of sound that comes with the onset of dusk, as if the world itself is tiring of the sun, and ready to bed down.

Aunt Kiki hugs me goodnight and says, 'Dele, you're getting too wide for me to put my arms around you properly.'

The door slams shut behind her. My mother turns to me, her eyes searching my body, probing, asking.

'Is it true?' she says.

We are sitting in the quietest place in the house, on the quietest day. On Sundays, we have no one in to help cook or clean. When visitors come, we prepare things to serve them and make them feel welcome. My sisters and I wash the dishes, we light the charcoal fire, we sweep floors, we cook. When visitors leave, we tidy up after them.

I don't reply right away. I busy myself with piling things onto the tray: bottles of Guinness, empty glasses, chewed ends of chicken bones. Then: 'Is what true, Ma?'

'Are you taking me to be a fool? What have you been up to, child?'

I keep my quiet, still trying to form words in an answer.

'I never thought it would come to this,' my mother says. 'What did I do to God?'

She answers her own question. I deny nothing. She starts to plan a response. 'Of course, I'll have to talk to Kiki about it. For now, the only thing I need to do is find a doctor, a reliable and quiet one, who can keep things to himself.'

I feel a rush of release, relief. My secret was as easy to crack as a ridge of mud tunnel built by hopeful, blind termites. I hadn't quite decided up to this point. I knew the options. I knew how having a baby would not get me back to university, how it would mark me apart, how it would take my life in directions I'd not previously contemplated.

'I'm keeping it,' I say. A bitter, slashing rancid taste washes my mouth. I feel giddy from saying it.

My mother *cheepooes*, sucking spit between her teeth. 'Don't be silly.'

My decision stokes an anger, a rage that she is deciding for me, telling me what I am to do. 'Have you asked me how I am? Do you know what *I* want to do?'

'It's obvious, isn't it? What else is there to know? You're a young girl, you're only eighteen. Become a mother? At your age? It's unthinkable.'

My mother's right, but I don't concede the point. I've had a term of misery. And after all, not everyone goes to university. Remi's gone with Kojo, but not to study. Moira's here, working. I close my eyes tight for a second. Many of the others have gone, though – to Nigeria, England, Italy, America. In my obstinacy, I know that with this choice, I'm making sure I'll stay here.

'Of course it's thinkable. It's my body and I can do with it what I want. I want this baby.'

'Who is going to help you bring it up? The child's father?'

'It doesn't matter. I'm old enough to look after myself, I'm old enough to look after a child.'

'Sometimes,' my mother says, 'I want to wash my hands of you. No gratitude, no sense of shame, no sense of obligation, of the right way to do things, to be.' She flaps off to talk to my sisters, leaving me at the doorway of my new beginning.

My mother rants. On Monday, it's mostly about the kind of example I am setting for my sisters. Kainde and Taiwo skulk about when she's around. When she's out, they both come into my room, their eyes bright open with curiosity.

Kainde says, 'Are you all right?'

I nod.

Taiwo says, 'You'll have to do as she says in the end. You know Ma.'

I reply, 'I made up my mind only when Ma told me what *we* were going to do about me. I knew what I needed to do.'

Kainde says, 'But what about finishing university?'

I shrug.

On Tuesday, my mother wants to know which boy did it, so his parents can take some of the responsibility and not leave her alone in her shame.

On Wednesday I am an absolute disgrace to my family.

On Thursday she asks Aunt Kiki to talk to me. She is willing to let me do what I want, even if I want to ruin my life. But I must say who the father is. With a name, at least the blame will be shared. Even if the boy does nothing to help to support me. Aunt

K asks to be left alone with me. 'Come on, child, if you insist on becoming a mother, try not to do it alone.'

'Ma thinks she can boss people about, however she likes. I am old enough to do this.'

On Friday, in the face of my continuing strong-headedness, my unwillingness to answer her questions about my pregnancy, my mother calls together a conclave of her second-tier friends. This time Aunt K is excluded, as she has not been able to accomplish the mission and other tactics are now required.

Ma asks me to pick stones out of the rice.

She and Aunt Hetty and Aunt Bola are sipping ginger beer, in the midst of the delicate task of dividing up the four baskets of dried fish they've bought together. The conversation meanders over the various merits of Cousin Evelyn, who is about to go to Fourah Bay College and study accounting, and famously clever Abisatou, who is off to Cambridge on a scholarship – 'What a delight she is to her mother, who would have thought that such an unlikely marriage would yield such a clever child?' They skirt Tunde Brown – getting married at Easter to Matthias Njie who is en route to a posting at the embassy in France: 'at least she's only marrying a Catholic'.

Having de-stoned half a bag of rice, I get up for the bathroom. My fingers are covered with rice dust. I have been concentrating as hard on finding little beige pebbles amongst the creamy grains as I have on blocking out their conversation. The twinge between my eyebrows foretells a headache. I am not yet out of earshot when, into the air stilled by my departure, I hear Aunt Bola say, 'Ah, you did your best with that girl. You can never blame yourself for how they turn out.'

My mother says, 'I guess she's satisfied with herself now, when everyone can see her condition and know how she got there. What did I do to God?'

'Yes, *walai*, the shame of it,' goes Aunt Hetty.

'I wonder how she did not think about the consequences when she opened her legs to that, that man.'

A deep hmm, by someone.

'Man indeed.'

Finding a rhythm, my mother continues, 'And who was it, eh, who? Can't be that hard to remember.'

Aunt Bola slaps her talking drum, *'Ah, dem pikin tiday.'*

After her friends leave, I end up in a shouting match with my mother.

'Ma, I don't like you discussing *my* life with *your* friends.'

'If I didn't discuss it with people who'd help me bear my burden, how do you think I can manage, carry on? At least with their advice, we can all help you do something with your life.'

'I don't need you to tell me what to do. I'll look after myself and I'll take care of my child.'

'Look at you. Eh, think you can solve everything just because you are young. Well, unless you think about the future, you'll end up bringing up that poor child in a gutter.'

'Well, at least it would be a gutter I make myself.'

'You ungrateful child. Can't you see the shame you've brought on all of us?'

'If you don't want to live this close to shame, I'll go and find somewhere else to be.'

Anger blurs vision. The only thing I can do is to go to my room, pack a bag and leave. I hear Taiwo and Kainde whispering away in their room, scared by the tempest of emotion in our house. I shove the few things I can still fit into and a spare pair of slippers into a soft cloth bag to carry over my shoulder. Then I slam my way out of the house. My anger doesn't leave any space for a goodbye. Osman's at the gate. With all the shouting, he must know something's going on.

'*Foye dem? Defa gudi di!*'

I glare at him. I don't know where I'm going. But I do know it's late.

'*Ubile rek*. Just open up.'

The night is dark and thick with star twinkles, and I stumble my way to the main road considering what to do. The options are:

(a) Aunt K – she's already in trouble with my mother; it would be unfair to stretch her friendship further right now, best to leave her as a potential negotiator;

(b) Mrs Foon, my English Literature teacher, means taking it outside the family at too early a stage, no matter how kind I think she is;

(c) Tunji, the cousin who's always looked out for me – but lives in Yundum, too far away; and . . .

(d) Aunt Ellie.

I decide to do it as a just revenge. My mother will be furious, livid. Aunt Ellie is not a proper aunt, merely an inglorious extension of our family. She had two daughters with a married man – my father's younger brother, the elegantly promiscuous, liquid-eyed Sola. She is deeply despised by my mother. Aunt Ellie stands her ground when she comes to family dos and my mother is bristly around her. She's held her own, and over time my father's family has accepted her as part of them. Uncle Sola's other adventures have also yielded offspring. We know of two other children, fathered far away, who eventually acquired names: Fatou in Dakar, and David in Freetown.

I stand by the side of the road and wonder how I am going to get there. It will take half an hour on the main road if I really step it out, then another twenty minutes or so trudging through the sandy lane that cuts a thoroughfare to the Bakau Road. I pull my

mind to the task in hand. Sand in my shoes will be a trifle considering what a thick *domoda* I've landed myself in. It is dark, but I
keep my spirits up by stomping on the tarmac thinking that will
discourage any nosy, wandering snakes.

A pair of tawny-eyed beams from a car creep up behind me.
The erratic sway of light across the road is like someone carelessly
swinging a large torch in his hand – just as I used to when making
my way home after a quick errand to the Amet shop. I stop, turn
and stare as a car zigs and wiggles an uncertain, but slow, progress
towards me. I recognise old Mr Hochiemy, the father of Idris the
knicker collector, in his cream-coloured classic Mercedes. He stops,
but I am sure he does not have a clue who I am. I hop in, offer my
good evening and say I am headed in his direction. Skunk drunk,
he mumbles through wondering what 'a preecie lil gel lick you'
is doing around at night. As for him, he was 'jush haveeng a few
wish frens' and now it is time to head home. We zag our way some
more, following his nose. He needs both hands on the steering
wheel. I am not sure how well he can see. I point to the corner as
we come close to the sandy lane, and ask to be dropped off. He
immediately slams on the brakes, a good ten metres away from the
corner, taking us to the opposite side of the road, close to a mango
tree I loved when I was small. I scramble out with a thank-you.

As I turn into the lane, I see the lights swing out as he steers back
onto the road. The left fender catches on to a large tree root and the
engine groans as he stays in first and rams the accelerator. There is
a chorus of barking in protest at the noise. Then there are voices of
watchmen stirred from their sleep. Juddering lights from weak
torches begin to make their way towards the car. I continue on.

I am convinced it is only because I am at Aunt Ellie's that my
mother has bothered to help at all. Along Fajara's stretch of cliff
road, the bush telegraph functions amazingly well despite the lack

of working telephones in many houses. The very next evening, my whereabouts are confirmed. A little army of aunts, the blood connection loosely applied, come round in the advance party. That my shame should reside so closely to Aunt Ellie's shame of even bigger magnitude is too much for my mother. On her white flag are:

- paid rent on a two-room mud-and-wattle outfit in Latrikunda;
- a monthly allowance of two hundred dalasi;
- no contact with my sisters – my corrupting influence is to end in my new premises.

The two-room on offer is close to Aunt Hetty's house; she is a recently embosomed friend of my mother's who is likely to take up the role of Chief Spy. I agree because I know the house is in Mrs Foon's family compound. My old teacher visits her in-laws in Foon-*kunda* often and I can therefore hope for the occasional caring word.

When I am seven months gone, I walk into the National Library to look for a book on childbirth. I ask Miss Sanyang (receptionist), who directs me to Mrs Johnson (women's section), who then directs me to Mr Ndure (reference) who looks at the Chinese whispers note I've been given and directs me to the stack of *Encyclopaedia Britannica*. Here I find diagrams of a growing baby in the womb, and a description of the birth canal. I retrace my steps to Mrs Johnson,

'I'd like a book on how babies are born, please.'

She mutters under her breath, loud enough to reach my ears but not those of Miss Sanyang, 'Your mother would have told you all this, if you had not been in such a rush to find out yourself.'

Although old news by now, my pregnancy still adds lashings of moral chilli to conversations with anyone of my mother's generation.

Apart from Mrs Foon, only Aunt K is trying to help. She regularly ladles out *Satiday soup* and *fufu* for me, reminding me I need iron for 'strength to bear'.

Nothing prepared me for a stomach that balloons so much it shrinks my bladder and leadens my legs. When I am due to go into hospital, Ma goes to Dakar to visit a friend, leaving me to 'stew in my own mango juice'.

It is hot in the tiny delivery room. The oil paint on the walls gleams back bumpy light from fluorescent strips overhead. At about eye level a painted dado line separates beige paint, on the upper part of the wall, from the brown that meets the floor. Between the bulb strips is a wonky fan, which sways from the plasterboard ceiling. I double up, lines of sweat dripping into my eyes, and colour the room with throat-emptying swearwords. Whenever I feel the next spasm of pain I look up at the wildly circling blades and focus on the blur in their spin. I get through it all, with no fancy gas and air stuff, or any painkillers injected into my spine. I learn about birthing a child as I do it, and I learn about pain and how it cuts into you so that you are in your own bubble of hell, an infinity of pain.

I screech when Kweku Sola's head crowns. My child, with his un-named father, is born to a mother whose body is unequipped. I am not ready for breast-feeding and the tightness and the drips after being away from him for a few hours. Or the physical tiredness and my tears when dealing with his colicky screams.

The house that Kweku Sola and I share in Latrikunda is in a block of three rental homes, each with two rooms. The roof of corrugated iron sheets, coloured brown by rain and air, hangs low and wreathes the porch in constant shade. There is a low cement-covered mud wall with deep gashes that expose the brown bricks underneath. It is meant to keep the rainwater out. To get to my front door, I need to simultaneously lift my step and duck my head. Our rooms are on the right. A single woman lives in the middle – she works in a government office somewhere in town, something to do with sesame feed and cows. On the other end is a family with four children. The father's a tailor in the large-roomed workshop with wide doors that faces onto the main road.

I cut some jasmine from Mrs Foon's verandah. I put it into the clay pots I buy from a Serahule in Latrikunda. I add a rough wooden climber for the jasmine to sprawl on to.

The front room is roughly square, about ten foot each side, with lino that is well worn in parts. The walls are whitewashed in limed paint made from crushed oyster shells. Rough to the touch, the painted walls leave enthusiastic streaks on hands, legs and clothes. The ceiling is lined with cane mats, and double-lined with cheap indigo tie-dye to stop bats from making their home in mine.

My furniture is plain. I ask a Fula carpenter to make me a special order on a single-width *tara* seat, as the regular double is too large to fit through my door. To make sitting more comfortable for the guests I never have, I get a long piece of foam to put on it. When the Foons give me some of their old furniture, I re-cover the cushions on the two armchairs with matching indigo tie dye, which Ansumane my tailor neighbour sews for me at a knock-down price. Later I negotiate a barter transaction with him, so he makes clothes for me and Kweku Sola while I give extra tutoring to his fourteen-year-old son.

In our bedroom I string a rope across the short wall. I hang a curtain and keep our clothes behind it. Although air gets stuck in the room when the back door is shut, it's a struggle to reach the single window and prise it open. When I first moved in, I slept on the floor for a few days until I could buy a black-painted iron bed and a cheap mattress. Kweku Sola now sleeps in the bed with me – there isn't any room for a cot.

Our bathroom is shared. There's an open-air enclosure with a pipe sticking straight out of the ground. In order to bathe, I take a bucket outside with a cup for scooping out water. If I've remembered to leave the bucket out in the sun during the day, the water warms up a bit, taking the edge off its cold. We also have a non-flushing long drop in a dark, stuffy hut that buzzes with huge flies. I only use it when I absolutely have to, preferring to pee when I have my shower, straight through the fat pipe from which the occasional toad has to be poked out, into the little suckaway behind the cane matting walls.

Moving away from Ma's house has allowed me to create a cocoon for myself. It means I don't have to remember the how or the why of me getting here. I can choose to cover the memories of fumblings behind our garden shed or in the cramped discomfort of a car. News of my school friends trickles through snatches of conversations with Mrs Foon, who revels in their success, yet tries hard not to hurt my feelings by seeming too pleased. Yuan, Reuben, Idris, Amina – they've all gone to university, in West Africa, Europe or North America. Moira got married soon after we got our A level results and stayed here. I don't try to search out friends who are still around – I doubt I can pick up the carefree talk you can have when there's a free future in front of you. By choosing to have Kweku Sola, I have set myself on a path different to my friends. I am on the other side of knowing, yet the answer to the mystery of how to make my life has been in me all along.

My days pick up a new rhythm. Mothering Kweku Sola on a

begrudging income from my mother deserves all my ingenuity. I borrow matches or a bit of hot coal for my fire off Ansumane's family. I ask Warrage next door to listen out for Kweku Sola while I rush to the Amet shop for candles. My reputation for cost-effective lessons to the children of exam-conscious parents grows. My fees are good value as they include the inconvenience of frequent interruptions from a gurgly baby. I start to tutor head-weary students about to take primary school leaving certificate examinations.

I am learning my freedom in making do.

Aunt Kiki comes to visit late one afternoon when Kweku Sola is asleep and I am catching up with housework. She wants to patch up my relationship with my mother. I offer her tea with powdered milk and a couple of cubes of sugar.

'How can you do this all on your own?' she says. 'Surely any help is better than none?'

'My mother's helping enough by paying my rent and feeding us,' I reply.

'This isn't good for either of you. Every time I see her, she mentions you somewhere in our conversation. She misses you.'

'It's more likely she misses someone to boss around and arrange.'

'You two are more alike than you imagine.'

When Kweku Sola wakes up, she jiggles him on her knee, making his face glow with pleasure, his dimples deep.

'Do you hear from any of your friends?' she asks.

I shake my head, 'The ones who've gone away don't write. I know Moira's around, but I don't go out much.'

'Hmm,' is her reply.

'I'm fine really. There are other people around to help. Ansumane next door, for example.'

'Family's different. You've lived with them a long time; they forgive more. Also friends you've known a long time understand you better. You need your family and friends right now.'

How to explain why I prefer it this way? How can I say she only knows one layer of my truth? The other layer may remain hidden until Kweku Sola grows up and his face becomes stamped with someone else's. Maybe my half-secret will break loose then. How can I tell her I don't know who my son's father is?

15

Polygamy

Mrs Foon happens to be talking to Madame LaFarge, the wife of
the French consul, who is fed up with her husband's complaints
about how bad his assistants are. On my old teacher's assurance
that I can actually *speak* some French, Madame LaFarge suggests
to her husband that I might be suitable. He has just fired the last
administrator and tiredly agrees to take me on, telling me on my
first day, 'I hope you can conjugate verbs.'

My job pays enough for me to snub my mother's allowance.

One day, Monsieur LaFarge walks into my tiny anteroom off the
reception area with a portly man in his wake. The visitor is luxu-
riant in his girth; his stomach precedes him into the room.

'Bonjour,' Monsieur LaFarge says. 'This is Mr Sisoho. He needs
a translation of his new agreement with his Peugeot distributors.
I hope you'll be able to do that for him.'

Amadou nods a head topped with a white embroidered prayer
cap. It's Friday morning, and an indecisive sun is flashing weak
light through my louvred window onto his blue gown, whose

neckline is embroidered in silver. His cheeks are shiny. When he smiles, his mouth squashes his eyes into little round holes of mirth.

Monsieur LaFarge flaps a sheaf of paper in my face, creating rivulets of air over loose, light things on my desk.

'I promised to do some filing for the library next week, but I'm sure I could do the translation first,' I say.

'*Bon*. Please see to it,' he replies, settling the matter by strolling back out the way they came.

By Wednesday the following week, I am done, surprised at how different the world of legalese and financial transactions is from my usual diet of French – culture and cinema, language and exchange visits.

I ring Amadou, calling him Mr Sisoho, to ask him to send someone to pick up the translation.

I think it odd when he turns up himself instead of his driver, and asks whether I can help him craft a response to the contract. He takes a piece of paper off my printer and starts to write down points to be mentioned. He holds the pen stiffly, his middle finger bends awkwardly as he concentrates on writing. He is slow, and the letters he forms are jerky, angled and large.

I don't feel anything in particular. No taut elastic band gripping us in a tight circle for two. No twang of recognition of a fellow soul. Amadou is simply a middle-aged man, a familiar acquaintance of my boss who I am doing some translation work for.

He is already married, his business successful. He is twice my age.

When Monsieur LaFarge comes back from his holiday, he calls me into his office.

'I see you've made an impression on Amadou Sisoho. He is offering you a job at twice whatever your salary is here. I hate to lose you after only three years, but it's my fault for introducing you in the first place, after all.'

When I start to work for Amadou, he asks me to learn German also, so I can help translate his business dealings with the Mercedes Benz suppliers. I buy myself a *Teach Yourself German* book from the Methodist Bookshop, encouraged by its optimistic cover in yellow and purple stripes. I *Achtung* my way through *den Zug erreichen* to Munich; Berlin can only be got to by *Flugzeug*.

Amadou not only has a Mercedes he drives himself, he also employs a driver who takes his children to and from the International School, and carts huge quantities of food home – bright yellow barrels of oil, sacks of rice, onions and potatoes, huge tins of tomato paste. His prayer gowns are always crisply starched and richly embroidered at the neck.

There's a constant stream of visitors to the office. Some are besuited, others have shoes made of tyre off-cuts. Over time, I learn to distinguish faces – know who I have to immediately offer tea to, who to tell he's busy and can they perhaps phone instead, who to give a ten-dalasi note to from the brown envelope of cash Amadou asks me to keep in my drawer as his offering for the poor.

I notice his eyes linger on my face, my fingers when I bring him a stack of letters to sign in the evenings. Then I pick Kweku Sola up from the neighbour who looks after him on workdays, and go home to my two-room house. I walk past Kweku Sola's bicycle chained to an outside post, into my front room with a chest of drawers for his clothes, into my bedroom with a window I can no longer open. I want more for my child. I'd better do something soon.

A year later, Amadou proposes. He does not consider me being a single mother a problem. At this stage in his life, a new wife in addition to the old is like adding *ranha* to a large bowl of *benachin* – you can do without it, but it adds another flavour to the experience of eating. It is a sigh of relief at future comfort for me. I accept.

Amadou has three children with Rohey, who will become the senior wife. Her house is behind a high white wall with broken bottles stuck with cement on top. A heavy piece of axle, tied behind the door with a length of fishing twine, lends its weight to push the door closed after Amadou lets go. The metal gate clangs. The outdoor area is concreted around a single mango tree sitting in a circle of free earth, a rough *bantaba* seat hammered around it. The forecourt has been swept clean. There is no one in sight and the house seems suspended in a breath. A radio somewhere twangs out a Super Diamano song, 'Mariama'.

Rohey sits in her front room with her children who have shiny vaselined faces, arms and legs. She is wearing a feather green lace boubou, with a matching scarf twirled on her head and a few strands of braids left to trail on her back.

'Rohey, this is Dele.'

'*Naka ngon si?*'

'*Alhamdoudilah.* Thank God.'

The tips of her fingers are long and dark and her hands have recently been hennaed. Her hand feels thin and cool in the quick seconds I have a grasp on it.

Her eyes, heavily lined with kohl, focus on my chin. 'Come and say hello to your new *tante*,' she says to the children. They come forward and extend lanky arms, wrists jiggling with thin stranded bracelets. Each child murmurs a greeting. They will call me Auntie Dele.

'*Kai len togg.* Come and sit down.' Rohey extends an arm towards a tray beside her, on which are a jug of deep purple *wonjor* and some clean glasses: Arcoroc, made in France, bought from Chellarams supermarket. Beside it sits an elaborate tin with Gem biscuits and tiny white saucers stacked alongside.

Amadou fills his seat, rearranging his boubou. 'It is getting hot, there's hardly any breeze today.'

The smile on Rohey's face sits tightly, her *jamm* mouth shadowed dark blue with indigo tattoo. 'Isatou,' she says, 'pour some drinks for your father and our visitor.'

Isatou's white shoes peek underneath her lace wrapper, and her heels tap out her few footsteps on the stone-tiled floor as she walks towards the table. She pours and comes towards me with both hands gripping the glass. She looks at the floor as she offers me the drink.

'*Tante.*'

'*Jerreh jaiffe,*' I reply.

Rohey continues, 'And serve some biscuits, too, eh?'

Isatou traipses back to the table and opens the tin. All our eyes are on her, any attempt at conversation suspended. The edges of the room vibrate with the things we cannot say.

Isatou brings me a plateful of tiny beige rounds with scalloped edges. They are slightly stale.

What must they see as they look at me? Presentable enough in my long white skirt, made out of imitation linen, which fits well because it is cut on the bias. I have on a high-collared Chinese-style top in navy blue silk splashed with spreads of large white flowers. On my feet I wear a pair of leather flipflops I bought in the craft market by the beach. My hair hangs in wisps past my ears. I am not wearing much makeup, just a dash of unobtrusive brown lipstick. Tiny studs are in my ears. No rings. Do I pose a mosquito-sized threat that will soon be swiped away?

As we sit and scratch around empty heads to find things to talk about, my fingers float to my mouth and I start to nibble on a fingernail. Amadou asks the girls about school. They squirm, point shoe tips towards the floor, sit on hands and bob their heads. I glance at Rohey. She isn't looking at me. Her face is carefully erased of all feeling. The set of her mouth reveals nothing. Her elbows rest on the chair's arms and her tendrilled fingers dangle down. She looks neither content nor angry. I move my hand away from my mouth to let it linger around my glass of *wonjor* instead.

I take in the details in the room. The curtains are pulled back to reveal shields of netting. The pot of greenery in a corner looks stiff, too uniform. My eyes slide past Rohey. This time, I find her looking at me straight in the eye. I try to recover from the shock of catching her gaze. In the short time I have to read her eyes, I can only find disdain. Her face stays empty.

'Yes, papa,' I hear one of the girls say.

Rohey's eyes sweep towards a door that is slightly ajar. 'And now,' she says, 'maybe I can get you some food.'

She disappears into the corridor behind the door. The father–daughter conversations continue. There is a clatter of tin against tin. Rohey walks back in.

The househelp follows her with a bowl of water, a bar of soap and a dish towel. We wash our hands. Rohey offers us *chereh*. I cannot refuse the dish she places before me, piled high with chunks of fish and wrinkled chilli peppers. One of her daughters places a side table in front of her father and a similarly full plate is put on it for Amadou.

After we've eaten, I smile and lean forward, trying to speak mostly to the girls. 'I got you some presents. I hope you'll like them.'

The eldest one slides a glance towards her mother, testing emotion. The answer remains a face wiped of reaction.

I give the eldest of the girls a shiny made-in-Taiwan notebook with matching pen; the second-oldest gets a T-shirt with the words *Born to Roam*; the present for the youngest is a dainty straw basket with embroidered flowers. The fringed cream-coloured scarf, imported from India, is for Rohey. There are enthusiastic thank-yous from the girls. Amadou looks around at his expanding family and taps the sides of his stomach with his hands.

That weekend, I get diarrhoea.

When I try to talk to Amadou about Rohey, he says, 'Well, it's not as if it's the first time I'm taking another wife. I married a girl called Zainab a few years ago. We weren't suited to each other and got divorced soon after.'

'Aren't you scared that could happen to us too?'

'She wasn't like you. She liked to socialise a lot more than me, wanted to go out almost every night.'

'Well, but there's still Rohey and . . .'

'She's not the only wife who's had to learn how to share a husband. She has to live with it.'

Kainde challenges me about my impending marriage. 'Are you sure you need to do this, Dele?'

I have a reply ready. It has been formulating in my mind for a while.

'Look at the story of Uncle Sola,' I say. 'Someone on the side hidden from your wife and family is worse than a marriage like this that is in the open.'

'Yes, other women can do it, but can *you*?'

'One can get used to things. There must be something to be said for a husband who, to be fair, has to spend half his nights with his other wife.' I make a joke of it. 'After all, I'll get some time in my head that I can keep for myself.'

I don't mention the other reasons. About never worrying about having enough to pay school fees. Being able to cook a meal with meat more than twice a week. Access to a car filled with petrol every day. Comfort. Security.

*

What does my mother think? Our relations have gone way beyond discord to something bordering on constant rage. Even with my sisters around, there's an undercurrent that snatches at my shoulders and claims their muscles for its own. By mutual consent, my mother and I make a great effort not to talk to the other about anything of importance. When I bring her news of my marriage, I make sure at least two people, who are used to our family, are around. She never gets the chance to present her views directly to me, undiluted. They eventually filter through anyhow – the extended family is pretty good at circulating opinions, especially those expressed with deep emotion. So I get to know that she's not surprised I end up being a second wife. I've pretty much messed up my life.

Aunt K continues to do what she can to patch things up between my mother and me. She says, 'I know this is a hard thing for your mother to tell you. She's relieved that you've finally found someone who can take care of you. She's heard Amadou Sisoho is a good man, a family kind of man.'

Officially the ban on contacting my sisters is lifted. I invite Taiwo to the wedding. She sends her excuses, saying, 'You know Reuben got a promotion just this past month. He's been planning a dinner party at our Sanyang beach house. He's invited his boss as well as the regional head based in Abidjan. I need to spend time making sure everything's perfect.' I haven't given Kainde enough notice, she's off on a work tour in the Far East and won't be able to come. 'Send me a few happy snaps,' she says over the phone.

The wedding is on a Friday. I have nothing to do with the bit that takes place in the mosque. The day feels like any other, except that I have an expensively textured outfit on with the gold earrings and necklace Amadou gives me as a present. Kweku Sola looks smart in his *mbaseng* gown but his five-year-old self cannot resist kicking a ball against a wall. By lunchtime, the gown is off and he's running around in a vest and the trouser bottoms. A few people drop in during the day – the LaFarges, Aunt K, Amadou's daughters. We eat bowlfuls of *mbahal* as the *tam tam* drummer from next door comes round to sound out our news. We give out plastic bags of *beignets* and bottles of soft drinks to the children who live along our street.

With my marriage official, I work fewer hours at the office, where everyone takes to calling me Mrs Sisoho.

Kweku Sola asks me one day, 'You told me to call Amadou Pa, but he's not really my father is he?'

'No, but he treats you like a son,' I answer.

He pauses and in the space, I watch him hesitate, fight his curiosity, but then ask, 'Who is my father?' His voice is quiet. I could choose to ignore it.

I let in my own pause before replying, 'You'll have to take Amadou as your father now. When you're older I'll tell you.'

What I should say is, 'When you're older, maybe your face will tell me.' The secret has stayed hidden. His father's features haven't been stamped on his face. Instead, there's me all over him and nothing of his two possible fathers. There's my hairline that starts too high on my head, leaving a drift of forehead to slope to my eyebrows. There's my nose that would crowd out my face if it weren't for huge, open eyes, edged with long lashes. All of me, and nothing of either of them.

To the question that remains on his face, I try to excuse myself, 'It's much too complicated to explain to you right now. Maybe you'll understand better when you are older.'

Trust flickers and calms some of the questions that remain in his face – but not all.

*

217

I know I have to work at Rohey, make an effort to befriend her somehow. I want to foster a level of mutual tolerance, I do not want a new war front. I make *nanburu* and send her a huge bowlful at Easter. At Christmas, I do likewise with chicken *benachin*. At odd times, I buy her some kitchen towels, saying I found them cheap at the stores. I never take them round to her house myself. I ask the driver to drop them off, and give him a message to pass on. He usually comes back with simple thanks.

Rohey allows her daughters to visit on Saturdays, even when their father isn't around. She has to let them come so she is not regarded as a poor loser. The girls sit stiffly in perfect clothes in the sitting room the first few times. As the months pass, they take to skipping outside, playing *paginyadi* on a rough chalk-drawn diagram in the courtyard. Rohey and I learn to live with each other. So do our children.

One wet Sunday evening, raindrops pelt a dance of marbles on the roof. Amadou is in Dakar to clear some Peugeot orders from the port and won't be back for a week. Rohey rings me with a sob in her voice: '*Walai*, Dele, they've taken it all.'

'Who? And what have they taken?'

'How can I explain all this to Amadou? How can people be so wicked? God will have to pay them back.'

She dissolves into tears on the phone. She was out with the girls all day and they have just come back home.

'Do you want me to come over?'

'Yes, come and see what these wicked people have done.'

Kweku Sola and I drive to Rohey's. The rain thins but the car sloshes in scattered puddles. When we arrive, there's a mini-crowd at her metal gate. Snippets of incredulity catch my ear as I *salaam* and walk past.

'*Nganeh!*'

'*Yaype?*'

'*Walai!*'

I want to hear the news from Rohey. She is sitting on the steps leading up to her verandah. Her children are next to her in a protective triangle, one on each side and the littlest on the step below, right in front of her mother.

'What happened?' I ask.

'Go in,' Rohey replies. 'Go in and see for yourself.'

There's no furniture in the sitting room. There are no curtains on the rails. No rug on the floor. No vibrantly green plant on a corner stool. I come back outside.

'But, what happened?' I repeat.

'That's not it. There's more. Go through. Go into my bedroom. Look at the kitchen.' Rohey's voice is smothered by the arms covering her head which is now settled into her lap.

I walk into the corridor and peer into the rooms. The bed frames are there, but nothing else. Wardrobe doors are open. Windows are bare. In the kitchen, the fridge groans and shudders. It and the cooker had been too heavy to carry so they'd left those behind. There are no pots on the shelves. There are no groceries in the tiny store off the kitchen.

Back outside, I ask Rohey, 'Who could have done this? How did they get in?'

'It was Kikoi, my gardener, and Kumba, the girl from my village who my mother sent to help me.'

'How do you know?'

'The children next door. They saw them. Go and ask them.'

I walk down the steps, across the cleared slab of concrete, past the mango tree to the metal gate that swings itself shut weighted by a Peugeot axle. Outside, I throw a question to the assembled crowd, 'Who saw what happened?'

A babble of voices. A truck. A pickup. White. A Peugeot. No, a Toyota. Twelve o'clock. Possibly five.

'Let me go and ask next door,' I say, leaving the voices behind. I do not have far to go. A woman is in the front yard, tending a charcoal stove on which she is roasting cobs of corn.

'The children saw them,' she says. 'In a white pickup. They came twice, and loaded up high each time.'

'Did you see anything?'

'Not much. I popped out to the Amet shop to buy some matches, and the pickup was half full. But I didn't think much of it at the time. I thought it a bit odd that Rohey had not mentioned she'd be moving, but that was all.'

All Rohey's clothes are gone – her grand boubous, her shoes, her gold, everything. The space under the children's bed, which had their new Koriteh things in suitcases, is empty. Everything movable is gone.

The next morning, I pause outside Kweku Sola's bedroom instead of bustling in as I usually do to wake him up for breakfast. With weak daylight edging the curtains at his windows, I can see the tip of his dark head poking out beyond the pillow he uses to cover his ears at night. I move in, walk past his bed and the shadowy triangles formed by his elbows on the white sheets. I push his curtains apart, drenching the room with early sunshine.

He's covered the cork board on the wall above his desk with his still-life pencil drawings. When I suggested he should try to do portraits, he looked at me steadily and said, 'Ma, people don't keep still, they move. When I put things together the way I want them to look, they stay where they are until I am finished.' I look at some of his recent drawings: a bowlful of mangoes, the dining room chairs in a tangle, cups and saucers after dinner. If we'd still been stuck in a mud-and-wattle, he could never have had this. I haven't forgotten how we got to where we are.

My househelp Bintou sits in my living room, legs splayed out, a huge chunk of bread in her hands with oil dribbling onto her fingers.

'*Mangai aingh rek*. I'm eating now. *Ham nga tei si suba mburu amout on*. There was no bread this morning.' She says it as if I really shouldn't mind. She gets up to amble towards the kitchen. I let my eyes pass over her stout frame, watching her fleshy arms jiggle.

'I've got some fish in the car for Amadou's dinner this evening. Ask the driver to take them round to the kitchen for you.'

She turns around at the door to ask, 'And what do you want me to do with them?'

'I'm making some *chereh* this evening. You know how he likes his *bonga*. Make sure you season it with fresh chillis. And you need to make a salad to go with it.'

'I'll get started right away.'

I plop into an armchair and get out a notebook from my bag, meaning to continue with the list of things to do that I'd started earlier. Instead, I let my eyes wander about. I'm proud of this house, and how I've made it feel a home for all of us. I like my armchairs – they're solid, yet comfy. I pull a leather pouffe closer to rest my legs on. The rug takes up a fair amount of floor space. Cleaning it is a bit like picking stones out of rice, but I like the close weave, the deep wines, the swirls of pattern in it. At this time of day, with the windows open, there's a cross-breeze blowing through the verandah and in through the front door.

Next thing I know, there's a *Salaam aleikum* and Rohey's here.

'Ayodele, sorry to wake you up. It's so hot today, I'm not surprised you fell asleep.'

'Come in. Kweku Sola said you might pop in sometime today.'

'I'm here to ask a favour. Before I start, shall I tell Bintou to make us some tea?'

To my nod, she heads for the kitchen and I hear the murmur of their exchange. When she returns, she takes a little brown plastic container from her bag. 'I got some *churrai* from my neighbour Saffiatou who has just come back from Mecca. It's a new incense she found there.'

I sniff at it. 'Smells good, as if it's got cinnamon in.'

'I thought you'd like some,' she says as she flaps her light blue gown about, her thin gold bangles rearranging themselves on her wrist as she settles in her seat. 'Since Saffiatou came back as an *Ajaratou*, she's always dropping into our conversations how this or that person called her Aji Saffi. I must do the *hajj* myself, or I'll never hear the last of it from her. Ayodele, I need you to speak to Amadou for me.'

'But Rohey, you could always ask him yourself.'

'I've already tried. He thinks all I want to do is spend his money. That I can't go shopping in Dakar for Koriteh and also go to Mecca. The *hajj* is different – people take you seriously afterwards, and anyway it's a good thing for all Muslims to do. Do talk to him for me, I know he will listen to you.'

'But . . .'

'Look, if the topic comes up, put in a good word for me. There are lots of gold jewellers in Mecca. I'll buy you some nice gold as a thank-you.'

'I'll see what I can . . .'

'This is a hard thing for a first wife to say but, you know what, you've been good for him. You've helped him in his business more than I ever could.'

Bintou brings in some tea, only narrowly avoiding spilling the sugar all over my rug.

When she leaves, Rohey continues, 'You know about Amadou's other wife, Zainab, don't you? His second marriage that didn't see the year through?'

'Well, not exactly . . .'

'Zainab left school at Form Five, so she had O levels and all. She was pretty, but *goggg*!' Rohey rolls her eyes and puts her hands on her waist, expressing Zainab's feistiness. 'Anyway, Amadou would spend and spend on her, take her wherever she wanted to go. But she wanted more. At first, I didn't believe what people were telling me, and it wasn't right to carry rumours to Amadou. One day, he found out for himself when he got back from a business trip.'

She takes a sip of her tea. 'There she was, in *his* house, *their* bedroom, with one of those guys who do the tourists on the beach.'

'Did Amadou tell you all this?'

'No, of course he didn't. I found out from the househelp. She heard all the shouting and saw this man hopping out of the bedroom with one trouser leg dragging on the floor.'

Bintou breaks into the pause by coming back with a tray of biscuits.

'Did you know about the new underwear at the Hochiemys'?' Rohey asks. When I shake my head she says, 'Why don't you come with me, I'm going there now. You might find something you like.' She sees my hesitation and presses her point. 'Amadou might like it too.'

'All right then. Let me make sure Bintou understands what else to prepare for his supper.'

Bintou is sitting on a stool outside the kitchen door, singing a lilt from her home town in Cassamance. I launch into instructions. 'Don't forget to get the *chereh* before dark. Start the sauce for me in the large pan. Leave the fish in the fridge and I'll finish it off when I get back. Get me some limes from the garden. This floor needs doing. And you need to make sure these surfaces are clean as you go along.'

Life is different from my best imaginings. I am about to go off to buy underwear with a woman who shares another bed with my husband. 'Don't you think we're lucky?' says Rohey, as we head for her car together.

16

Religion

Moira, with the familiarity of a friend from childhood, visits every week after Amadou dies, usually laden with plants – ferns, orchids, a lady's-slipper. She stays and cooks with me – fish *chereh*, oxtail soup, *akara* with a fiery chilli sauce. Kweku Sola is often out when he's not in his room studying for his O levels. Soon, I start to look forward to Moira's company. It's the doing that helps mostly, someone to chat alongside. One Friday, she says she can't come to visit me because she is hosting a church supper at her house. She invites me along. I meet Brother Paul, who extracts a promise from me to attend his next Sunday evening service.

I go to the service three times before I offer my life to Christ. The church is in Brother Paul's house – a tidy verandahed bungalow off an untidy smelly street in Churchill's Town. Twenty of us meet there, in the combined sitting/dining room. We move the dining table to the front, as a preacher's desk. We edge the sofa and armchairs around the room, and dot the dining chairs between them.

Brother Paul has a round face and wears round glasses. He is balding on top, with hair around the side and the back which he shaves to match the hairless circle at the front. He favours brown safari suits. He and his equally round wife Acy huddle me into a new family and provide comfort with explanations.

Brother Paul preaches with power, his face mirroring the energy in his words. His voice changes tone, direction, volume. It lowers to a whisper, heightens to a roar. Sweat pours off him. He uses a large white handkerchief to mop his brow. On the Sunday I join the clump of two at the front of the room, the sermon is about a peace that passes all understanding. A peace that can become mine if I believe. It makes sense without me knowing why. I choose to go up and be prayed for with the laying on of hands. I turn to it all with relief. I choose to believe.

Amadou has been dead for six months. I knew the businesses and how much each one could make. Rohey did not. I knew that although the Mercedes distributorship had a smaller turnover, it also gave higher returns – more money for far less work. The Peugeot business was bigger, busier and brought with it a lot more hassle – more angry customers, more staff with hospital or school fees to settle. I knew which I preferred. I showed Rohey the figures. She chose the Peugeot saying she prefers a business with a lot of activity – she wants to keep herself busy.

We go out on church picnics at a spot way beyond the tourist beaches, past the young men who sell their bodies to wizened European tourists, to where the sand sparkles with glitter treasure from the sea. The water here moves with varieties of blue, the waves froth and spill onto the beach. Lagoons often get abandoned by the sea at low tide, and the water in them is still, reflecting palm trees against sand so sunbeaten it looks white.

Brother Paul says, 'Look at God's creation. Look at the things around us. See how God's hand is in the blue of the sky. See how restless the sea is, how green the palm fronds. This is all God's doing.'

I can see what he means as the breeze that sways the trees also blows through my head, whisking away the whys crowding it out.

He says, 'When I used to think I was clever, clever with the knowledge of science, I batted God away. I made up chemicals in the laboratory not knowing that their beauty was part of God's creation. Now my cleverness is based on how much I know of His word.' He holds up the Bible in his hand. He sounds certain, as if he knows the truth from deep inside his gut. He unfolds the teachings in the Bible like the careful peeling of a Sa'lone plum, with each strip letting loose dribbles of sweet tangy juice. Eating the soft, firm flesh is a delight that needs practice – in the middle is an energetically spiky seed. As he puts it, 'The word of God is sweet and tears asunder.'

Our church grows. We move out of Brother Paul's house. We rent the school hall by the Latrikunda market. It is convenient and easy to get to – the main taxi park is close by.

One Good Friday, we decide to have a celebration. We sing with passion: *Freely, freely, you have received, freely, freely, give / Go in my name and because you believe, others will know that I live.* Brother Paul challenges us: 'We are going outside right now to share our faith. Set yourself a goal – to witness to one person. Just one. One person to give a tract and encourage to come to our service.'

I feel rather useless standing in the line of us outside the school. People walking past seem busy – intent on getting somewhere. It being Friday, many are walking past with the ends of their long gowns trailing up dust. They carry prayer mats and a few hold plastic kettles full of water. They are heading for the nearby mosque which is already belching out the call to prayer from two loudspeakers set on the minarets.

In the end, we provoke anger with our proselytising booklets. The imam comes to the school the Tuesday after Easter to complain to the headmistress. As Brother Paul tells us the following Sunday, the headmistress said we should not be a nuisance in the neighbourhood. The imam said he is prepared to let our flock be. We should return the courtesy and allow his worshippers to attend to their prayers without harassment. He believed in his Allah, and that Mohammed was His Prophet – he wasn't about to change his mind. The headmistress let us off on a stern warning.

As Latrikunda High School hall is not only cheap but convenient, Brother Paul advises us thus: 'Remember that the seed of the Word of God can fall on hard ground. All we can do is to be patient, and pray that by our very lives, others will be encouraged to know this God of ours, and that the ground of their hearts will become prepared.'

Three years on, I am voted onto the church council. We meet once a month at Brother Paul's house to discuss things that concern us all. This month, there are several issues on our agenda. First, though, we pray and we sing.

Hair covering is item number one. Sister Moira mentions the sayings of Saint Paul in 1 Corinthians 11:5:

And every woman who prays or prophesies with her head uncovered dishonours her head – it is just as though her head were shaved.

The church is changing in tiny ways. This is one of them. If a headscarf matches my dress, I don't mind having one on. But if I have to carry one in my bag in case someone is stricken by an urge to pray . . . It's as if they don't realise that short hair and shorn heads are fashionable in women these days. My sister Kainde cut off her dreads in favour of hardly any hair. In our meeting today, uncovered heads are crowned with short black hair, or various shades of brown skin glistening with after-singing sweat. All these heads belong to men.

Brother Tani smiles at me with teeth that are stained, but not from too many kola nuts. He walks through the dining room into the bathroom. Later, I know, he will sneak past us quietly into the kitchen and out of the back door for a smoke. He will clutch his phone in his hand and wave it at whoever catches him. We all have our burdens. Where would the freedom be otherwise, if I marched up to him and told him off for pretence? He's doing his best and that's all that God requires of us.

Indeed, *the truth shall set us free*.

Item number two is on home visits. I put in my report. 'I visited Mr Bright last night. I took him a cane food basket with Ovaltine, Gem biscuits, cans of Peak milk, *nanburu*, some bread I made at home, and some imported apples. We chatted. He was full of memories of his wife. He said to me "She's now passed over to the other side, but she used to make the best *nanburu* I've ever tasted." These home visits are an important way to show we care for each other.'

Brother Paul says, 'How good it is to give, as well as to receive. Well done, Sister Dele.' I smile at the praise, casting my eyes down at the floor.

For Any Other Business, I propose the following: 'Um, I remember when we were having a picnic at the beach once, and Brother Paul talked about the beauty of God's creation. I wonder whether we can start to put flowers in the church on Sundays?'

'That will be expensive, won't it?' says Brother Tani.

'I don't mind increasing my tithe to cover the cost,' I reply.

Moira chips in, 'It will be good to increase your tithe. But the church should use the money for slightly more useful things than flower decorations. We need to help the mentally ill at Campana. We support the orphanage at Farafenni and there are many more things to do than we have the money for.' Moira is changing.

'I wouldn't mind using flowers from my garden instead.'

She puts up her right hand. 'Excuse me, but don't you think,' she says in that high-pitched girl voice of hers that can send barbs into the ears of all who don't prepare themselves, 'that the two hours you spend putting the flowers into vases could be used more productively on your knees? Remember,' she continues, 'how beautiful heaven will be. You'll have flowers there to your heart's content. While we're here,' and she turns to smile at Brother Paul, 'we need to be as useful as we can.'

I don't give up easily. 'Different things for different purposes. We can celebrate by bringing nature into our church. On days with communion especially, I wish the front of the church looked a bit more *festive*. When I was little, my mother's church always looked beautiful on Easter Sunday, flowers everywhere.' I could add that the breeze played through the windows and the sea sparkled against the sun beyond. I am changing too, but crossways.

Everyone stays silent. Except Moira.

'You keep talking about how things used to be in your mother's church! Well, they are different in this one. Those churches with orders of service and polite prayers are dying. Our kind of church is where the Lord chooses to do new things.' Her face is shiny with rightness. 'Not so?' she says to everyone clustered around the room, turning her eye on each one and daring them to contradict her.

Moira is wearing black patent leather strappy sandals that show off her bunions with style. She has on some straw hat with a wide brim and what seems like an even wider ribbon attached to the rim in tight ruching. Brown hat. Beige ribbon. Her high-necked dress has large pink and brown flowers on a beige background. It is low-waisted and at the seam are three giant pleats, unevenly ironed, curving out stiffly over the chair she is perched on, bum so dangerously near the edge, I wonder how she will stop us all from seeing her knickers if she tips off the chair.

I give up.

We stand together and hold hands, then bow our heads for prayer. Brother Paul intones, 'Search our hearts, Lord. Let anything that can come between us and serving you properly be stamped out.' He stops to wait for the Holy Spirit to act.

There is a snuffle. I do not look up. We are all prone to the occasional public confession when God rests among us. The snuffles get louder. Brother Paul continues, 'Dear Lord, thank you for working in our lives. Thank you for shining your light and showing up the dross. We ask for forgiveness, and ask that you set us on the path to righteousness.'

We open our eyes but Brother Isaac is bawling now. Tears run down his face, his shoulders shake. 'I need to confess before all of you. I have sinned with Aina. May the Lord forgive me, forgive us.'

Moira shakes her head in disbelief. Aina! Aina used to come to church in tight trousers. Moira, who's appointed herself our watchwoman of virtue, took her aside to recommend dresses. Aina did switch to dresses, but they also were tight, fitting as closely to her body as a stocking. It was as if she spilled out of her clothes. Moira says, 'It was just like I told her. What she wears only encourages young men to have sinful thoughts.'

Brother Paul says, 'We'll end here for tonight. Brother Isaac — you can stay behind for counselling. You'll need to clear your soul before God.'

We amen and hallelujah, say our goodnights and leave.

*

It's good to stay in fellowship. I wish it continued into all areas of our lives. I do not struggle alone. We are individuals, each with our own place in the body of Christ, and the body has to work together to stay whole. I wish I knew for sure whether I'm meant to be a little finger, and at least given a reasonable role to play, or whether I should be content being an eyebrow hair. Bubbles of discord arise like the ripe farts I get after eating too many slices of green mango dipped in chilli and salt.

I turn thirty-five on a Sunday. I ask Brother Paul to come and mark it for me with special prayers for the coming year. Moira invites herself as soon as she gets wind of the party, but of course I did mean to ask her. She phones me the night before to discuss the arrangement of songs for the Sunday evening service. To conclude our conversation, she says, 'I'll be coming round to yours after the service of course.' Then she titters.

She brings me a small earthenware pot with a tiny aloe in it. 'It's quite hardy and won't die even if you don't water it for a month.' It's almost her back to her old self. However, her commentary on my life begins soon enough.

'I see you've kept the white Benz. It can't be cheap to run. We could do a lot for the orphanage in Farafenni with that kind of money.'

I grit my teeth and distract myself by asking, 'Now, how many people would like Sprite?' I rush to the kitchen to get some from the crate, and walk out with the bottles clinking against each other on my tray.

Everyone is in the backyard, huddling next to charcoal burners I lit to warm the air. Moira welcomes me: 'My dear sister, you shouldn't buy charcoal, it destroys too many trees and is against the law. We must render unto Caesar that which is Caesar's and unto God that which is God's. Luke 20:25. This is a good law we must obey. The word of God is our sword – we apply it in our lives to guard against the Evil One. Isn't that right, Deacon John?'

I'd asked Bintou to take Saturday off so she could come and help me serve today. Moira does not hold back her comment when Bintou comes out with the first hot dish, 'Hmm, you're not even giving your house staff a rest on Sundays. Genesis 2:3 says we should all rest on the seventh day. Even the heathen.'

I find myself protesting, 'Bintou is practically family and she wanted to help anyway.'

There is a lot of chat, but my heart stays cold, dry. And bitter.

She preaches at me all evening. Back from a trip to the bathroom, she announces – out loud to everyone – 'I noticed your Senegalese batik of two women holding pestles over a wooden mortar. I'm surprised you've put it on such a *nice* bit of wall space. Surely a plain dark-varnished cross would be perfect there – just the thing you need to declare your witness, for we must use every opportunity to share our faith, must we not?'

When we move inside to stand together for final prayers, she casts her eyes over the books on my shelf. She picks one out and holds it up, 'Palace of Desire? *Na-gwib Manfous?* What kind of books are you reading, sister? We must all guard our minds and keep them clean, you have to watch what you read.'

At the goodbye, she says, 'Thank you my dear for a lovely evening.' She edges in for a hug. At the hint of my perfume she stands back and grasps my shoulders with hardening, clasping hands, 'We are the odour of the Lord, we don't need any props!' As she makes her way to the door, she flings her final salvo, 'I really must watch my sister in the lord, I have seen many revelations about her life tonight!'

How she plays her devotion. And what intense attention she gives to the details of other people's lives.

*

As usual, I wake Kweku Sola up early to get ready for the first church service. We have a quick argument about what he chooses to wear. We settle on dark jeans, belted up around the waist, and a plainish T-shirt. I ask him to comb his hair.

God is Good, we sing and shout it, God is Good, we celebrate.

I am a 'Welcoming Friend'. I stand at the door of our church and give out photocopied sheets about the week's events and shake hands with everyone who comes in. Kweku Sola is at the front – he will fiddle with the buttons on the electronic equipment until it is time for him to go and help out in the Sunday School. When we go home and I ask, 'How was church today?' I can only expect him to use his standard response: *Boring*, the single word accompanied by a *tut* and a resigned sigh. But how else is he going to learn what I believe unless I bring him with me?

Just after we open the building, it is quiet, ugly even – a large dull space with empty air above rows of flat plywood seats that stand unevenly on the floor. Then it starts filling up, with church members coming in to do their various duties – preparing for communion, setting up instruments, selecting overhead transparencies for the choruses.

I walk outside with the sign we put up each Sunday:

Church of Christ Brethren
Welcome to our international congregation of worshippers.
Come and receive your own miracle today.
Open Sundays: 9am to 12 noon; 4pm to 8pm

A man in dirty, dirty clothes walks in, smelling strongly of drink. He's been before and usually hunches up in a seat right at the back and goes to sleep. We welcome everyone, we don't turn anyone away, for we are all lost sheep in need of a Saviour. I shake his hand and smile as good a welcome as I can. With all these people you don't know coming from wherever, I was glad when the Deacons decided to switch from using large aluminium communion cups of Vimto to the kind of little glasses used at my mother's church, passed along in a wooden tray with holes to fit them into. Much healthier. I recommended the change and paid for the glasses and holders. There's absolutely no need to pass germs around in a place of worship.

The church has grown a lot, to more than three hundred regular worshippers now. We have bought things to help us to grow even more: musical instruments, a public address system, stackable chairs, a mini-podium, and overhead projectors. As Brother Paul says, 'We are multiplying indeed by His grace and His goodness.'

Other regulars are arriving now. Aunty Therese shuffles in. She is bent over in a voluminous old-style Krio dress, with carpet slippers and her hair firmly tied with a length of cotton print in the season's colours – blue for the rain and green for the springy growth all around us. Rivers of age show in the stretches and folds of skin pulling off her face. Her eyes are alert as she turns towards me.

'The best of God's morning to you,' she says.

'And to you too,' I reply.

The taxi driver who brings her in every Sunday morning stands behind her like a sentry.

'I'll pick her up at the usual time,' he says to me, handing over the green canvas bag she brings with her each week.

'Let me take you to your seat,' I offer. We walk to the very front, where I take her cushion out of her bag. I also get out a square blanket in bright pink-and-white acrylic, with a waffle imprint, and settle that on her knees after she sits down.

'Don't forget my water, please,' she says.

Her bottle of water has a sports top, and its clear plastic is emblazoned in bright red with *Heartbeat – we'll keep your pulse.*

'Are you all right? Can I leave you now?'

'Yes, my dear. Thank you.'

She pulls at her pink acrylic with hands which her skin claws to hold onto. I let her be.

I spot Brother Isaac up at the front, looking busy with the mike and speakers. He is on one knee, with his generously sized behind gloved in brown suiting trousers, the kind modestly dressed men wear to remain indistinguishable in a crowd. He can't see me, but I see him and remember. Aina turned up to service perhaps three times after their involvement was made public. She never looked sorry. Her lips stayed strongly outlined with dark red pencil, and slobbered over with gloss. Her eyes stayed mascaraed, and her braids were shot through with bright extensions of gold and blond. The last I heard of her, she'd emigrated to Qatar and was rumoured to have accompanied one of the German engineers who built the Farafenni–Fatoto road.

By the time I get back to the door, Brother Paul is squatting next to Aunty Therese, holding one of her hands; their heads are bowed in prayer. Brother Isaac taps and blows into a microphone. His voice is rough with a slight rasp: *Testing, testing, one two three*.

Brother Tani walks in with a jean jacket huddled close, sneakers with a jaunt in them and a stale drift of cigarette smoke.

As the church fills up, it seems like God Himself comes to rest among us. Indeed He does say, 'Where two or three are gathered, there am I, in the midst of them.' People hug as they greet each other. The laughter, the hellos and the energetic waving of arms across the room all create a warmth, as if in sharing these little things of ourselves, we become linked one to another. There is a buzz in the air, and an expectation of blessing from the Lord – the happy sound of heaven, people lifting their voices together and praising God.

'. . . how sweet the sound, that saved a wretch like me . . .'

Moira trills away, delivering her solo on the mike, hitting the high notes clearly and springing sighs and amens from random corners of the room. How a voice so honeyed could possibly cope with a heart with so much poison . . . I start a silent prayer: *Dear Lord, forgive me but that woman has become my personal thorn. Please give me patience, so I hold my tongue instead of retorting to her sharp remarks about my ways and habits.*

The service has started. Aunty Therese hobbles along to share her miracle of this week. The microphone is adjusted to her height but as soon as she starts to speak, it protests with a screech about being too close to the drummer's mike. Brother Isaac rushes to fiddle with wires and adjust the synthesiser.

'I thank God. Some of you may know I am a widow, and that the money I live on is the pension my dear husband worked for all his life so I could continue to live without charity after his death.' She pauses, 'Last month's cheque never made it into my hands.'

Her voice cracks like the sharp snap of hard-set sesame sugar snacks. She clears her throat, but it wavers as she continues, 'And it's God, only God, who helped me track it down.'

In the pause that follows her sniffs, emotion runs down her cheeks.

'These days the people at the Post Office cannot be trusted. The whole country suffers from dishonesty. The place is full of thieves but I thank God for His deliverance. The thief took it to the Standard Bank, where the cashier recognised my name. She did not pay it out straightaway, but instead asked her boss to verify the cheque. The man was caught. I got my cheque back, and my money for this month. Praise God.'

Her joy spins free into the air like a loose balloon, nudging the sky with its nose and waggling its string tail in glee. In response, we murmur our allelujahs. There are a few scattered claps, forcing hand-dampened air tight and letting out hiccups of holy applause.

237

Next, Brother Hassan shares a vision. 'Just now, when Brother Paul was praying, I received a picture in my mind. I saw a gate in a walled city. There were lots of people pushing forward, shouting, trying to find their way out through the gate. At first it was hard for me to understand why we were all there, as I was near the back of the crowd and could not see. After waiting for what seemed like ages, someone shouted – 'There he is, the one who could not save himself.' I did nothing. I said nothing, but felt shame creeping up on me, because by choosing to stay in the crowd and not trying to find out more, not trying to insist on knowing what was going on, I knew I had failed him. When at last I got to stand at the gate, I saw the greenest hill up ahead, with fresh bright grass. I remember thinking it was odd that the hill looked like half a calabash and not like a proper mountain. For a minute a cloud covered the sun, yet provided some light in the background. I saw the outline of three crosses. My shame was so great, I clung to the gate and could go no further.'

He explains, 'I saw Jesus' crucifixion on a green hill outside Jerusalem. God was reminding me that I put Jesus right there, on that cross. We all put him there. I am grateful that He thought I was worth the sacrifice. Amen.'

Throat-clucking praise and the odd echoing amen accompany him back to his seat.

When Brother Paul stands up for the main sermon, he takes up more space than the tiny podium has to offer. His voice hardly needs the boost of the microphone. The thrust of his message is this: 'Money is the root of all kinds of evil. Rather than let money control us, we should control the money. Money is all part of God's design. He gave us humans the ability to invent a way of sharing wealth. But we must guard against money becoming our master. For it is then that we call it *mammon*, a curse of faith.'

The main announcement today is for a wedding. Brother Tani to Sister Yetunde. We are all invited to the ceremony in two weeks' time.

My silver Mercedes has not lost its new-car smell. I am in its cockpit, with cushioned air around me, beige leather seat under me, and a panel of lights on the dashboard to tell me about trouble before it comes. I turn out of my house, heading for the Banjul road, where I'll be meeting Rohey for lunch. The engine murmurs under my acceleration and the wheels swing this way and that to my slightest touch.

This car is the kind of model I can sell on in a couple of years to a politician, industrialist or diplomat. It has every kind of modern convenience: cupholders, a sun roof, a glove compartment that can stow an emergency wardrobe, and wing mirrors that are adjustable from the inside. My Merc talks to me if I leave the lights on, the keys in the ignition, or if my petrol gets low, providing the comfort of an electronic caretaker. It cuts a dash on the highway, being one-of-a-kind in town, stretching my tanks of petrol, soothing over bumps in the road.

Money is not a headache for my clients. All the government ministers have Mercedes, and I have supplied our president with ten models in the past couple of years. Yesterday, a Mr Oguntola from the Nigerian High Commission rang to put in an order for two new black series E. Mr Mboge rang to ask me to look out for a 'solid second-hand'. It is not always clear to me where people get their money from, but I can't exactly turn my back on God's blessings and start to ask stupid questions.

Count your blessings, name them one by one.
Count your blessings, see what God has done.

My good luck has all been in God's hands.

Rohey and I meet for lunch at the SeaFront Beach Bar and Restaurant. We greet each other the way we've been doing since we first became friends.

'*Awor*,' I say, giving her the respect of the senior wife.

'*Sate*,' she replies, acknowledging me as the newest wife, the recently favoured.

We kiss and two lots of big-sleeved boubous embrace. She's in a lemony gold and I am in a purply pink. We ease ourselves onto the cushioned concrete benches and order our drinks. I started drinking the occasional light beer after Amadou died, but Rohey has kept to the teetotal principles she was brought up with. She orders a mango juice.

'Now, tell me how life is,' she says, as she puts an elbow on the table, making her gold bangles slide down. When she smiles, the glint thrown from one of her rings is mirrored in the gold that covers her incisor tooth.

'*Ehyey*, when did you get that put in?'

'Just last week. I kept the gold nuggets I bought when I first went to Mecca all those years ago. I decided it was time to use them.'

She turns sideways and smiles again to give me a better view.

'Where did you get it done?'

'Dentist Tabbal. Do you think it suits?'

'Very well.' I add a *huhunh* in additional admiration.

We natter on.

Good news! Good news! Christ died for me!

Last Sunday, Brother Paul talked about how we need to share our faith more often. I feel blessed, but I tend to keep to myself the source of this blessing. I decide to give it a try.

'Rohey, I have something for you to look at,' I say, handing over two credit-card-sized tracts: *Blessings of Creation* and *Left Behind*.

She opens one slowly. There are cartoons of the end of time: volcanoes erupting in the distance and tsunamis bulging over islands. On the final day, the sky thunders open, and Christ returns to collect his own, who ascend with him into a palette of blue and white sky.

'Dele,' says Rohey slowly, 'I see you believe in all this.' She pauses, taking her time to put the words of her next sentence together. 'You changed when you started going to this church of yours.'

I nod. More drinks arrive. I am still on beer. Rohey has moved on to green tea.

She continues, 'You were a better wife to Amadou than I ever expected. You also did all you could to make my daughters feel your house was their second home.'

'Which it still is,' I interject.

'They know that. When Amadou died, you were strong and organised. Without you, I don't know how I could have sorted out his businesses or even thought I could run one myself. I have learnt to be strong too, but using beliefs I was taught when I was small. We don't need to try to change each other's religion now.'

'I was completely mixed up when Amadou died. I acted strong, but I wasn't sleeping well. This church helped me find a way to be. That's why I want to share my faith.'

'That's all well and good. I think it best if everyone were left to follow what they feel inside. I admire what you have found. But your life and your ways cannot be my life and ways. I read my Koran, but do not understand all this talk of a world that is to come. What I really want is to live the life I can see now as best as I can.'

After we pay up, we walk to our cars. Rohey gives me a quick hug before she gets into hers, and says, 'Remember, we are lucky.'

241

17

Inheritance

Kainde is forty-two and her lover is at least ten years younger. They have something I never had with Amadou. There isn't any of that excessive screech teenagers make to the outside world: *Look at us! We're in love!* Instead I see them acknowledge each other's entrance into a room. I see them pat a hand as they share a joke. I hear them chatting away in their room late at night. Laughter. The enjoyment of two people who each thrive in the company of the other.

The night before they leave for Canada, I remark on their ease with each other.

'Yes, it's funny, isn't it? Remember what I used to say?' Kainde's face quietens and her eyes drift into the past. I follow her memory.

Kainde at fourteen. Donald Bah at sixteen. He kept sending her notes. She'd get home and find he'd slipped another letter into her school bag, swearing love to the death, quoting Shakespeare's Romeo, declaring that family would never keep them apart. We kept it to ourselves, not involving the grownups. He started

phoning at odd hours. Kainde avoided answering the phone.
Because their voices were indistinguishable to Donald, whenever
Taiwo answered she'd get an earful of adolescent passion. He got
angry if she said he'd got the wrong twin. It wasn't a passion any
of us understood. Months later, it was defused by the new Namibian
girl who came to our school; overnight, Donald switched his
affection. Kainde declared at the time that if love could be so
wrongfully blind, then she wanted no part of it.

Now she tells me, 'Since then I've never been able to understand men. I've dated them, I've even kissed a few. But I stopped
trying and thought that I might prefer to be on my own. Until
now.'

I see truth in her face. Me, who's never known anything more
fiery than a grateful holding of another in the dark. All right, but
less. Less than what I needed. I don't like where my mind is
leading me.

'You have made your house into a den of iniquity,' Brother Paul
says to me. 'It would shame Jesus to see what you are allowing
your sister to do in your house. Would he not act as he did when
he went to the temple and saw the moneychangers? He threw up
their tables in anger. Righteous anger that knows its place and
when it is to be shown. You have to tell them they are living in
sin.'

My muteness is my response.

'If you cannot witness to your own sister, you do not stand a
chance of becoming a deaconess in this church,' he concludes.

When I am half pushed out of the Church of Christ Brethren for
overquestioning authority, I go. My leaving gouges a hole in me,
making me feel as light as a sunbird's feather, all iridescent and
flashily pretty, but weightless, able to be pushed any which way. I

do normal things – go to the office, shop, arrange what to cook. Inside, I am angry. I find I cry easily. I droop around the house on Sunday mornings, unable to place myself anywhere. I feel alone, cut off. After nine Sundays, I go back to the church my mother took me to as a child, the one where they have flowers on Easter Sundays, where breezes blow wave-soaked wind through the louvred windows, and there I make my kind of peace.

Away from books and films, what would love feel like if it happened in real life, my life? Superlative sex? A guaranteed Song of Solomon type heaven?

Instead of the daily reading suggested in my *Food for the Soul* guide, I pick up my Bible and find myself wanting to read the Song again. I want to prove to myself that earthly love is but a reflection of the love that exists between a creator and the created.

Let him kiss me with the kisses of his mouth / Your name is like perfume poured out.

I try to imagine how it would feel to be intoxicated with the smell of someone you want to melt into. An intensity I have sometimes sniffed at. I have dreamt, I have wondered, but I have not felt.

Just as well I have my God, and this desire to seek ecstasy with my body can be safely locked away. The texture of my faith has changed. I no longer expect everything of it, I no longer let it swirl me up the way it used to in Brother Paul's church. Yet I find I still believe.

I set my breakfast table for one. Perky brown birds chirrup and hop about on the guava tree outside. I hear pedestrians talking in descants to each other as they walk past my open windows. My Sony radio is on. To the background of the ills in the world and the slow death dance being played out in Israel and the West

Bank, I get a bowl and some cutlery. The drawer sticks in its wooden frame, sliding out jerkily as I tug at it. The news is sliced into chunks and delivered by a voice trying to make me understand how it all fits together. Today there is no shocking tragedy – no typhoons in Bangladesh or starving children in Ethiopia – but peace talks have gone stale and the Dow and the Footsie are jiggling up and down, the euro and the dollar are heading for all-out war.

Yesterday, several giant grapefruits fell off my tree. I slice into a chilled yellow one and concentrate on separating the skin from the tears of juice. The news roundup fails to hold the shreds of my thoughts together. Instead my mind runs off with a skittish skip. Words drift through it.

My lover is to me a sachet of myrrh resting between my breasts.

To have a scent stuck between breasts constantly keeping your Other in your thoughts. You think about him without pause and carry his scent as you move through the day, doing normal things. What did Amadou and I have? It started off being this exchange of his comfort for my skill. That bred familiarity. We ate together when he stayed with me, chatting about this and that over supper. We hardly ever quarrelled. When he was at Rohey's I had space in my head for myself. It seemed balanced, that kind of life, that kind of sharing. I never wanted our lives to be so entwined that we suffocated each other. We made our marriage work, and that was enough. All this scent carrying never crossed my mind then.

I hear Bintou at the door. I walk over to let her in. She and I know the curves of each other's mornings now. With Kweku Sola gone, and less and less to do around the house, we have adjusted our hours. She comes in later now, and leaves earlier. That's why I have all this extra time to sit around thinking and making myself yearn for things I could never have had anyway, even when I was young.

With relief, I find something else to shunt these thoughts away. I discuss food.

'You could do me some fish *mbahal* today,' I say.

'If you're going to the market, I'll need some parsley and garlic for the stuffing. How many cups of rice should I cook?'

'Four. Might as well. Kweku Sola will be coming later and people may drop in.' I open the fridge to check on the tomato paste.

'That boy can eat – remember how high he used to pile his plate with my *benachin*?'

I turn round to look her up and down before reminding her, 'And who needs *two* extra cups when we do *mbahal bu tilim*, as a late-evening snack?'

Bintou laughs with a bubbly gruff from her middles which makes her upper arms jiggle. She slaps her thigh loudly and says, with a touch of pride, 'I have an excuse, I need the fat. It helps to pad my knees for scrubbing floors.'

She waddles off to get the bucket and cloths from the broom cupboard, and I hear her bustle into the bathroom as her workday begins.

I walk to the market. On the way, I wave to people I know in the cars going past, and several stop to offer me a ride. Each time, I insist that I need the walk to strengthen my bones. I wish greetings on family, household and assorted relatives and continue on.

The market is full of activity – and flies. It's ten o'clock and the women who dry fish for a living are gutting the morning's catch. I edge past stacks of rancid beige fish curled into irregular cardboard. My mother would have said: 'Oh, look at you – without *gayja*, your *mbahal* will lack that undertone. Just put perfume on your wrists before you go. Hold your breath if you need to, but just buy it, you hear?' Now I can choose to cook *gayja*-less *mbahal*, changing her recipe to suit my nose.

I bump into Reverend Sillah at the market, idling by a fish-monger's stall.

'I was wondering,' he says, 'what the difference is between squid and octopus, and whether it matters which one I get for supper tonight.'

I dither about the amount of detail I should get into. He has been a widower for five years, and several members of our con-gregation regard that as time enough for his heart to have mended.

'It really does not matter,' I assure him. 'Get whichever is cheaper by the kilo.'

I have noticed that he often sits next to me at our church's social events and I'm not yet sure what I think about that. Especially as church members have been dropping hints as plentiful as a swarm of flying termites after the rain.

'Do you think I should fry, or grill?'

'Squid pockets are easier to clean and quick to grill.' Seeing that he may well stretch out our discussion, I excuse myself with: 'In a bit of a hurry. I need to get my fish home, fresh without ice.' I move with a speed and purpose that make me grateful for healthy bones.

Kweku Sola does come to visit, just as he always does on Fridays after work. While we eat, we usually chat about politics, goings-on at his office, how my business is doing. Today, as I dish out a mound of glistening rice onto his plate, he's quieter than usual. Eventually I ask, 'What's the matter?'

He lets his fork clatter onto the table, takes in a wide breath and lets it puff out again. 'Ma, do you remember after you got married and you said I should call Amadou Pa?'

'Yes I do.'

'You also said there were things you couldn't explain then but would explain when I was older.'

'And now you're ready to ask your questions again?'

He nods.

'Who's my father?'

We both wait for the years from long ago to come crashing into the present.

'I made certain choices when I was young, younger than you. Those choices created you.'

He shakes his head. 'I want to know whose face I've got.'

'You've got my eyes,' I say and touch one of his. 'If your ears were just a bit smaller they'd be exactly like mine. I see nothing of anyone else in you.'

'You're not giving me a straight answer, Ma.'

I pause. And think about how wanting to know what a skin that was allowed to sing felt like. And about wanting to know how much rougher it could be standing up behind a watchman's hut. Not things I can explain, not now.

'Once you make some choices, they stick – you can't shake them off. They cling and shape you.'

His face is full of questions. My head has no better answer. The call for prayer from the mosque a mile away rises and fades.

'I'm no longer a child, Ma. I can handle the truth.'

Truth. What truth?

'Amadou *was* your father. He brought you up.'

'When, if, I have my own children, what do you want me to tell them? That Amadou is their grandfather, even though I know it's a lie?'

'What could your father have done for you that he didn't do?'

'Ma, do you remember when I refused to draw people's faces?'

I nod.

'I did a charcoal drawing of myself once. I know the distance between my eyes. I know the shape of my ears. I remember faces. There's nothing in mine that came from Amadou.'

It's my turn to shake my head. 'Not today, Kweku Sola. My choices still affect many lives, not just yours.'

'Amadou is dead, Ma. Nothing you say will hurt him.'

I shake my head again. No. No.

'The bank have offered me a trainee manager's post in Ghana.'

I can't blame him for this. He's free to choose himself out of my life.

'Will you go?'

'Maybe.'

We sit at the table while the *mbahal* goes cold.

Amina comes as the sun is layering longer shadows on hard-packed brown earth. Her wine-coloured lipstick unreliably edges her mouth.

We clatter in the kitchen heating up the *mbahal*. Amina chatters away, bringing me up to date with local gossip, including a summary of the recent turn of events in a long-standing marital dispute in which husband and wife have not exchanged a word for over fifteen years.

When we sit down to eat, she tosses her wig onto a nearby chair and massages her weathered hairline. 'I need to let my head breathe. Should I get my hair braided for the wedding?'

'I'm not sure. What does Jainaba think?'

Amina's youngest daughter, Jainaba, is about to get married.

'She said I should do what I want. I ask her for advice and she gives me backchat. Oh, modern children. She doesn't know how lucky she is to have me as a mother.'

'Has she decided on her wedding dress?'

'Doesn't care what I think. Yellow she says. Girls in Spain

marry in yellow apparently. I said how would she feel if I wore black?'

'And what did she say to that?'

'That if I wanted to mourn at her wedding, I was welcome to. This silliness has to stop somewhere, why doesn't she listen?'

'Better to let her marry as she wants.'

She screws her eyebrows together and sends a slanted, slightly hurt, look my way.

'Don't you think she should let me enjoy being the mother of the bride?'

At this point, we are tucking into Bintou's excellent *mbahal*, which Amina comments on. 'This Bintou of yours, she learned in the end, didn't she? How to cook, and clean.' Without pausing for much breath, Amina picks up her previous topic. 'We came back here for nothing. I thought it would calm her wildness. All that effort I spent trying to get her to respect her elders.'

'Jainaba is very much like you were. She knows her own mind.'

'But just once in a while, to listen? I have some good ideas for the wedding.'

'I'm sure you have, but you'll have to give in this time.'

She moues her mouth as she considers what I've said.

'You've been so lucky with Kweku Sola. He's sensible and, I hear, doing well at Standard Chartered. You've done well by him.'

I blurt out, 'He wanted to know who his father is when he came round earlier.'

Amina's spoon stops halfway to her mouth.

'And what did you tell him?'

I shake my head.

'You know something, Dele? Lie.'

When Amina leaves, she leaves a space empty of air, as if her energy has sucked it all up, carving her shadow where she had been sitting moments before.

To allow myself to ignore her airless shadow, I put on some of my old music. What should I tell him? The whole truth or a slice of it? If a slice, what do I leave out? I lie on the couch and stare at the ceiling. It is white, not a single rain-blemished dot. It can tell me nothing.

I try to write out a note to him: 'I think your father is dead. He used to work for my mother.'

My lover thrust his hand through the latch-opening; / My heart began to pound for him.

'There was no love. His name is Osman Touray. He came from Mansakonko. I never had anything else to do with him.'

I stare at the words. I scratch out 'I think'. At the beginning I add, 'This is not easy for me to say'.

I keep the rest of the slices of truth to myself. It is best to be certain, best not to dangle two possibles before him. Best not to say how I chose. And how it led to him.

I take a clean sheet of paper and start all over.

Daughters of Jerusalem, I charge you: / Do not arouse or awaken love until it so desires.

These driftings breed discontent. They bring memories of being a girl. Being eighteen and full of hope. I should rest easy – passions like these would never have worked in my kind of life. Better this way, this kind of living, grabbing at contentment whenever I can.

The phone rings and creates diversion. It's Reverend Sillah.

If the Church of Christ Brethren never noticed my departure, my mother's old church has certainly noted my entrance.

He says, 'When I saw you at the market, I forgot to mention the new fundraiser for refugees.'

'How is it going?' I ask, stirring up some inner bravery but not really wanting to know, at least not right now.

'Excellent. Excellent.' I can see him rubbing his cheek in enthusiasm. 'At this rate, we'll be able to support twenty of them in all.'

'You've worked hard on it. Well done.' I give credit where it is due.

'I was wondering whether you have time to come round and see the petition I am sending to the United Nations refugee office. My grilled squid turned out really well. I could cook you some more.'

How do I say no? Is it impossible to say yes?

I am a wall to some in this community. I am a wall because I choose to contribute to as many causes as I can, sit on the many committees I am asked to join. With all this love talk and wedding talk and Solomon thinking, today I see myself as a mirrored wall, where others see their own reflection but think it's me. Or maybe a tinted pane in one of those high-bumpered four-wheel drives in which the passengers can see out, but no casual passer-by can see in. Glass, anyway, because I know better than anyone else the many times in the past when I could have shattered myself into tiny little pieces, unglueable, destroyed.

18

Death

Tea works best at times like these, and I have in my hand an old mug, old from my thirteenth birthday. All of thirty years later, it has only one chip on the rim above the handle, and a tiny crooked crack down the side. The handle is white, the inside navy blue. My hand curves around it, and it returns diluted heat. On the outside, white polka dots puncture dark blue. My mother died today. It is evening and I am sitting on her verandah drinking tea.

Sprigs of golden showers hang heavy on the vine that has worked its way over the verandah roof and down each pillar. As I breathe in and out, a cluster of the tube-shaped flowers, orange and free, moves slightly with my breaths. In. Out. I don't hear the househelp Nimsatu as she comes close. The tiles in the house have got used to her hardened bare feet traipsing over them several times a day. She stands at my shoulder and speaks. Her first words bite into my collarbone and some tea jerks into my lap.

'Missis said there were some things I could have. That big *awujor* pot in the kitchen. I was wondering whether I could take it home with me tonight.'

I turn to stare at her. Her words don't make sense. My mother's body was taken to the mortuary at lunchtime. We are having a family meeting at seven to discuss the funeral.

'What did you say?'

She repeats herself. 'There is a large *awujor* pot in the kitchen that your mother used when she needed to cook food for many people. It was one of the things she promised I could have when she died. I want to take it home now.'

Some words trickle in. There is a pot. For cooking for many people. To be taken home now. My mother has promised this. A pot?

'You mean that heavy pot? The metal one on three legs? The one she always used to cook *benachin* at Christmas?'

Nimsatu touches her headscarf and pushes it forward. There are tiny knots of hair at the back of her head, skimmed with grey.

'Yes, that's the one I'm talking about. She keeps it in the store beside the dining room. I mean she used to keep it there. But it's still there. Right on the bottom shelf, because it was too heavy to lift if we put it any higher.'

She has two *malans* on. The brown one underneath has the beak of a yellow duck peeking out under the scrunched flowers of the one on top.

'And you want to take this home with you tonight. You mean right now?'

Her hands move up again to her headscarf.

'Yes.'

There's a pot on three legs, desired by Nimsatu for many years, that she wants to take home.

'What if we need it for cooking here?'

'I can always lend it back to you. As long as everyone knows it's mine.'

'Why can't everyone know it's yours if you leave it here until we've finished with it?'

254

'There are many people who'll be coming and going. I've heard Aunty K talk about how well that pot cooks rice, because it moves the heat all the way to the middle. You know your mother bought that pot from an old man from Cassamance who worked metal. He died.'

And she's died too.

There is a low table in the middle of the room, squat atop a busy brown and white tufted rug. On it is a square of white cotton, embroidered at each corner with a convoluted nest of greens, oranges and reds. We are all sitting on thin-sponged cushions stuck into the low-legged, long-bottomed, wood-framed seats.

'I guess we should discuss funeral dates first. Once we're agreed, we can decide on the format of the service.'

Taiwo shifts to the edge of her seat and bends forward. 'Reuben and I were thinking maybe he should take charge of meetings and things. You know he has all the experience from work, being secretary to the Board.'

She glances over at Reuben with a face creased with pride. 'I could take the notes and then together we could make sure everybody does as they are supposed to.'

There are two rows of three chairs, facing each other across the low table. I am opposite Taiwo. Reuben is next to her, their seats separated by a small stool for setting drinks onto.

I know I am going to give in even before I form words in my head to batten down the flash of irritation inside me. He *married* into the family. She was *our* mother. A few seconds pass.

Taiwo reaches out to pat her husband's arm. It is a good six inches away. Her hand touches air as she says, filling in the silence, 'That's all right, isn't it?'

'Over to you, then.' I nod to Reuben. Taiwo is prepared. She reaches into her bag and extracts a brand-new lined notebook with *Cahier* stamped on it. A smart new Biro is already slid into the spine of the notebook. They are ready to go.

Reuben clears his throat. 'Well, as Ayodele was saying, we shall first need to discuss the funeral date. However, there are several other related issues. What kind of coffin for instance? Will we have a wake in this house or not? After that, we will make suggestions on the order of service. During the service, who shall we reserve seats for in the front row? We shall need someone to make sure Kainde knows what we plan, so she understands what she has to do when she arrives.'

Taiwo scribbles.

'You have all those points, yes?' Reuben addresses his wife, who nods hard enough to move her headful of bobbed weave. He continues, 'There's the catering, of course. We shall also need to set up a roster for who needs to be in the house, this house, I mean – your mother's house – to welcome mourners and ensure they have refreshments. Finally, central to all our planning, we have to discuss the unfortunate business of money.' His right hand orchestrates the air in front of him with his fingers splayed.

His hand stays up while Taiwo makes a final full stop and raises her head. 'Right,' she says, 'we have eleven items on our agenda. The first item is the funeral date.'

For each point, it is obvious they have already conferred, and their prevailing view passes. A Saturday of course. Luckily no one else notable has died this week, so we will certainly get first dibs for the cathedral in town. 'The day thou gavest Lord is ended' is on the list of dirges we are to sing. Appropriate verses will be read – Corinthians – their twelve-year-old son, Modupeh, is suggested as a reader.

'What a good idea,' says Taiwo. 'It will give him a lot of confidence in public speaking.'

'Yes, my dear, put some backbone into the boy. People will talk about how the grandchildren were included in the service. Never been done before, with children as young as ours. Will make history in this town.' Reuben's cheeks gleam with excitement. They stand high on his cheekbones, burnished a deep mahogany. His rimless glasses fit into two dents, and twinkle back strips of fluorescent lighting.

'I think we could get him to practise *O death, where is thy sting?* It will be a joy to see.'

Kweku Sola is selected as a pallbearer. I am delegated to communicate with Kainde.

There is noise at the gate. A door slams. The metal doors shake with thumps. Aunt K's voice booms a greeting to the watchman. I meet her at the main door.

'Ah these bones,' she says by way of greeting. 'It's getting harder and harder to move around. How are you all getting on?'

'Made all the major decisions, but your suggestions will be useful.' Then I shut my eyes, mouth out 'Help' before draping myself around her in a tight hug. 'It's good to see you. Come and tell us what mother would have done for food.'

Aunt K shuffles across the room, her cane leaving dampened circles in the rug. She sits in my mother's embroidery chair. 'Your mother knows I can't sit in those other ones. This is the only one my legs can get me out of,' she says as she settles herself. She turns to pick the embroidered headrest off the chair's back.

'I remember her making this,' she says, putting it on her lap and straightening out the edges. She touches the patterns as purples merge into blue, and dashes of yellow puncture the vine design. 'I shall miss her very much.' We watch, horrified, as Aunt K cries. It is the first time anyone has cried in public for our mother. Aunt K's shoulders shiver. She bends down to fiddle in her bag to find a handkerchief. We move our gaze away, to our fingers, our toes, the floor, the centre table, anywhere but at Aunt K, crying for losing a friend.

She wipes her eyes. She blows her nose. 'Now, then, how can I help?'

Aunt K is given responsibility for catering.

And the *awujor* pot is gone.

I choose not to sleep in my mother's house. I have not made peace with her. I do not want to feel her absence, her emptiness. I do not want to hear her slam the door of her bedroom and slap her slippers in the corridor as she walks past my room. I do not want to hear her voice telling us how we are arranging everything wrong.

Amina phones me at home late. '*Osh for berring*. I am sorry to hear about your mother.'

'You know how we were, Amina. I haven't been able to cry.'

'Remember she wasn't all bad. Maybe life happened to her, and she just coped.'

'Even if I could ever forgive her that, look at what she's gone and done now. Left me next in line to die in our family.'

'Give it time. And let me know whenever I can help.'

Under Any Other Business, I was assigned two jobs. I am to contact the priest, Foday Sillah, and discuss our order of service. I am also to look through mother's things and log 'anything of significance' that all the siblings should see or might be interested in keeping. I am to be fair, referring anything that can be quarrelled over to the company of sisters.

Knowing which I'd find easier, I phone Foday to ask whether he'd mind meeting to discuss the service. I explain about needing to be around my mother's house in case people call to give their condolences.

I sit on the verandah drinking my sixth cup of tea, having the next item on my list piled like a truck-load of rubbish in the middle of life's road. I would rather choose to lie down under the wheels of a Massey Ferguson tractor than put my hands into what I am sure will only bring up muck.

Eventually I make my way to my sisters' bedroom and stop at the door. My mother turned it into a guest room – it has two single beds, with a *tara* mat set between them. The walls are painted white, an old indifferent white. She had reused the old sitting-room curtains from our childhood – which hang in stiff lines of purple and blue. There is little else in the room except for my sisters' dressing table. I open a few drawers. They are swollen from disuse, and the two I eventually prise open are empty.

I walk out and stand outside my bedroom door. It became a storeroom in which she kept old things, things she did not use on a day-to-day basis. I try the handle. It is locked. Panic, then relief floods me. But Nimsatu comes up the corridor and says, when she sees me standing there, 'I'll get you the key. Your mother used to keep it in her bedroom.'

When she pushes the door open, damp air flutters out, laced with the dust of memories that have been laid down. The room is tinted by two slices of light let loose by the curtains to bang against the wall. A fresh-faced yesterday puts me back in here, scheming about how my life would go. Now, all that is left of that time are the walls, murky with dust, and the sunny yellow curtains I'd chosen when I was sixteen. My bed is gone. There are the traces of where my popstar posters used to be, a grinning David Bowie, wild Grace Jones and moody Marvin Gaye.

My mother started to keep her unwanted furniture in here, at least that's what Taiwo had said. I see a few stacked chairs she might have hoped to mend, and the new sofa that came with the set of chairs she had in her sitting room. She never used it, preferring people to sit singly, not forced into an artificial cluster on a shared seat. The furniture is stringed along the left wall, and on the right I find the trunks and the cartons marked with Marlboro in which she put her keepsakes.

I stand there, unable to decide where to start, unable to move. Nimsatu forces me to turn around. 'I don't know whether, as you are looking through things, you could remember to give me your mother's jewellery case. It's not much, but she used to say that even though all her gold and silver would go to you girls, she did not think you'd have any use for the case.'

'Fine. Yes.'

She hovers, expecting me to say more.

'If I find it, I will keep it aside.'

'But it won't be here. It will be in her bedroom. That's where she kept all her important things.'

'All right.' I repeat myself. 'If I find it when I look through her room, I will keep it aside.'

Satisfied, she announces, 'I'll go and tidy the kitchen. Check that food isn't going bad.'

'You do just that.'

With her gone, and me alone in my remembering, I sit down on the floor and push the door halfway closed. Here in my old room are all the things my mother wanted to keep. I pick out stuff with my eyes, a rolled-up rug, a pair of tapestried slippers. The facts of her living, how she lived, stacked up in the things that held either memory or hope of some future use. There are the marks still on the ceiling, but there's less of a future to read now, less I need to know about what life could be. Cats on my shoulder – my story is more than half told.

Nimsatu comes back a couple of hours later, exclaiming, 'You haven't even started! The priest is here.' Her eyes scan the room, take me in, take in how nothing has been touched. 'Shall I get him something to drink? I asked him to wait in the sitting room.'

*

'Ah, Ayodele,' he says as I come into the room. With one look at my face, he asks, 'Are you all right?'

'I am trying to go through my mother's things.'

There is a moment of silence while he does what religious people with a skill for helping others can do, stretches out and touches my feelings, testing, finding out how far he should go.

'Would you like to review the service now,' he continues, 'or would it be best to leave it for another time?'

'Now is as good a time as any.' I sit down. 'Um, one of the issues is where to have the service.'

'You want it at the cathedral, I understand.'

'My sister and her husband do.' My eyes flick to his face. I hope he understands what I am trying to say. 'But I think, without being sure of the numbers of people who will attend, that it will be best to have it at a smaller church. It's not like we're having a state burial or anything.'

'To make sure the church does not seem empty, you mean? That can be arranged. Is this something you'd like me to suggest to the others?'

'Yes, please.'

After that, it's easy. I do not mind the hymns, the organ music, the Bible readings, or the people chosen to read. As I didn't mind when Taiwo and Reuben decided on who is going to arrange the flowers, or what dress Ma will be buried in.

At the end, after my tenth cup of tea of the day, and his third during his visit, I feel ready to tackle anything. It seems that the calm, the laid-back energy all came from him. When I say goodbye, I grab his right hand in my two hands and shake it hard. My eyes stay dry, but my hands stay on his as I say 'thank you' several times over.

*

I open the curtains and encourage a decade's worth of dust to play with the sun's rays. The motes seem to hold the light, furrily soft as they dance about in yellow air.

I take down the first Marlboro box. In it are exercise books in various tones of dull – blue, green, beige. My sisters' names are scrawled on the covers. I pick one out of the pile and leaf through. *The circumference of a circle is 2πr.* I pick up another. A ghost story that starts: *It all began the day she knew she could hear things others could not.* The handwriting gets larger, more uncertain, as I make my way through until half the box is empty and there is a wobbly pile of books next to me on the floor. In a large envelope I find a sheaf of my school reports, ordered, intact – each term, from the year I started school to the year I left.

The second box has things we made at school – my wooden pickup truck which could be wound up by an elastic band connected to the axles. There's the baby cardigan Kainde crocheted out of thin blue wool with one sleeve noticeably shorter than the other. She'd tried to give it to me for Kweku Sola, but Ma had refused. Taiwo had made a set of linen napkins with decorative edging.

There is more. A box full of photographs and albums. Weddings of cousins, our school photographs. Visitors. Christmases. Church outings. I come across an album with a cream fabric cover, cushioned, and shot through with drifts of silver thread. It is inscribed:

To Millie,
for you to start remembering us together,
Love Bankole.

I leaf through black-and-white photographs, mostly of the two of them, my mother and father standing together in a studio somewhere in Banjul, with a painted background of sea, beach and palm tree. There are some photographs of themselves younger, with brown tinges at the scalloped edges of the prints. A few from the time they went to Italy for my father's agricultural extension course. Another time when he went to Dakar for a conference. Then me, an open-eyed baby with large cheeks and a frilly dress, on my father's knee as he sits in a studio chair. Half of the wall behind is panelled with wood, and the rest is wallpapered. Neither looks quite real. On the floor is a roll of loud diamond-patterned linoleum. The pictures stop. The album has six unused pages, their stripes of sticky adhesive crinkly against the polythene cover protector. The memories end.

I leave the album open at the first page, at that very first photograph of them together. The two of them turning towards each other for the brief seconds it took for the flash to blink and the darks and lights be written onto film. A few seconds on film that defined a start to their life. There's an energy in their shared look, but in real life, the fizz was too little to last, and it soon burnt itself out.

In a trunk with some of Ma's clothes, I recognise the dress in the picture. It is a tight-waisted dress with a wide skirt, and an underskirt with some ruches and soft cotton lace at the fringe. In the photo, her eyes turn towards my father who looks down at her. Her shoes have heels and one of her legs is angled in front of the other as she grasps my father's right hand.

The trunk has two other dresses, three pairs of shoes, three bags brimming with sequins and beads, and three scarves. Ma has kept one of everything for each of her daughters, her things, her young things that had all her hope for life – kept for us.

The air is suddenly too stale in the room, the scent of camphor too overpowering. The dust I disturb makes me want to sneeze. I need to leave.

*

At the tiny church on top of the cliff, where the sea waves throw themselves over the hard brown-black rocks, we sing:

The day thou gavest Lord is ended / The darkness grows at thy behest.

There are wreaths made of thorny bougainvillea, with taped areas for handles. Clumps of purple flowers with tiny heads of white stems inside them cluster together. There are some plain green ones, made of young casuarina stems, twisted together. Others have bell-shaped yellow flowers shot into them. I made my wreath from the trail of jasmine that grows outside my front door, twined around a woody stem shorn of leaves and forced into a circle. The flowers are white, with pink undersides. The wreaths lie on top of each other, busily lining the length of the coffin, which has been burnished a dark brown and trimmed with two brass handles.

Foday Sillah asks the congregants to make a Corridor of Condolence. Kweku Sola provides one of the shoulders that carry the coffin outside. We follow it, our faces quiet, walking past a wall of people, all the way out of the church. The coffin goes into the hearse. The three of us sisters sit in the back of the lead mourning car, a black Mercedes estate I borrowed from an old client who keeps several in his garage. Reuben sits in the front seat, next to the driver borrowed with the car.

I feel like I do when I stand on the wet sand on the beach, when the tide is turning, and try to guess which of the waves will reach my toes before their weight pulls them back. I often guess wrong. It's not the obvious ones, not necessarily the big ones that ride by themselves. More often than not, these waves never touch my toes.

People drop by the house in the evening, after the burial. Remi, Kojo and Frederick Adams arrive around eight. Remi says, '*Osh for berring*. I am so sorry to hear about your mother.'

'Thank you,' I reply. Then I pause the requisite number of sad seconds.

'Kojo and I came back last week. Every time he gets fed up with the country, he asks the bank to find him a job somewhere else. All of us get uprooted, but at least we get to see Africa.'

'Where have you come back from?'

'Swaziland. Far, high, cold. My father hopes we will stay behind this time. He says he's old and needs looking after now my mother's gone.'

I find nothing to say in reply, but Remi continues, 'Now, we're both the same – motherless.'

I remember how we used to be. So close we'd pretend we were twins, just like my sisters. We'd pretend we could transfer thoughts. We showed each other everything. Until I decided on my path of knowing.

I smile back at her, then past her to her father. 'How are you?' I ask.

'Getting old, as we all do. *Osh for berring*,' he says. 'Your mother was a fine woman.'

He shakes my hand then pats my elbow. It was all too long ago. Kweku Sola definitely does not have his mouth.

I continue: 'Come and have something to eat and drink.'

At some point in the evening, after the guests have eaten and she's helped to tidy up the kitchen, Nimsatu slides along to me, with my feet resting on a *tara* bench on the verandah, Kainde close by, both of us unable to chat, express or accept sorrow. Nimsatu whispers, 'You know, your mother also promised me the embroidery chair.'

Only a handful of diehard relatives and friends are still at the house. It's almost over. I prepare a plate for Ma as we say goodbye. I get portions of all the food we've had in the house that day. Cassava *fufu* and a fish-filled *Satiday soup*. I roll out a rectangular piece of *olehleh* from softened banana leaf. I add some balls of *akara* and peppery onion sauce. A feast for her that we want her to share with us. I will leave it on the table overnight.

I can hear her voice, right as if she were standing next to me and bellowing into my ear: '*Eh boh*, did you forget palm oil and fish give me heartburn this late at night?'

Warm pellets of moisture roll down my cheeks. My shoulders don't shake. My heart does not squeeze tight. It's the small waves that ride on several medium-sized waves. The ones that take their energy from underneath. Those are usually the ones that make it to my toes. I cry.

19

Wanting

A certain story was told us when we were no longer little girls but also a long way from being women.

'*Lepole*,' the storyteller would say.

'*Leepail*,' we would chorus back.

'*Amon na fi*,' the storyteller would continue. *There once was.*

There once was a mermaid who lived in the crashing ocean that you see when you go walking past the beach at Fajara. She came from a tribe of mermaids that lived further south, closer to the border with Senegal, right on the edge where the Diolas of Cassamance live. You know, don't you, that the Diolas can make powerful magic, incantations that can force the most strong-hearted of us to give in. Let me tell you this though: there is one thing that no incantation can force us to do. It can never force us to want something we do not already half-want.

There once was this mermaid who lived in the sea, among the huge rocks with eyes in them, where cockles live, right at the bottom where sand is made. As she grew up she learnt the names of the fish there – barracuda, sole, mbiscit and so on. She learnt to make the wind sing for her when she was happy and to force the waves to jiggle boats about when she was feeling mischievous. Her tail was silvery grey with flecks of pinkish red at the spine, with splodges of black along the rim of her tail fin.

A time comes when all mermaids have to choose where to live. The ocean is a big place. Some who hanker after different kinds of food, or a change of scenery, can choose to go far away. Others who like the comforts of home can find a cave just a few minutes away from their parents' house. It is up to each mermaid to choose.

Our mermaid, the one whose life we are interested in, cannot decide. Sometimes it seems to her that life in the sea is boring. On a night when the moon bathes the sea in silver, she kicks up her fin and swims on her back. On nights like this she wants to live in the sky. At other times, she looks at the fishermen in their tiny pirogues, with ebony backs and arms which pull in the catch and she thinks that a life on land, with the chance to visit the sea often, would be perfect.

One day, the choice is taken from her hands. The moon is peeking out a crescent of itself, leaving most of the dark to the stars, which trickle their light onto different parts of the sky. The mermaid is swimming on her back and is so lost in her imaginings that she does not see a net thrown from a boat nearby. On ordinary days, she would simply dive deeper and faster than the net and swim away. But today, her mind does not turn quickly enough. Barbs at the edges of the net catch in her tail. One sticks in her arm, another in her neck. She yelps with pain and begs the waves to smother the boat. But her song is weak, her voice is not true, and she is captured.

The fisherman is the son of one of those Diola medicine men I told you about at the beginning of this story. He has been sent out by his father to catch something in the sea whose eyes could be roasted and ground into a potion. He is to bring back the first thing he catches. The fisherman is afraid when he sees the mermaid he's caught. If he disobeys his father, he will get into trouble when the potion does not work.

The mermaid looks back at him and thinks about how she need not fight. She can let herself be taken. She need not choose.

'Now,' the storyteller would say, 'what do you think should happen? Will the son of the medicine man win because he is scared of his father? Will the mermaid let her world be taken from her without her approval?'

The story did not always end the same way. Sometimes the mermaid realises at the last minute what she could lose, and she opens her throat and lets out the most soulful of the songs she knows of the sea. And the wind comes to help. The boat sinks, the boy drowns, the mermaid goes free.

At other times, the fisherman hauls the mermaid in and takes her to his father. His father does incantations that change her fish legs to human legs that never learn to walk. He needs to make a potion for a powerful chief and so he uses her eyes, after begging her pardon. She marries the fisherman, she lives on land and can hear the sea, but she can never take herself down to it and swim with the freedom she once had.

The moral of the story is, if you want something, don't half-want it. Either want it properly and go and get it, or forget about it so you will not be drawn into someone else's magic and get the decision taken out of your hands.

'It's us next isn't it?' says Kainde on the day before she leaves for a Montreal she describes as stupidly expensive, and misty grey.

She chews off the tip of the nail on her little finger and flicks a curl of hardened calcium off her lower lip onto the floor, like an irritating insect.

I nod. Without parents, we are next in line to die. There's no other generation to insulate us against death. It's us next.

'Why do I stay there? Do you think it's only the money?'

'Life isn't all sugar cubes here either. Visiting is different from living here,' I reply.

'Life in Montreal feels unreal sometimes. I'm a tiny cog in this huge organisation, where little gets done and everyone wants to hang on to their jobs and their benefits. We're supposed to be helping the world, but all we're doing is helping ourselves.'

'I can feel petty here too, when life is a constant stream of unwanted interruptions. People want things around you, off you, all the time.'

'Nimsatu and the embroidery chair didn't help, did it?'

'And the thing is, she couldn't understand why we didn't just give it to her. How could Aunt K's need be greater than hers? She thought we were being mean.'

'What a time to choose to get annoyed over a chair. After working with Ma for forty years too. Perhaps being greedy is what defines us. We want and we take, without permission if necessary.'

We are quiet as we mourn the halves of our lives that have smothered our youth, and the other half that is stretching into a grave just like our mother's.

Most of the people I meet again at my mother's funeral quickly fade back into a mist of acquaintances, who will be occasionally sighted in the supermarket. We will kiss then and exclaim about how long it's been since we last saw each other. We will promise to keep in touch. We will say goodbye and then let busyness redo what it did before – blanket our lives with activity. There are exceptions. Remi tries to build on our teenage friendship. Perhaps she finds that, like me, there is comfort in keeping a link with a youth that we want to remember as long as we can.

*

Ma was buried a week ago. My sisters and I are trying to make some decisions. Already, the morning's heat is creeping across the sky, about to jump on and munch the last of the night's clouds. We're at the dining table, with tea, cubed sugar in a dark blue cardboard box, a tin of Peak evaporated milk sitting with two gashes in its top, and a large bowl of coos pap.

'I'm not sure what I want to keep. Maybe one of her dresses and one of the bags she left in the trunk. They'll help me think of her in happier times,' I say.

'I'll go through the kitchen and take whatever will be useful in mine,' says Taiwo.

'I'd like a dress too, and when we divide the jewellery, could I please have the silver shell? Remember how Ma used to wear it at Christmas saying a shell made far more sense to her than a star. And that if she'd been one of the wise men, she would have given the most perfect shell she could find on the beach,' says Kainde.

'We can look through the clothes in the trunk and the jewellery before you leave. If you do the kitchen next week, Taiwo, I shall go through her bedroom and pack it up to give away. I think her memories are in the storeroom; she did not leave them where they could nudge her every day.'

'What do we do with the house itself?' asks Taiwo.

'I'm not ready to let it go yet,' says Kainde.

I nod. 'I agree. There's too much of us bound up in it still.'

'Shall we rent it out then?'

'Perhaps. We'll need to tidy up the house, disturb our history a bit, but it will let in some fresh air, so that the next time you come,' I say to Kainde, 'we will be able to talk about it again.'

'Will you two sort it out when I'm gone?'

'I think Reuben might be able to help us here. He knows people from work who might need to rent a house. And he's able to tell us how much to charge,' offers Taiwo.

271

The stray cat I sometimes feed comes streaking past us. From its favoured position on my doorstep soaking up the sun, it heads for the kitchen. As it leaps out through the gap in the flimsy bars I have on my windows to protect me from night-time burglars, a plate slides off my dish pile straight for the floor.

After the crash, Taiwo says, 'That was definitely Ma, saying she's heard us talking about her.'

There are sharp, quick footsteps on the driveway. Amina walks in with high-heeled slippers.

'Hope I'm not disturbing anything. I heard the noise of something breaking. You're not throwing things at each other, are you?'

We laugh. Kainde says, 'Taiwo says that was Ma who got the cat to push the plate over.'

'Might well have been. I came by to drop off something for Kainde to take back.' She turns to Kainde. 'You were saying at the funeral how hard it is for you to remember home, right? Here's something you'll be able to use every day. It will keep home closer to you, tugging at you, urging you to visit more often.'

The leather bag, burnished a deep brown, has the simplest of decorations around the clasp and the ends of its long straps.

'What about us, the ones who stay behind the whole year round?' I protest.

'You live, breathe and see this all the time. She doesn't.'

As she hands it over, she notices the coos pap. 'If you don't mind me, can I join in the breakfast, I'm in no hurry.'

I take the serving bowl to the kitchen to pour back into the saucepan and heat it up.

When I get back with it steaming again, Amina says, 'And look, all that time you spent running away from the kitchen. Did you *krawoo* yourself? Or buy it?'

'Did it myself, in that large calabash over there.'

'You know life never ends – if you still want a husband I'm sure there's someone out there who would treasure a wife who taught herself to cook so well.'

Taiwo has started to fuss around the table, clattering together our used bowls, collecting the spoons, loading up a tray for the kitchen.

'Don't be silly, Amina,' I protest.

'Silliness has nothing to do with it. It's just the way life is.'

'I have to be going,' interrupts Taiwo. 'I promised Reuben I'd get him some *chereh* for lunch tomorrow. I'll let myself out through the kitchen door.'

'Watch out for any bits Ayodele missed when she swept up the broken plate,' says Kainde as Taiwo hurries into the kitchen with the loaded tray.

'Sorry, don't have time or I'd do it myself to make sure. But must rush,' she replies. The key turns in the kitchen door, and she pushes the door open.

'Whatever will I do without this kind of talk on a quiet Saturday morning to liven up my life?' says Kainde.

I ask them: 'Do you remember the story about the mermaid? Do you remember how Aunt K would change the ending when she told us her version?'

'She even changed the beginning didn't she?'

'Hers went: *Una siddon goodwan?* And we'd all go: *We siddon goodwan.*'

'Then she'd continue: *Una yais opin?*'

'*We yais opin.*'

'And her magic came from the Mende, not the Diola.'

'You remember how we'd all gasp when he fell into the water, or click our tongues when she stayed on land.'

'How did it make you feel?'

'Dreamy. It seemed as if the story warned against being too

273

dreamy, about wanting what you shouldn't be wanting. Yet that is exactly how it made me feel.'

'I loved the idea that it was all in the mermaid's hands. She could decide what she wanted to do. And it meant my life could be full of possibles too.'

Talk meanders through to late afternoon. Kainde has to pack. I feel like a walk on the beach.

'Come with me, Amina,' I say.

'It's too bloody hot. What do you want to walk for at this hour,' she grumbles. Then she picks up her bag. 'Come on then, what are you waiting for?'

'Didn't you just say . . .'

'Of course I'll come. I felt like complaining, that's all. Bye, Kainde.'

More often than not, when I come to the beach now, I turn right. Today, we go the other way, intending to walk past the hotels to a stretch of dune and orphaned sea.

'What happened to us?' I say.

'Life?' says Amina.

'Were you happy in Italy?'

'Sometimes. But bad things happen wherever you are.'

'Mostly things happened the way you wanted. You seemed to be in control.'

'To some extent, yes. But I couldn't shape everything exactly as I liked. I'll never grow up, Dele, I'll never learn enough.'

There are many things I want to say to my friend. About this stupid life when we choose things that breed unhappiness, and then know that we have ourselves to blame. This constant following of the perfect life leads to wants that cannot be satisfied, like a *mamiwata* longing for legs and a life on land, when all of the ocean is open to her, free to swim in, free to claim.

There's a man ahead of us, with a dog on a leash. By the time we are past the busiest three hotels, I can make out his footprints in the sand. The heels sink in far deeper than the toes and the strides are wide. When he lets his dog off the leash, the pawprints race off into the distance and then double back to meet up with his, before looping off again. Then the dog stops, at a largish pool that will join up with the sea at the next high tide. There is a palm tree standing at its post, wagging its ears at the wind. The dog barks, runs back to its owner and then back to the pool to bark some more. When the man reaches his dog, he crouches down.

We soon catch up. Amina walks up to the pool to pat the dog and say, 'Hey, what did you find?'

Without looking up, the man points at the shallow water and says, 'That.'

That is a fish, about a foot long, curving and flapping its tail, smacking the water with each flick.

'It looks tired,' I say.

'And the water must have got hotter during the day,' he says.

'I guess you could try to catch it and drop it back in the sea,' I say.

'I was just thinking that myself. But how?'

I offer my flipflops, 'If you angle them in a V, you'll be able to scoop up the fish.'

He manages to put the fish back after four tries. Amina stands by the edge of the water and chats to him. I look out to sea, to the line where it meets the sky.

There once was. A girl called Ayodele. Her story can be told in many different ways.

My eyes catch what looks like the flick of a tail, sprinkling splashes of water high above the surface, slicing cleanly back into the ocean. Then it's gone.

Acknowledgements

Disorderly thanks for:

Reading the book and remembering home,
Vibrant introduction to the American short story and the magic of
    creating fiction,
The knack of helping me out of sticky writerly corners,
Spreading nice rumours about my novel,
Enthusiastically taking me on and getting me published,
Listening to the mermaid tale and pronouncing it brilliant,
Early and practical encouragement,
Amazingly attentive editing,
Egging me on by always asking whether I'd met my deadline,

to the following wonderful people:

Caroline Lightowler
Binyavanga Wainana
Rupert Heath
Joshua Snow
Jane Katims
Rochelle Venables
Musabi Muteshi
Danda Jaroljmek
Muthoni Garland